# PiXELS and PAiNT

# PiXELS AND PAiNT

## KRiSTi ANN HUNTER

Oholiab Creations
Georgia, United States

To the God whose grace is made perfect in our imperfections.
2 Corinthians 12:7-10

And for Blessing1.
Thank you for changing my life. Your quirks are a gift.

And to everyone who told me to go for it when I said I wanted to write both contemporary and regency novels, thank you for believing in me.

**EMMA**

A bag of peanut butter M&M's is not worth the agony I will endure over the next hour as the sights before me burn through the backs of my eyes and imprint themselves in my brain. There is little doubt what my nightmares for the next few nights will consist of.

I should have known I was in for torture when the bag my sister used to bribe me into coming tonight was the reclosable party size. She'd better be prepared to support me when I tell our mother that I am counting this as next month's Family Artistic Culture Outing, even though it's only been two weeks since they made me sit through a presentation of Shakespeare's *Cymbeline*.

That apparently wasn't enough of a mind bender because tonight—a mere fortnight later, as the Bard would say—I'm standing here looking at the most unexplainable painting.

*The Silent Wanderer* by Richie Reynolds according to the plaque on the wall and a work of incomparable genius according to my twin sister.

All I see is a cat in a dancing costume.

I think.

It's a little hard to say because the cat is not actually dancing. It is sitting completely still, staring off into space as cats so often do. Unlike a normal cat, however, this one seems to be wearing a swirly dancing costume like the Romani wear in video games.

Maybe it's dreaming of wearing one? While the cat itself is a rather lifelike rendering, the dress is, well, not.

I squint, blink, turn my head to the side, step back, step closer, and still I can't find whatever is inspiring the awe of the people around me. Should I try standing on my head? If I lean enough to have a perpendicular view of the painting, will it make sense?

Experience tells me no. It also tells me the other patrons wouldn't appreciate such an action.

Although, if what they appreciate is a decent painting of a tabby marred by swirling smears of pink and yellow that vaguely resemble a skirt and cropped top, my idea of appropriate might be off the mark.

"What is that?" My twin sister's voice is a low hiss near my ear.

I blink. Is it possible she thinks the painting is as weird as I do? Have I completely misread her earlier enthusiasm? If she brought me here so we could bond over not understanding the appeal of something in the art world, I'll send her a box of those expensive bonbons she treats herself with on special occasions.

"I think it's a cat." I grin at the person who looks as different from me as two sisters can look despite entering the world a mere seven minutes apart.

Her gray-green eyes blink at me slowly from beneath a frame of animated-princess-worthy blonde waves. "Of course it's a cat. I wasn't referring to the painting." She points at my arm before widening her eyes in horror once more. "What is *that*?"

I hold up my arm and inspect the sleeve of the silky, clingy, uncomfortable blouse she considers ideal for events such as this one. Not a stain or a stray thread in sight. That shouldn't be a point of pride for a twenty-seven-year-old woman with a job and her own apartment, but life's full of little quirks like that. "It's a blouse? At least that's what you labeled it in the *Look Book*."

Every year, my sister, my mom, and my aunt gift me a styling adjustment for my birthday. They come in, clean out my closet, add a few trendy pieces or accessories, and leave behind a binder containing details for every ensemble, from shirt to shoes to makeup suggestions to coordinating earrings. All of it organized into neat, tabbed sections.

I drop my arm and look down at the pants that looked like they were going to be exceptionally comfortable but have enough fabric flowing down from the wide, fitted waistband to make two normal pairs of pants, a matching vest, and a pair of socks.

"This was behind the *Evening Out* tab," I say.

She rolls her eyes. "I know that, silly. I was the one who put it there. What I did not do was put that watch on the approved accessories list."

My gaze drops back to my wrist where, yes, my smart watch is fully visible beneath the cuff of the sleeve. I tilt my arm and the blank surface lights up with a generic black and silver analog clock. "But I changed the band and the face."

According to the dimly glowing watch, I've been in this art gallery for eight minutes and thirty seconds. I'm already losing my mind and desperate to leave. This may be a new record.

Amy frowns. "You don't always use the black leather band?"

As what I normally attach to my watch is a comfortable, stretchy green nylon, I decide not to answer.

She moves on with a quick shake of her head. "Never mind. We placed an appropriate bracelet watch in your jewelry drawer."

I frown. "That watch face is perhaps a quarter the size of this one and doesn't light up."

"Which is why it's appropriate for formal events."

"This isn't formal." I jut out my leg and the extra fabric drapes down. So far, I've only come close to tripping over the extra fabric twice, which

I consider an achievement. "If it was, you'd owe me far more than a bag of M&M's."

She rolls her eyes and crosses her arms over the fitted top of her sleek, burgundy dress. "Semi-formal, elegant, chic, it doesn't matter. I know I didn't include that watch for anything that wasn't work, lounging, or casual wear."

"Do you badger your other customers when they veer away from your prescribed plan?"

My mom and aunt own a popular fashion boutique in Benson, the same affluent Atlanta suburb the art gallery I am currently standing in caters to. My sister joined their team after design school and expanded their offerings to include styling services for everything from an event to a closet overhaul with an outfit suggestion binder.

It's popular and expensive and honestly, they should probably give me credit for the idea. Mom and Amy have been doing some variation of this service since I could put on my own pants.

Amy gives one of those delicate, tinkly laughs that don't draw attention from outside her conversational circle and shakes her head, sending her blond waves dancing around her shoulders. "Those customers actually pay for our services and cherish the advice and guidelines we give. You, my ungrateful twin, don't seem to appreciate the value of your annual *Look Book* refresh."

That's where she's wrong. I greatly appreciate the *Look Book* because it means every time I see my family, I can be sure my outfit won't be one that leads to a fight at the dinner table.

If they saw what I wear when they aren't around and how my straight brown hair is normally piled into a sloppy bun, they'd disown me.

Amy hooks her arm through mine, a frown puckering between her eyebrows. "I think it's your job."

While I am grateful to follow her away from the painting, I'd rather not journey down this path of conversation. I know where it leads. I clear my throat. "My job is fine."

Her free hand lifts to give my upper arm a comforting pat. "Oh, I know it is, but it must be confining, sitting in your apartment, putting together other people's ideas and designs. You're disconnected from the beauty of the big picture." She turns her frown my way again. "I really wish you'd join us more than once a month. There are so many fabulous things to see in the city."

"Amy, you promised." College had been an eye-opening experience for me and when I'd moved into an apartment twenty-five minutes away from the rest of my family after graduation, I knew I'd need boundaries to maintain my new freedom and life in addition to my family relationships.

My compromise is one cultural outing a month, two of which can be formal over the course of the year, and a monthly dinner at Mom's house. Tonight's visit to the opening of a new exhibit at an art gallery falls outside those boundaries and I am deeply regretting the breach.

"I know, I know." Amy sighs. "But wouldn't you be happier surrounded by the exciting buzz of actual creation?"

"I can go into the office whenever I like."

"Just remember that the boutique could always use a competent technology person. We have to hire services for everything from the website to social media scheduling. If you want a more fulfilling job, we'd bring all that in-house and you could have a hand in some of the creative portions as well as the implementation."

Right. Because being the senior programmer at an award-winning immersive technology company couldn't possibly be a fulfilling career. At least, not in my family's eyes.

She squeezes my arm. Two short pulses and one long compression. It's been our code of support since we were children. Whether it was me reassuring her before a math test or her letting me know she believed in my ability to walk across the stage at high school graduation and not forget to shake everyone's hand in my rush to get off, it has always been our gesture of solidarity. Time to preserve familial unity and redirect this conversation.

"So, why am I here?"

She gives my arm a tug. "Come see my favorite one."

Okay, that was a disturbing non-answer. How does she already have a favorite? Did she study the catalog before we came? I hope not. That would mean she's deliberately subjecting my eyeballs to this bizarreness.

We trot past several people, all of whom are gazing at the paintings with varying degrees of rapture. If any of them are as skeptical of the art as I am, they don't show it.

Hopefully, I'm not wearing my feelings on my face either. A lifetime of museums, theaters, and exhibits have done nothing to explain to me why anyone would want to truss up in clothing that can't be thrown in the washer and requires special undergarments, then stand around pretending they don't want to eat the available food. Add in the fact that the point of the evening is to find meaning in someone else's emotional unburdening, and my state of confusion is complete.

We skirt around a small group of people chatting and pointing at a skeleton in what I think is a wedding gown. It looks like the ancient remains are being swallowed by a vortex of shredded tulle.

Yes, I know what tulle is. I listened when my mother explained what was scratching the skin off my legs when I was six.

"Just wait." Amy adjusts her grip so she can squeeze the blood out of my hand. "Tonight will unlock the secret understanding you need to get promoted to the design team."

As I already report directly to the owner and president of the company, who happens to be my best friend that I met in college, I don't think I can be promoted anywhere. And when did Amy start speaking of mystic unlockings? I scrunch up my nose and consider my sister. We have decidedly different views on spiritual matters, but this is new. "Why are you talking like that?"

"You'll thank me when you understand the pull of artistic expression."

"I'm not certain that's possible."

We pass a realistic tree painted over with wild strokes that might be some form of deconstructed swing set and I shudder. It's as if someone took the projects from an advanced art class and reused them during preschool craft time.

Maybe Richie Reynolds is actually a daycare instead of a person?

Amy meanders gracefully between the art lovers and I trip along behind. I'm not a clumsy person, but someone else is driving my body and they aren't using any turn signals.

Also, these pants.

I tuck my elbow in close to avoid knocking into a tiny plate of food one person is holding as they walk around. So there *is* food here. I'd been beginning to wonder. My head swivels to look around the room because once Amy finishes showing me this painting, the food is my next destination. The tiny portions at the fusion restaurant Aunt Jade selected tonight did not fill me up.

There. Along one wall of the gallery is a table draped in a white cloth that reaches the floor. Artfully arranged trays of little bite-sized foods cover the top. Either some secret staff member is constantly replenishing the food, or it's barely been touched.

Given that everyone I see is holding a champagne flute but only three are holding plates, I'm going with the latter.

Maybe I can spend the rest of the night by the table, pretending to admire the nearby artwork while I scarf down whatever canape is within reach.

The painting above the food table is a field of corn covered by ... is that meant to be a hamburger? Maybe a container of French fries? New plan.

I can stack up a plate—maybe two, because those plates look tiny—and hide under the table while I eat them. No one would be the wiser.

It's a nice dream, but I'll never do it. I don't have the skills to convince anyone I'm not just biding time until I can be anywhere but here if I were to get discovered. If my family knew how much I hated everything they love, it would break their hearts.

We come to a stop in front of another painting, and I can't help but think that maybe bruising Amy's heart just a little wouldn't be so bad. I want to look away, but I can't. My eyes take in every stroke and line like a person watching a car crash in slow motion. Amy, however, is looking up at the wall, hand over her heart as if she needs to hold the organ in place.

The painting inspiring such awe is of the wall of a shed covered in garden tools and other farm supplies. At least, that's the part that's clearly identifiable through the strokes of green and yellow and black that I believe are meant to be a tractor.

Should this be over with the fast food and corn painting?

"Don't you just love it?" Amy breathes out.

I shift my head in a tilting motion that she can take as a nod if she so chooses. "I am without words."

"Give it a moment before telling me how you feel. Let it sink in and resonate."

What is she wanting from me? Amy has never been in a tool shed. She faked a stomach bug rather than attend the agricultural field trip when we were in fourth grade. I'm not even certain she's seen the inside of a farmer's market.

I've been to dozens of these art events in my life, though. Surely I've heard something in those hours that I can spout off now to make Amy happy.

"The artist really—" I wave a hand toward the canvas. *Has a lot of paints* is not the correct answer here. Even I know that. "Er, knows how to change styles."

That must appease Amy, because she's all smiles and giddy giggles before hooking her arm with mine once more and pulling me toward a corner.

"You have to meet him," she says breathlessly. "He is amazing."

Ah. There's a *him* I have to meet. The artist, presumably.

Like the job discussion, I know how this will go. Amy will introduce us, Mother or Aunt Jade will appear and suddenly need Amy for some reason, and I will be left to make small talk with a stranger because my family is convinced I need to date more.

But no, Amy is not wearing her crafty, determined-to-improve-Emma's-life expression. She's looking ... dreamy.

I am no longer here to earn my peanut butter M&M's. I am a younger sister and I need to make sure this guy is worthy of the googly eyes my sister is making at him.

We come to a stop in front of a lanky man dressed entirely too casually for this event in a gray V-neck T-shirt, dark jeans, and loafers. Amy drops my arm and snuggles up to his side, hugging the man's elbow.

"Richie," Amy says, "this is my sister, Emma."

I can do this. I know how to do the small talk thing. I have a system.

"Nice to meet you, Richie," I say, even though technically Amy never introduced him to me. Small talk question one: ask about their career or hobby. I clear my throat. "Have you been painting long?"

"A painter is born," Richie says, averting his gaze to something over my left shoulder. "When he finds his brush, he is discovered."

Did somebody suddenly change the rules of small talk? I look to Amy, hoping to exchange that twin connection of confusion, but she is staring up at Richie in complete enthrallment.

Then she turns her dreamy smile and dazed eyes toward me, and I fear she's looking for some form of revelation brought on by her man's extreme depth.

"How true," she breathes out.

I open and close my mouth. Nothing comes out. I have no words. There *are* no words. I gave up babysitting as a teenager because I couldn't handle conversing with toddlers, and they'd made more sense than Richie just did.

*God, a little divine inspiration would be great about now.*

Even if the man is spouting unfathomable proverbs, he's the first guy Amy has seen fit to introduce to the family in a couple of years. I have to support her, at least until I can confirm that I need to knock some sense into her. I refuse to be the first person to step away from this conversation.

What had he said? Something about painters finding their brushes? I can work with that. "How, er, fortunate for us that you found yours."

Amy sighs. "Richie discovered his muse when his father left them. It is such a tragic story. He went to strike his father from the family portrait and discovered the beauty of abstract against refined." She giggles and hugs his arm tighter. "Isn't he a genius?"

Richie shakes his head. "The viewer finds their own genius. The artist is merely the avenue to enlightenment."

I blink. Amy gives another slack-jawed, wide-eyed nod. A prickling sensation forms in the back of my head. Is this what it feels like when brain cells choose to shrivel up and die instead of attempting to process the bizarreness the world is feeding them?

"Everyone sees different, er, enlightenments from your work, then, huh?" My laugh is cringe-inducingly awkward, but I soldier on. "I guess that makes us all in this room alone together."

I wish that statement was as nonsensical as Richie's had been, but I am all too aware of what it feels like to be surrounded by people and yet alone. One might say that's far closer to my default state than a sense of belonging.

In this moment, I definitely feel like the odd man out as the appreciative murmurs continue behind me. If any shred of reasonableness is left in the world, at least half of them are faking it. If a green smear of a turtle over the shoes of a marathon runner means profound things in this world, then I want to get off.

His gaze lifts to the corner of the ceiling and his eyes seem to focus on nothing. Is he trying to look like some sort of otherworldly guru, or does he truly think the secrets of life come to him in cryptic bombs delivered by trance-state planes?

"The exposure of the inner self is effective armor against the ridicule of the critic. One can only be truly known when the doors and windows are open."

I take that statement and twist it this way and that. Maybe it's a puzzle and I'm meant to rearrange the words? Was Yoda his elementary school English teacher?

No matter how I look at it, his statement is utter rubbish. I am close to my family, my friends, and even my colleagues, but each of those groups needs different things from me. If I just put myself out there with everything on display at once, I wouldn't fit in with anyone, and that would hurt.

Maybe people are like plug adapters. Some have one set of prongs and wiring that make them suitable for one type of plug. Other adapters have prongs to fit the plugs for different countries and the ability to carry different levels of current.

God made me one of those adapters that have different prongs on each side and you twist and turn it about depending on what sort of plug you need. It used to be confusing, but I've gotten it down to a decent routine now.

Amy, however, nods along as if every word from this man's mouth is illuminating life enrichment.

Yet she rolls her eyes when I mention church, God, or faith.

The problem at this moment, though, is that I've allowed Richie's nonsense to throw me off my small talk script. I open my mouth to move on to question two by asking him how he's enjoying the event.

Instead of my own voice, though, I hear Amy's. "Oh!" She releases her death grip on Richie's arm—the one attached to a hand he has yet to remove from his pocket—and points behind me. "There's Greg."

So this is an introduction *and* a set-up. No wonder Amy found it worth feeding my preference for something as unrefined as M&M's.

I'm not sure why my family persists. It's not like I *never* date. I went to the movies with a guy from church just last month. Or was it two months ago? No matter. The point is I went. Just because no guy has attained boyfriend status since I was in college doesn't mean my life is lacking.

For three people who have never been married and can—at best—be considered serial daters, they have an inordinate interest in the state of my love life.

"Ahoy, Greg!" Richie slides a hand from his pocket to wave.

Now he can be bothered to lift his arm? And who uses the word ahoy? Sailors have probably even given that one up.

I don't turn to look at Greg, far more concerned about the couple in front of me. Are they truly together or have they formed some sort of act for the benefit of the gallery showing? Theater was the one artistic endeavor Amy never excelled in, so I have to believe her sentiments are real. Richie's not selling anything I can buy.

Figuratively speaking. Literally, he's selling over a dozen paintings that I could drain my savings account to procure, but that's not the point.

"Greg is Richie's agent." Amy gives me her cartoon-villain smile, the one that says she's got me right where she wants me. It looks a little strange with her wide eyes, delicate features, and bouncy cloud of hair.

The man beside me, who I've yet to look at, says, "Things are going well, Richie. The gallery tells me we've sold a third of the pieces already."

Richie sniffs as if the sale of art is beneath his notice. "The art finds its way. I release it to fate, and she gifts me in return."

I steal a glance at Greg, but he's nodding and humming in agreement.

Is it possible my family is normal, and I am the one who is weird?

"Greg," Amy says with a smile diabetics should stay away from, "this is my sister Emma."

I turn to the man beside me. It's not his fault Amy is insufferable. "Hi, Greg. How long have you been Richie's agent?"

**2**

## *CARTER*

T hirty-one is too young to be jaded, but the fact that the only thing I find fascinating in this entire art gallery is a woman whose body language is screaming how much she doesn't want to be here is proof I've spent the past six years descending slowly into apathy.

I'm actually relieved to feel a spark of interest in anything related to art. Watching her look at the paintings as if they might be a secret portal for an alien invasion is like that first breath of clean air that comes when you step outside of a bowling alley or a club or even a crowded restaurant that hasn't been properly vented.

She'd entered with three blonde women, but I wasn't certain she knew them because they'd immediately dispersed about the gallery like seasoned professionals. They knew who to greet, wore expressions of proper enthrallment, and were clearly as on display as the artwork.

Given how the youngest blonde just pulled the brunette through the gallery, though, they are closely acquainted. My mind churns with even more questions and possible scenarios.

There are always people who don't want to be at a showing, exhibit, or gallery, but they're usually capable of hiding their displeasure. I can't remember the last time I enjoyed one, but no one but me is aware of that.

She, however, either doesn't know how to properly channel her less than impressed reaction or she doesn't care. The third, and possibly more interesting, option is that she thinks she's hiding it, but she disapproves so much it can't be contained.

Does she not like the art or the people who came out to look at it? It's impossible to tell as she seems to be wishing herself away from everything in the room.

I can't blame her for wanting to get away from Richie. Somewhere along the line the man decided to develop the personality of a fortune cookie.

She stands out from the carefully directed spotlights, thoughtfully arranged paintings, and swarming mass of art connoisseurs. It isn't so much her attire as it is the way she seems disconnected from the crowd's core commonality. I'm transfixed. My fingers itch to paint it, to find a way to convey the idea I'm seeing to others.

Should I use people? Perhaps animals would create a better depiction of the idea. A dog among a bunch of cats or a chicken being herded along with the pigs going to slaughter. No, not that last one. It needs to be something the larger group as a whole would actually want to be doing.

"The turnout is fantastic." Frank, the gallery owner, steps into the shadowy alcove where I've been lurking all evening and interrupts my mental sketching.

"Your concern over having a large opening like this for a solo show-ing was understandable." I clap my hand on his shoulder and give it a squeeze. "All the parties involved should be happy, though. I'm glad."

He elbows me in the ribs with a grin. "Thanks for coming tonight, even if we ended up not needing the push."

"You took a similar chance on me and that paid off. I owe you."

Ten years ago, Frank had been the first one to believe in me, giving me a solo showing much like this one. I don't sell my work through his gallery anymore, but he remains in my life as something even more important—a friend.

"All the same, I know this isn't your normal scene anymore."

"We all have to play the game some, whether we want to or not." I slide my hands into the pockets of my trousers and look around the gallery. "This isn't your normal acquisition."

Frank blows out a long breath. "It was a risk, but I need the gallery to gain a broader reputation." His expression turns pleased as one of his employees quietly places a discreet *Sold* marker next to one of the name plaques. "It looks like it's going to pay off. We even had the art critic from *The Gazette* in here at the beginning, gathering quotes for a write-up."

"Congratulations." My gaze slides to the brunette, drawn by a pull I can resist only so long, even while conversing with a friend.

She seems to curl in on herself even as the blonde clinging to Richie's arm seems to grow bouncier. Talking to Richie is an exercise in discombobulation and the bored, aloof mannerisms he cultivated after selling his first five-figure painting make him unapproachable.

"Promise me something, Frank."

"Yeah?"

I nod toward the grouping that now includes Richie's agent, Greg. "If I ever become that absorbed in my own success, shove me in a lake."

"Gladly." Frank winces as he looks across the room. "I'm still not certain if he expects to get his portion of the sales as a check or a truckload of watermelons."

"The bounty of creative harvest?"

Frank chuckles. "You've heard it before?"

I nod. "Once. It was memorable."

Frank's smile remains as he steps away from me. "I need to mingle. It doesn't look like I need you to make the rounds, so feel free to slip out the back if you want to."

He gives me a small salute and returns to working the crowd.

Twenty minutes ago, I'd have already had my keys in hand and my feet halfway out the door, but now I can't quite bring myself to abandon the first real inspiration I've found in longer than I care to remember.

She'd likely find it creepy if she knew I was standing here, watching her, but she'll never know. Despite my hyper-realistic style of painting, I never depict actual places or people. I create scenes that represent an idea or a concept, such as a lone person standing among a group of admirers asking why they are all enthralled.

Meeting her would likely destroy the illusion, but watching for a few more moments won't hurt. The various body languages from the small grouping of people are giving me idea after idea. Should I do a series of paintings depicting people out of step with the world around them?

My brain floods with exciting ideas to put into my sketchbook when I return home. Any of them will be better than the meaningless perspective paintings I've been putting out just to stay active in the art world.

Greg adjusts his suit coat and shifts his weight to his toes. He is excited to meet the brunette, while she's tossed at least five furtive glances at the door, as if she's merely looking for an excuse to leave.

Eventually Greg turns and gestures to a table of artfully laid out hors d'oeuvres. For the first time all evening, the brunette shows a glimmer of enthusiasm.

Greg puts the requisite three items on his tiny plate and proceeds to ignore them as he talks. I sampled a few items before the doors opened and he is missing out on some delectable food.

She seems determined not to miss out, though, as she takes two of everything until her tiny plate is filled just beyond what could be considered polite. After biting a small fruit tart in half, she gives Greg a small nod of attention and glances from the watch on her wrist to the door.

The softly glowing face of her watch makes me wince. I accept the benefits of modern technology. At this moment, a cell phone is resting in the pocket of my sport coat. It's last year's model, too, not a minimalistic flip phone. It's also turned off.

Harsh lights and graphics don't belong in a gallery setting where they would distract and detract from whatever connection the art is making with the viewers.

I tilt my head and consider her. Is that why she dislikes the paintings so much? Does she need her art to dance and beep and burn her retinas?

Her foot is now pointing toward the exit and her smile is tight. Everything about her begs for a rescue.

Before I can think about it, I step out of the shadow and make my way across the room. This urge is nonsensical. I am an observer of human nature, not a knight in shining, or even slightly tarnished, armor. It's not as if she's in danger. Greg likes to collect controversial artists who create conversation pieces, but he isn't a bad guy.

Maybe it's because the emotion she displayed earlier, even if unwittingly, is now blocked behind a polite, stony façade. Maybe it's because I want to know if there's more to the picture that I'm not seeing, more to her that can inspire me.

Whatever the reason, it's compelling enough to have me crossing the room. I move slowly and keep my face averted from the other attendees. No one notices me until I'm passing the corner where Richie has stationed himself, as if he, too, is an art installation.

"Mr. Anderson," he says in the monotone he's adopted for this public persona.

The art world is too small for me to outright ignore him, so I give a small nod of greeting. "Mr. Reynolds."

The pretentious formality of the exchange nearly makes me roll my eyes. As if we've never met before. Five years ago, he attended one of my hyper-realism workshops. He'd been Richard then, and I'd been Carter and there'd been no indication what direction he wanted to take his, er, talents.

"I didn't realize you'd been invited," Richie drones.

Is he worried my presence will decrease the value of his work or concerned people will think I had a hand in making tonight a success? As the plan is for no one to see me aside from Greg and the brunette, I hope to avoid anyone making a public connection between myself and Richie.

"Frank is a friend of mine." Hopefully that connection is enough to tell him I'm not here for him as either fan or critic.

He nods slowly before shifting his gaze up toward the corner. "A friend will pull favors in the pursuit of greatness."

I ... what? How can I respond to that?

His gaze drifts back down but never quite meets mine. "Favors are not necessary. I have great respect for your abilities. If you wish to observe my methods, I could arrange a time for you to come by my studio."

I glance at a painting of an abstract car atop a gracefully running horse. "Such a unique style could never be emulated."

Nor would I want to try. The horse is decent. If he wanted to, he could make a decent living selling paintings of such quality, particularly if he took on portrait commissions. Does he care more for notoriety than financial stability?

Or does he truly think his work is that exceptionally groundbreakingly brilliant?

"Is this a friend of yours, Richie?" The blonde sends a beaming smile my way before gazing adoringly up at Richie.

"A colleague," Richie answers. "The elevation of greatness is a hill far too difficult for friendship to climb."

And that is about all of that I can take for an evening. With any luck, the blonde will read between the lines there and learn Richie wants nothing from her but arm candy.

"Congratulations on a good opening," I say with a smile and a nod for both of them. "Please excuse me. There is someone I need to speak with."

I stroll away, leaving Richie to tell the woman how I fear I will fade away as I bask in his glow or some other such nonsense. Redoubling my effort to draw no attention, I make my way to the food table. Fame isn't something I deal with on a regular basis, but here I stand a high chance of being recognized.

I would rather not have my name attached to Richie's if I can help it.

I slide a plate from the stack and busy myself with placing a tiny sandwich, three grapes, and a cookie on top of it. Slowly, I ease into the space where Greg and the brunette are standing at the end of the table.

Though I am a constant student of human nature and body language, it is possible I have misread the situation. She might be perfectly happy spending an evening with Greg, though if she is, I'll have to question everything I thought I'd observed earlier.

"Good evening." I give them each a nod as I reach for a fruit tart.

Greg's eyes widen slightly but his professional demeanor quickly slides into place. "Carter, what a surprise! Richie's having a splendid night."

An answer from me is unnecessary as Greg falls into a one-sided discussion about art patrons and pieces sold, and the upcoming write-up in the newspaper from the nearby city. What he's not doing is introducing me to the brunette. Intentional slight or just poor manners?

She's frowning down as she pokes at the cookie on the edge of her plate, so I lean close to her and whisper, "It's a palmier."

Her frown turns my way, and I can make out details that weren't available to me from across the room. Her makeup has clearly been applied by an expert hand, but it hasn't been touched up. The lip color is now uneven as if no care was taken to reapply it after dinner.

"The cookie." I nod to her plate and lift my own cookie as if in a toast. "It's a palmier."

"Interesting." She slides the cookie to the other side of her small plate. "I tried one earlier."

A portion of another cookie lies beneath a fruit tart. "Did you not care for it?"

"Why do you ask?" She looks up from her plate and blue eyes briefly meet my gaze before shifting to Greg.

The brief connection slams into me and the urge to find a pencil and sketchpad burns through my chest. I'll even take a ballpoint pen and a cocktail napkin.

For the first time in months, I can see a painting in my mind. Darkness and shadows with mere streaks of light to show the details. I'd remove all the makeup from her face, but her clothing would become finer, fancier, the kind of dress worn to galas and shown off for the press. There'd be jewels winking in the darkness. I'd give her every trapping that normally catches people's attention, but it would all fade as the viewer is captivated by her eyes. Bright, blue, glowing depths that would make it impossible to look anywhere else.

Greg leans in until his shoulder brushes against mine. "Carter, you know better than to question a lady's eating choices."

Likely—hopefully—the agent means for the whispered admonishment to go no farther than my ears, but the brunette obviously hears. I don't know how she interprets the statement, but her eyes narrow and she glares at Greg as she shoves the entire cookie into her mouth.

I can't say anything. If I do, laughter over the way she is attempting to cover her clear revulsion while managing her overly full mouth will spill out.

Someone is not a fan of cinnamon palmiers.

She's even less a fan of Greg, at least at the moment.

Her eyes dart about as she chews. Greg snags a flute of champagne and offers it to her, but her face twists as if she is considering spitting the cookie into the pale, bubbly liquid instead of drinking it.

I don't blame her. Alcohol is a terrible choice for washing down unwanted food unless a person also wants to be dry-mouthed and tipsy.

Setting my plate on a nearby tray, I gesture to the back of the room and the shadows I'd recently been inhabiting. "If I may, there are bottles of water in the employee lounge."

Those bright blue eyes meet mine once more, this time with an emotion I can't pinpoint. Regret? Gratitude? Concern? Her neck convulses through a series of quick swallows before she sets her plate beside mine and chokes out, "Please."

"Right this way." I swing my arm out in a grand invitation.

Greg pats her awkwardly on the shoulder. "I'll ... go speak to some people until you come back."

Her tight smile makes me think she has no intention of returning and I plan to assist her with that goal. Now that I've interacted with her, I need to know more about her. My motives are admittedly self-serving, but I'm certain every rescuer of distressed damsels is motivated at least a little by a selfish reason.

I lead her to the darkened portion of the gallery and push open a door marked *Employees Only*. She follows without pause, and soon we're in the more practical section of the building where all the business actually gets done.

A handful of workstations are positioned to our left and beyond them sits a cluster of couches near a credenza boasting an empty silver platter and a single-cup coffeemaker. I lead her through the room and down a short hall into the break room.

The dark-flecked white tile, small brown Formica table, three armless blue chairs, standard white fridge, and cream-colored counter with a metal sink and a rack of mismatched coffee mugs are far more office building than elegant gallery. Will her demeanor change along with the atmosphere?

I pull two bottles of water from the fridge and extend one in her direction. She nearly snatches it from my hand and twists it open. She gulps down half the contents while I slowly sip from the second bottle.

Finally, her eyes slide closed, and she sighs in grateful bliss. Such elemental enjoyment of something as plain as a bottle of water is a strange idea to me. Does she have strong feelings about everything? Richie's art is horrific, bottled water is blissful, etc.?

"Thank you." She sighs. "Those cookies were disgusting."

I can no longer resist the urge to laugh. "Noted."

"You didn't make them, did you?" She glances around the break room as if expecting to find an oven and a pile of dirty cookie sheets.

"Ah, no. I'm not a baker. Frank has a standard caterer he uses."

She grimaces. "I can't see Richie Reynolds using standard anything."

I take another drink, delaying my response to such a personal statement. Does she know Richie? Have I misread the discomfort? Is it possible she'd been jealous of the blond woman? "Do you—"

"Thank you." Her words cut off my question as she flops into one of the armless chairs and sets her almost empty bottle on the small table.

"You're welcome?" We've already discussed the water, so what is she thanking me for now? Rescuing her? That would make a good conversational opening, but before I can take it, she continues.

"You probably can't leave me back here alone, can you? If I promise not to touch anything aside from this chair and this bottle of water, could you make an exception? I don't want to keep you from your work, but I just can't go back out there right now."

"I can stay—"

"I promise to leave in"—she glances at her watch—"twenty-five minutes."

Thinking I work here is a logical conclusion. I should correct her, but the last thing I want to do is talk about myself. I already know about me.

I lean back against the counter. "As it happens, they don't actually need me here tonight. Frank told me I could leave when I was ready."

That's a true statement, if a slightly misleading one. The flicker of guilt fades quickly since my chances of seeing this woman again are slim to none. Far stronger is my inexplicably desperate need to understand her better before she slips away into the night.

I clear my throat. "We can stay hidden for a while. There's even a back exit you can use."

"Wonderful." She pulls out her phone and unlocks it with her thumb. A few taps and several quick swipes of her finger and she sets the phone aside with a sigh.

I can't help but smile. "You're that desperate to leave? You've been here barely half an hour."

A light pink flush spreads over her cheeks as she considers me. "Were you watching me?"

No denying it now. I give a short nod. "It was my job to keep an eye on how many people arrived to ensure there was a decent turnout for the event."

She laughs. "As if you could magically make more people appear?"

I could, actually, but that isn't what I want to talk about. I never want to talk about that. The only part of me that enjoys my little niche corner of fame is my bank account. "So, you weren't appreciating the showing?"

With two fingers she pinches the loose corner of the wrapper on the water bottle and tugs at it, making the bottle crinkle under the slight pressure.

She sighs. "I never enjoy art." Her eyes widen and she slaps a hand over her mouth. Her voice is muffled as she gasps. "I'm so sorry."

Not just showings, but all art? I've met many a person who only saw merit in particular styles or mediums, but never someone who would willingly sit in the back room of an art gallery and proclaim they didn't care for any of it.

Goodbye, curiosity. Hello, obsession.

## EMMA

Perhaps my family is right to worry about my dating life. After all, I did just tell an attractive man who was gracious and observant enough to save me from a very awkward social encounter that I hate the very thing he has chosen to surround himself with. I mean, no one would apply for a job in a gallery unless they liked paintings and sculptures and whatever else gets displayed.

A surge of light-headedness makes the room spin around me, but thankfully the plastic chair keeps holding me up. What if he was the one to approve Richie's work?

Despite the embarrassment flooding my body and possibly my cheeks, I can't pull my gaze away from his. No matter how hard I search, the handsome face looking back at me doesn't reveal a single clue as to his reaction.

*Handsome* is such a pretentious-feeling word to use, but there are too many waves of sophistication rolling off this man to call him anything else. Words such as *cute, hot, good-looking, a straight ten,* or any other description I've seen or heard my friends use absolutely give off the wrong impression.

Is it possible I'm a biased observer right now? Could the bizarreness I spent the past half hour perusing have altered my perception? Maybe. But I can easily picture him lounging against the counter in my favorite coffee shop, and that mental image does not spark a different reaction.

This man appears as comfortable in a jacket and slacks as other men are in sweats and T-shirts. Even the brown hair that is long enough to brush the open collar of his dress shirt is lying like it was edited for a magazine cover.

And I just told this six-foot-something man of casual, elegant perfection that I hate the core of what he does for a living.

*Good job, Emma.*

How long has he just been staring at me? Can I backpedal? Pretend I misspoke? It feels like I've been drowning in his direct hazel gaze for several minutes, but it's probably only been a second or two. I'm not that great at maintaining eye contact.

Time to take a stab at salvaging this situation. "I, er, I mean this art, or rather—"

His impassive expression breaks as a low chuckle fills the room. "You don't have to apologize." He shakes his head, somehow still holding my gaze. "Art is subjective. I would say, though, that if you don't like any of it, chances are you've never been introduced to it properly."

"I'm sure you're right." Actually, I'm sure he isn't. Art's been thrown at me in every way imaginable. Agreement is an easy path out of this discomfort, though.

I take a drink from my water bottle and glance in the direction of the gallery. "Do you like it?"

*Do you like it?* That's my brilliant transition out of an awkward discussion?

This is why I created a script for conversing with strangers. Without it, I inevitably stick my foot in my mouth far enough to gnaw on my knee.

Should I laugh it off? No, my best friend, Jason, says my fake laugh sounds like a deranged parrot. More backpedaling it is, then. "What I meant was, um ..." How close can I get to my normal Question 1? "Do you like your job?"

He considers me through narrowed eyes as he, too, buys time by taking a drink of water. After he sets the bottle down, his skepticism seems to clear as he gives a slight bob of his head. "Most of the time, yes."

I shift my weight in my chair, careful not to lean forward in anticipation. Anyone who takes the time to truly think before answering a question is more interesting than someone who gives a pat, practiced, socially expected response.

"I don't suppose any job is good all the time. Even one you love has mundane parts." I dreamed about having a job like my current one while I was sitting in college classes, but there are still days I want to chuck it all and try my hand at making it as a video game streamer. "If nothing else, there's filling out tax forms."

He laughs, face splitting into a wide smile and revealing straight white teeth and dimples.

I wrap the fingers of my left hand around the edge of the seat beneath me to make sure I stay where I am. Handsome has left the building. Gorgeous has taken up residence. They should clear out all the paintings from the other room so people can simply stand around and gawk at this man laughing.

Of course, then he probably wouldn't be laughing.

The last thing I need is for my brain to travel any farther down that particular road, so I search for something else to talk about or even think about. All I can imagine eclipsing that captivating smile is the bizarreness in the other room. I wave a hand toward the door. "So, you ... understand all that?"

"Are you referring to the patrons, the gallery, or tonight's displayed works?"

I blink as the confusing environment I'd recently escaped slides into different mental groupings, like objects in a piece of code. The context is more comfortable but doesn't bring sense to the idea. "Any of it, I suppose."

He picks up his water and takes a drink, once more seeming to give real consideration to my question before answering it. "A gallery is a business." One finger starts tracing through the condensation on the bottle. "You acquire a product with a potential audience. If it sells, you make money. I've been around places like this for fifteen years and I can tell you there's nothing more noble to it."

Fifteen years? Either he *really* appreciates art, or he aged like cheddar cheese.

"As for the art itself ..." His gaze lifts to meet mine before shifting to the wall. "Every form of art has someone who appreciates it. Personally, I prefer the nuance and context of realism."

I can't stop the conspiratorial smirk from forming as I say, "Does it mean more to you when covered in abstract household appliances?"

He shakes his head, one side of his mouth tilting enough to bring out that dimple again. "No, but that does bring me to the patrons. Richie could make a living taking commissions and doing portraits and other true-to-life paintings. He's got the skills for it."

I suppose I can see some appeal to the old-world idea of having a portrait of the family pet or hanging your family above the fireplace, but wouldn't it be faster, easier, and cheaper to get a large print of a good photo?

Probably best not to ask the art guy.

"By adding something unique," Carter continues, "Richie is limiting his audience, but he also increases his potential value. Not everyone appreciates it, but when the right person does ..." He shrugs.

My nose wrinkles into a frown as I try to imagine finding enjoyment in seeing those pieces every day. I don't think my failure to do so is completely the fault of my lack of creativity.

"See?" Carter points his water bottle at me before taking another sip.

"See what?"

"You responded. Art is as much about evoking a response in the viewer as it is providing an outlet of expression for the creator."

"Are you saying he wants me to hate his work?"

Carter gives another shrug. "No, but revulsion is a response. For an artist, the further someone is from stoic disinterest, the bigger the success. It doesn't matter which direction the emotion goes, although positive feelings tend to pay more."

He settles deeper into thought and crosses his legs at the ankles as he looks up at the ceiling. "I suppose that's why I like showings no matter what is on display. Patrons are their own exhibit."

"What do you see?"

"Well"—he gives me a grin—"sometimes I see people who need a bit of assistance."

And I am right back to the heat of awkward embarrassment.

"If you prefer, we can pretend I developed a sudden craving for tiny sandwiches."

Did he come over out of pity or from a desire to meet me? Which is better? Either idea has heat building in my ears and threatening to flood my face.

Thankfully, he comes to my rescue again by asking, "What is it you don't like?"

That it's paint on canvas and I'm supposed to look at it and become connected to some deeper meaning in life? Not even historically inaccurate paintings of Jesus do that for me. "You said you didn't like it either."

"My reaction was not as, shall we say, visceral as yours. I can appreciate the skill if not the final product."

"That probably comes in handy working at a gallery."

He says nothing as he watches me, waiting for an answer.

Since tonight is the first time I've admitted to a living soul that I dislike all forms of art, I've never taken time to articulate what it is I don't like about it. Do I have an actual reason? Does this feeling of distaste bother me so much because it doesn't have an explainable cause?

"I suppose," I say, dragging out the words as I try to gather my thoughts, "that I don't see the purpose."

"And you like everything to be practical and efficient."

My eyebrows shoot up. That had been a firm statement, not a questioning observation.

He nods toward my arm. "Your watch."

My watch? I turn my wrist and the face lights up, telling me I have fifteen minutes until my promised hour is up.

"No one, at least none of the ladies, wore one tonight. It is a practical accessory but not a fashionable one."

I try to swallow the mix of flattery and discomfort. "How long were you watching me?"

He smirks. "You weren't exactly hiding your distaste. It was instantly noticeable."

That doesn't answer my question, but as I'm not certain I want to know the truth, I don't press him. "I don't believe everything has to be practical, but I do think it needs a purpose. Fun can be an impractical purpose. So can relaxation."

"Beauty isn't a purpose?"

"That"—I point toward the gallery—"is not beautiful. It's weird."

"To you."

"I concede that some people might like that art, but if you go in there and ask them why, none of them will say, 'Because it's pretty.' They would spout some sort of nonsense about existential crisis and sociological displacement and transcendental warfare."

Water splutters from his mouth as he laughs around a sip of water. "Pretension is a purpose as well."

"Why, Carter, are you implying those people out there came for their own egos and not the great Richie Reynolds?"

I think my joke is funny and in line with the conversation, but his smile immediately fades, and he considers me with a hard look. Gorgeousness must make me stupid. That's the only reason I have for why I keep speaking without thinking around this man.

"Uh, I didn't mean ..." I swallow and try to dig my way out of one more verbal blunder. "I have family out there. I was just thinking of them, and, wow, that doesn't sound any better."

"You know who I am?"

The amount of disappointment in his voice makes me want to cross the room and give him a comforting hug. Although my just-shy-of-average-sized self would be nose to shirt button and I don't know how comforting that would be.

"I, well, no." I grip my nearly empty water bottle tighter. "Greg called you Carter, so I assumed that was your name." My nose screws up. "That's probably odd, isn't it? Having me use your name because I heard it somewhere? I'm usually talking to people I had an online connection to first and I'm just accustomed to learning a name and using it."

Never before have I considered the dangers of meeting people via email signature.

He considers me for a moment before the small smile returns to his face. "Do you have a business card or something I can learn your name from? I'm afraid I'm more accustomed to formal introductions."

My social skills are as vague as the car Richie smeared atop a running shoe. I try to smile. "I'm Emma."

"Nice to meet you, Emma." He inclines his head with a smile, making his dimples crease and crinkles form beside his hazel eyes.

My mind is a complete blank even as I press my tongue to my teeth in preparation for continuing the conversation. The buzzing of my phone saves me, and I pick it up to silence the alarm I set to use as a fake emergency text. "It appears I have fulfilled my time obligation and can now make my way home."

"Does it count if you spent half the time in the breakroom?"

"I spent an hour at the gallery, which is all I promised to do." I shrug. "Besides, I already opened the bag of bribery M&M's my sister gave me so she can't take them back."

"You were bribed into attending with M&M's?"

"Yes. Peanut butter ones." Although, I must admit it was the best possible introduction one could be given to the man who is Richie Reynolds. I can't imagine trying to put context around his demeanor if I'd met him in Mother's living room.

If this relationship progresses to the point that he attends our monthly dinners, will I get to hear him speak like a normal person or will it just be more random banalities?

That's a worry for another day. For now, I just need to get out of here and out of these uncomfortable clothes.

I push the chair back from the table and stand. The miles of extra fabric in the loose pant leg catches on the chair and bring it skittering after me as I step away.

Stupid fancy-named pants. Jeans and yoga pants do not betray a girl this way. Carter steps forward to help me extricate myself from the chair and I give him a tight smile. "I'm not clumsy."

"Okay."

"Really. I'm not. See?" I toss the empty water bottle toward the trash can and it drops right in.

"You could have recycled that." He points to the blue bin in the other corner.

"Well, that's just silly. Why wouldn't you put them beside each other so that a person knows recycling is an option?"

"Because everyone back here is supposed to already know?"

"Fair." I sigh and look into the trash can.

The bottle rests atop a lone, closed takeout container so I scoop it back up and toss it toward the recycling bin. It swooshes right in, thanks to many nights spent working in a computer lab and being too lazy to cross the room.

He nods in appreciation before letting his gaze sweep over my person. It isn't one of those creepy check-out-the-little-lady sort of scans. No, he appears to be looking for evidence of my real personality.

I hate to tell him, but he won't find it in anything I am currently wearing. Even my underwear is the fancy kind because my normal ones looked weird under the pants.

I glance down. One pant leg is still bunched up from the chair incident. The droopy yet clingy shirt is twisted, and a seam is now arching from beneath my right arm to the vicinity of my belly button. At least my shoes match each other.

He may indeed think he's learning something about me right now, but it isn't a favorable impression.

I sigh. The ability to wear nice clothing gracefully must be attached to the genetic quality that provides creativity and an appreciation of art. It's not from a class, because my mother made me attend those as a teenager and I still don't possess the skills.

"Thank you for the water and the rescue, but I hope you won't find it too offensive that I am more than ready to leave this event."

"Understandable."

I return his long last look, though mine is committing him to memory. While I do not want to think about how he might remember me, I know I'll be remembering him as the good-looking guy who got to see me in my least impressive setting.

If we ever meet again, I pray it will be while I'm doing something I'm competent at and wearing clothes I don't want to burn. He could watch me work and be impressed with the consistent way I name my variables, or log in to *Wizard's World 3* and marvel at the kingdom I've built up, or see me strategize my way to a win during board game night with my friends.

Most of those things happen in my apartment, though, so more likely than not, I'll never see him again.

**CARTER**

**4 Weeks Later**

I've often heard it said that the Lord works in mysterious ways, but I've never truly experienced it until the past few weeks.

After two years of praying for God to renew my passion for my art and seeming to receive not a single answer, the past four weeks have been almost overwhelming.

Ideas come at me with such regularity that I've taken to carrying my sketchbook with me everywhere again. I haven't done that since my first year living in New York City, where it became easier to simply mull over the idea during the day and then lay down the sketch in the evening. At the time, I'd thought it was because I'd gotten mature enough in my painting that I could cull through mediocre ideas without exploring them on paper.

Now I have to wonder if I'd already been losing my inspiration.

There is no question that I'm inspired now. A piece of trash on the ground, a person laughing too loudly in a quiet coffee shop, or even a near crash when a car stopped at the yellow light of an intersection and the car behind them had to swerve into the ditch because they'd been intending to keep going. The smallest moments in life make me think of ideas.

They make me think of Emma.

How had less than an hour with a random woman made such an impact on me? The results can't be denied. My sketchbook holds several pages of quick doodles and nearly a dozen partially fleshed out sketches of groupings that don't quite work. There's always one item that doesn't seem to belong and it's more than replacing the depth I've been missing in my work.

The burn to draw is fading some and becoming containable. It's probably a good thing. A fire that hot isn't sustainable. Fortunately, I'm nowhere near the chill of fearing my art career is going to die at an age as absurdly young as it began.

Still, it would be nice if I had a way to spend more time with Emma to see if that fuels the intensity a little longer. She's become an almost mythic creature in my mind, but that imaginary version of her isn't as compelling as the real one was.

I shift the strap of my leather messenger bag so it rests more securely on my shoulder and stroll through the quiet museum. It's after public hours, but as long as I'm out before the offices close, no one cares.

When I was a boy, I'd found drawing in the shadow of the masters to be inspiring. Over the years, I've dropped that habit as well. Reviving it hasn't seemed to make as much difference as the fresh inspiration did.

"Ah, Carter, I didn't know you were still here." Carl Leonard, the museum director and head curator, strolls into the lobby of the Mc-Grady Museum of Art from the wing opposite the one I'd been strolling through.

I give him a nod. "Just a little quiet inspiration from those who've come before me."

He gives a pleased sigh. "It can't be beat. I'm still amazed that I get to work with such beauty every day."

A person dressed in the almost formalwear of a professional caterer enters the wing Carl recently exited.

I nod toward the wide archway. "What's happening?"

"Private event. A celebration of a new fashion line from the daughter of one of our patrons."

"Catering?" I try to subtly lean around him to make sure the ropes have been put up in the gallery. It makes me nervous when food and drink are brought into the gallery spaces.

"Relax, Carter. The cocktail tables are in the center, the perimeter cords are in place, and the catering staff has been briefed on how high to fill the drink glasses and to keep the flow of food slow." Carl gives me a pointed stare. "You're not the only one who respects the art, you know."

I should be a little embarrassed over his admonishment, but I'm not. I give a small shrug. "You asked me to be the artistic representative for a reason."

He claps me on the shoulder and walks with me toward the staff exit. "That I did. Not that our board doesn't have reverence and respect for the works in our care, but it is nice to have an idea of how the creators of the work would view our efforts."

When the museum had asked me to be a consultant, I'd thought it a needless position. I was mostly correct, but there have been a few times I've been glad to point out how an artist might wish their work to be treated or displayed differently.

"You'll be in the board meetings for the next few months, right? We're starting to cull through the options for the new self-guided tour."

"I'll be here." I restrain a sigh, but can't keep my resignation out of the words.

Carl chuckles. "Not everyone wants to sit in front of a Caravaggio for hours and let it speak to their soul, you know."

I hate that he's right. I want art to be accessible to everyone, but I also want them to experience the deep, powerful connection to it as well. I've never wanted a guide in an art museum since I'm there to experience the art, but I can see where other people might need the assistance. For most, the museum's old style of a printed brochure of highlights isn't enough anymore.

Emma pops into my head once more, sitting in that plastic chair designed for efficiency and value instead of aesthetics, declaring she hates art.

"Whatever you choose," I say as I reach for the door, "it needs to highlight the way we connect to art. Even someone who hates what they are looking at should be able to respect that emotional pull."

Carl nods in thought. "You want them immersed in the art."

"Exactly." That's how I felt when I looked at particular pieces. Immersed in the world the artist created, connected to the idea, and inspired in my own life.

In a way, that time with Emma was like a piece of art. I stepped into a different view of the world and was inspired by it.

What a shame I can't revisit it like I do the Caravaggio in this museum that I would stare at when I was a kid.

"Do you want to stay for the party?" Carl gestures back toward the gallery being set up. "I've an extra tie in my office if you feel the need to dress it up a bit."

I shake my head. "Thanks for the invitation, though."

One step outside, and my mind immediately changes. To my left is the staff parking lot and my car. To my right is the museum's main entrance, where people are already arriving for tonight's party.

I immediately recognize the blonde standing to the side as a valet drives away in a red Mercedes. Her hair rolls in artful curls past her shoulders, highlighted against the sleek drape of the black dress. The two older blondes from the art gallery are there as well, already preparing to enter the museum.

Nowhere is there a head of sleek brown hair, but even the possibility of her showing up tonight has me changing my plans.

A silver hatchback hybrid purrs up to the valet next. The uniformed driver opens the door and offers an arm of support to the driver. My heart speeds up a little when I see the heavy black square on a black leather band wrapped around the wrist of the hand that emerges.

One foot appears wearing a strappy sandal, the heel of which is caught on the hem of a green skirt. With more expedience than grace, Emma emerges from the car and sets herself to rights. Beneath her black wrap is a blue and green gown and her brown hair is ensconced in a twisted updo that leaves her face fully visible.

It takes me a few minutes to stash my satchel in the car and return to the museum, swinging by Carl's office to take him up on the offer of a tie. My gray sport coat and pale blue shirt aren't exactly formal, but as I'll be more of a lurker than a true guest, it should be all right.

I don't immediately return to the gallery room where the party is being held. I want to observe Emma again, which means a lot more people need to arrive before I make an appearance.

The party doesn't officially start for another twenty minutes. A half hour after that, I slip into the gallery room through an employee door tucked into a corner.

My gaze immediately tracks to Emma. Her dress is a gradient of blue and green, sleeveless, and elegantly draped. Now that she's standing somewhat still, it doesn't look the least bit awkward, aside from the watch on her wrist. That hand holds a tall, cylindrical glass that she occasionally sips from as she smiles and nods at the people talking to her.

Several models stroll the room in clothing bearing similar shades of blue and green to the ones in Emma's dress. She couldn't possibly be the designer.

No, people seem most interested in talking to the blonde in the black dress. I accept a glass from a passing waiter so that I look the part of a guest, then find a corner to observe from.

The art on the wall is given nothing but a passing glance by the party attendees. That one of my pieces is among those being ignored adds a little salt to the wound.

I sidle around the room, trying to get close enough to Emma that I can hear her conversation but not draw her notice. Does this make me a stalker? We've only met once nearly a month ago. If caught, I'll just pretend I was trying to recall where I know her from.

I wince a little at the duplicity of such a statement, but wasn't I just asking God to prolong the excitement of this new direction for a little while longer? Emma's presence is an answer to prayer.

When I get within hearing distance, Emma is talking to an older woman with an abundance of sparkling jewelry, in addition to a sparkling dress. If those gemstones are real, the security guard in the far corner might be here for her as much as he is for protecting the art.

"She's an utter genius." The woman raises her glass in a toast and Emma copies the movement with a tight smile on her face. "I always knew she was going to accomplish great things."

Emma seems to frown a little at this, but she covers it with a sip of what I strongly suspect is water.

"I've been visiting the boutique for years, you know. When Amethyst started offering stylist services and custom designs it took a fabulous store to an exceptional one."

The woman stops smiling indulgently at the blonde across the room and turns a critical eye toward Emma. "Is this one of the early designs? It looks similar to the one I was admiring earlier, but it doesn't have the pretty sleeves."

"Amy made this one just for me." Emma's smile is almost wooden now, and her gaze isn't focusing on the other lady.

"You should have had her add the sleeves. It looks better."

I search the room for a model wearing the dress the woman is referring to. Once I find it, I have to admit the light tiers of fluttering fabric that make the sleeves bring an impressive addition to the look, but it doesn't stop me from wanting to come to Emma's defense.

"The official design with the sleeves will be available in the boutique next week."

The only reason I know its Emma's voice is that it matches the movements being made by her lips. She doesn't sound at all like the charming woman I talked to in a breakroom a month ago.

Is there a way to paint sound? Could I represent such a change visually?

"Your mother tells me you are going to be joining the boutique soon."

The wooden expression on Emma's face gives way to wide-eyed panic as she chokes on the sip she just took.

Her free hand slaps three times against her chest and the older woman takes a half step back in alarm.

"I'm sorry." Emma gives that tight smile again but with her eyes still wide, it looks somewhat manic. "What did my mother say?"

"It was after they had that social media scheduling issue last week. She said you were going to be coming in as their technical support since you worked with computers. Might as well keep it in the family."

Emma blinks three times. "But I'm a programmer."

The older woman frowns. "That's not with computers?"

"Yes, but, um, will you excuse me? I need to find my mother."

I'm not certain what Emma's thinking—I'm not even certain Emma knows what she's thinking—but she presses the glass of water into the other woman's hand and moves to cross the room.

The woman looks at the water in complete befuddlement until a passing server takes it from her and offers a partially filled flute of champagne instead.

My lips curve into a smile as I watch Emma move across the room. She isn't strolling or gliding like most of the other occupants. Nor is she striding with great strength and purpose, though I think that might be the fault of the shoes. Her walk is a little unsteady—again, the shoes—and somewhat hesitant as if she's trying to hurry without looking like she's hurrying.

She stops near where the group of people have congregated around the blonde but doesn't infiltrate the cluster. Instead, she stares at a nearby painting.

I shift until I can see the side of her face. She isn't just biding her time until she can break into the conversation. The view has completely captured her attention.

I can't handle not knowing what she's thinking right now.

Because the painting she finds enthralling is one of mine.

## 5

**EMMA**

As I wait patiently for my mother to be available so I can try—again—to convince her that doing IT support for her small business isn't a fulfilling job or even a full-time one and certainly not what I spent years of my life studying to do, I stare at the nearest painting.

It's of a jail cell, the kind with old, rusted metal bars that can only be seen now in pirate movies and Revolutionary war documentaries. The reality of it is disturbing. Part of my brain is convinced that if I were to reach beyond the velvet cording and drag a finger across one of the bars, slight flakes of rust would fall to the floor.

A tightness crosses my chest as I stare. From where I'm standing, I feel as if I am the one trapped in the cell. The door covers the large vertical canvas, forcing me to examine everything through the confining bars. A large padlock is holding the door shut but all I can see is the back of it. In the distance, beyond the shadowy depths of other cells and a jailer's table strewn with the remains of a dinner the cell's inhabitant will never see, is a glimmer of sunlight on a rough set of stone stairs.

The relatability of the image is unsettling. I'm not in some sort of cell, even if the custom couture dress reminds me of a torture device. My life is a carefully managed set of relationships, yes, but it's created that way on purpose. No one trapped me into it.

I tear my gaze away from the painting and step into my mother's peripheral vision so I can grab a moment of her attention.

"You know I'll need a different skirt with it though," the woman beside Mother is saying in a gravely serious tone.

Mother nods along solemnly as if they were discussing a medical diagnosis instead of a dress.

The woman's eyes grow wide. "I tried to look at some of your past customizations, but the gallery wouldn't load on the website."

Oh no. I know where this conversation is going next, and I want no part of it. I step back, intending to flee to the food table, the bathroom, maybe even a lockable closet. I'm not fast enough, though, because Mother turns to me and places a hand on my arm.

In another twenty years or so, this is what Amy is going to look like—wide smile, perfectly coiffed blond hair, just enough wrinkles left untouched to appear like she isn't trying too hard.

"Darling, Melinda here was just telling me our website doesn't seem to be loading properly."

This is what I came over here to talk to Mother about, but doing so in front of this stranger doesn't feel appropriate. My lips press into a slight frown that I hope looks appropriately commiserating. "Sounds like you should contact customer support."

Mother's eyes widen. "But it's Friday! While I'm certain everyone is going to flock to the boutique Monday to scoop up Amethyst's designs, we have many customers that are going to want custom variations and we want them to inquire while this event is fresh in their minds." She looks me up and down. "Did Scott get a good picture of you tonight? We'll definitely want to include this one in the gallery."

"Yes, I've been appropriately photographed." At least, I smiled at a man with a monster of a camera earlier.

"Excellent." Mother clasps her hands together. "So you'll take a look at the website this weekend?"

Ever since Amy convinced Mother and Aunt Jade to expand the boutique's virtual presence, they've been after me to come work for the boutique. Creating code for virtual, augmented, and mixed reality experiences is far more interesting to me than making sure their website is user-error-proof.

Not to mention the stress that would come with seeing my family day in and day out. Somehow, I don't think they'd accept my preferred daily attire of leggings and oversized hoodies or the general vibe of chaos I create while I work.

"Your website company has 24/7 support," I remind her. I'd made sure of it when I helped them select it. "You just enter a ticket on their website, and they'll get right on it."

Mother frowns. "I don't have to call?"

"Not unless you have a hankering for hold music."

Mother looks like she's about to make another argument for my coming into the fold. It's not happening. I love my mother, but I long ago accepted my fate as the disappointing twin. "I'm going to see how Amy is doing," I announce before spinning away, intent on escaping to my sister's side.

Except she's a mere four steps away, clearly having been caught by someone on her way to join Mother's and my conversation. As I step over to her, the wrinkles of tension forming at the edge of her smile come into view. I reach out and grasp her fingers, giving them two short squeezes and one long one. Her shoulders lower a little.

She wraps up her conversation and turns to me, her free hand joining our already clasped ones. "I think it's going well. Do you think it's going well?"

I don't know what to say, as tonight is supposed to be a celebration, not a critique. "I . . . yes?" People seem happy, so that means it's a successful party, right?

She looks me up and down before giving a sharp nod. "I was right to change the color for you. This is absolutely your shade. I'll need to remember that on our birthday."

I make a non-committal grunt. The green is pretty enough, and, objectively speaking, this is a nice dress.

It's just not for me.

Mother and Aunt Jade join us and for a moment, it's just my family, the way it's been my whole life. My father had been long gone from Mother's life when she discovered our existence and was more than happy to provide a check while Mother moved in with her sister.

With Amy being the woman of the hour, our familial solitude doesn't last long.

"Congratulations," an older man says as he steps into our loose gathering. "The gowns are works of art unto themselves."

"Thank you." Amy's gracious society smile is far warmer than mine. That might be because she means it. "And thank you for letting us use this space. I just love the McGrary Museum."

"Of course." Everyone looks around the room as if we haven't been staring at the same paintings and people for the last two hours.

I go to sip my water, but my hand is empty. Where did I put my glass?

"You'll have to return in a few months." He leans in and whispers, even though he is obviously excited. "We're in the process of soliciting pitches for a new self-guided tour system and the selected prototypes will do a small test run in this very gallery."

"Oh really?" Aunt Jade turns to me. "That should be interesting for you, Emma."

"Mmm." I don't give a committal response even though my mind is churning. How had I not heard about this? My boss and best friend

Jason has been wanting to expand into the educational realm. This isn't a school, but the idea would be the same.

His sincere gaze swings my way. "Are you interested in the blend of art and technology?" The man chuckles. "I admit our board is struggling a little with the concept, but modern times and all that."

"You should give him some ideas," Amy says.

"Or have your boss contact him." Mother places a hand on my arm. "Do you need Mr. Leonard's card?" She looks to the man. "Emerald just does the manufacturing part. She's not one of the creative design people."

It isn't anything I haven't heard dozens of times before. My family equates being a programmer with being the stitcher who puts Amy's clothing designs together. Usually, I can pretend it doesn't bother me, but this time, possibly because this could be a good contact for my company, I can't let it slide.

"I design solutions," I say. Because I do. The aesthetic design of a program only matters if the underlying code is functional. The design team tells me what they want, and I figure out how to make it happen.

It would be more along the lines of Amy saying she wants a shirt with giant sleeves that won't deflate and someone else having to figure out how to make that possible.

"Are the specs for the project still available?" I ask.

I'm expecting a business card, a website, or maybe even instructions to call the office on Monday.

Instead, I get my mother's fingers wrapped around my arm until the pressure threatens to cut off my circulation. "Oh, darling, congratulations on your promotion."

"I . . . what?" I look to the other people in the circle, hoping they can make sense of Mother's statement.

Aunt Jade and Amy have looks of equal excitement, though.

"You didn't have to save that announcement," Amy says with a wide smile. "It's always fun to share the spotlight with my twin."

"We should make another toast. Let everyone know we're celebrating a promotion in the family as well." Aunt Jade presses a hand to her chest. "You're a designer now. I knew you had it in you. Blood will tell, after all."

Oh no.

"It's not like that," I say, trying to laugh it off.

"Nonsense." Mother turns to Mr. Leonard. "Emerald will be able to create the perfect design for you. I've immersed her in the creative world since she was a child. She's a true lover of the arts."

Apparently, I'm a better actress than Amy was in high school.

Mr. Crawford slides his hand into his pocket, pulls out a card, and extends it. "We're not officially accepting applications anymore, but your mother has been a longtime patron of this museum, and I trust her eye. If she says we need to hear from you, I'll slip your name onto the list."

Accepting the card is the only option, so I take it in my fingers. The paper is thick with raised print. I rub my thumb over it as I swallow and desperately search for a way out of this. "My company would love to send a team in—"

"Now, Emerald." Mother's hand is on my arm again, this time in a firm press that is probably meant to be reassuring. "Don't go doubting your abilities just because you're new to the design team. This is your chance to really show your boss you know what you're doing."

"We have plenty of other options if you don't want to join them." Mr. Leonard's smile is easy. He really doesn't seem to care one way or the other, which means the only way Digital World Solutions is getting its foot in the door is through me.

"Of course," I say, even though that doesn't really make sense in the flow of the conversation. "I mean, yes, thank you."

Mother is nearly beside herself with glee. "I'm so proud of you, darling."

Amy's hand lands on my shoulder and gives it three squeezes. Two short, one long.

"We should celebrate," Aunt Jade says, "maybe get you a new pant suit. We've got some lovely ones in the boutique this season."

"I'll make you one custom for the presentation," Amy adds with a small smile.

Mr. Leonard pulls out his phone. "Emerald, is it? I've added you to the docket." He angles his phone to show me the email. It instructs the receiver to add my name, not the company's, to the list.

He grins at mother. "Opal, you Trinket ladies really are jewels." His smile turns to me. "Emerald Trinket is a beautiful name."

Only if you've never had to hear the snickers at the doctor's office or had the DMV accuse you of trying to pull a prank.

"Are these board meetings open to patrons, by any chance?" Mother leans forward as if she's being conspiratorial.

I almost fall over as my eyes widen. She wants to come and watch?

This is too much. I make my excuses, congratulate Amy one more time, and make my way to the exit. As I leave behind the buzz of the gallery, I breathe a small sigh of relief. A few people are scattered through the foyer, putting on coats and waiting for cars. I join the line to retrieve my belongings from the coat check.

"Your hour is up, I take it?"

I turn to find Carter, the man from the museum, behind me. He looks out of a place, like a memory that has somehow worked its way into a dream and thrown everything off.

Finally, I manage a small wave. "Hi."

He looks over his shoulder at the gallery. "Anything tonight more to your taste?"

"Um, my sister."

It's his turn to look at a loss for words. I leave him to grapple for the thread of conversation as I accept my coat and bag from the girl working the counter and step to the side to extract my phone and valet ticket.

He steps away from the line and joins me without handing over a ticket.

I look from him to the claim counter. "You don't have a coat?"

"It's back in the office." He jabs a thumb over his shoulder toward a door behind the claim counter that says *No Public Admittance.*

I can't help my smile. "You must really love art."

"One could say I've built my life around it." His returning smile has an underlying emotion to it that I want to stop and explore, but my tangle of thoughts and feelings is taking up too much headspace.

Still, I can't bring myself to walk away from him. "You work here, too, then?"

His head gives a wobble that isn't a nod and isn't a shake. "Sort of. It's a part-time thing. Almost more of a volunteer position."

I try to imagine coming here, spending my free time here, devoting hours to whatever it is people do to care for the art in museums. A shudder runs up my spine, and I try to mask it by shrugging into my wrap. Seriously. Who decided that women in confining formal clothing should also tangle with a long piece of cloth when it's cold instead of wearing a proper, securable jacket?

He laughs as he plucks the valet ticket from my hand and nods toward the door. "Obviously, the museum's art isn't more to your taste than the art gallery's. You don't have to stay in here on my account."

I wince as I follow him to the door. He gives the valet my ticket and shoves his hands into his pockets.

He nods toward the museum. "Your sister brought you tonight? She was the one who dragged you out to see Richie, wasn't she?"

I can't help but frown at the mention of Richie. He has yet to make an appearance tonight, despite this being as much of an achievement for

Amy as his gallery opening had been for him. "You know how it goes. Family."

A more weighted statement has never been uttered.

"Was tonight better, at least? Any art you actually liked?"

The heavy presence of the locked cell door flashes through my mind again, but that had been more disturbing than appealing. I gave my head a small shake. "I'm afraid places like this just aren't my cup of tea."

They're going to have to be though, as I just got signed up to present a pitch for a job here. Maybe there's a way out of that one without making my family even more disappointed in me.

Carter looks at me for a long moment, seeming to study me. His gaze drops to my shoulder and one side of his mouth kicks up as the valet pulls up in my silver hatchback hybrid.

I glance down. It would seem this wrap is actually more of a very flimsy sweater type-thing and I've draped it over myself in a way that leaves the sleeve dangling down my back. Lovely.

"Well," I say as I awkwardly sidestep to the driver's door. "See you around."

"Not unless your sister and I keep having the same taste."

How true. And sad. Because I have to say it was nice to lay eyes on Carter again.

"Right. Well. I guess this is goodbye then." I give a little wave and slide into my car.

I drive away from the McGrary Museum just outside the Benson suburb I grew up in. Usually, my breathing would get easier as I make the twenty-minute drive to Eastborne, but tonight, the tight constriction in my chest grows. What am I going to do about this mess? My family thinks I'm a designer. The museum thinks I'm pitching an enhanced tour guide system, and Carter, well, Carter isn't expecting anything because I have once again confirmed my complete lack of interest in that which he holds most dear.

My clothes, which have been irritating since I put them on, seem to scrape at my skin as I climb the steps to my apartment and press my thumb to the sensor on my doorknob.

As soon as I'm inside, I shed the formal dress and shake the constricting feeling from my skin, but it does nothing to ease the feeling of dread. Even my coziest hoodie and comfiest yoga pants can't do the trick.

I shove my Bluetooth earpiece into position and press the call connect icon on my phone before flopping down on my couch.

"I hope you're calling to tell me you had a miserable time since you canceled game night."

My best friend Jason's voice is jovial as he doesn't actually mean what he's saying, but I dearly wish I'd been playing Settlers of Catan tonight instead of digging myself into a hole.

"Yeah, so I may have gotten put on the schedule to present a pitch to the McGrady Museum tonight."

There's silence for a moment, and then a burst of laughter fills my ear.

"Ugh." I grab a throw pillow shaped like a game console controller and smash it against my face.

"What happened?" Jason asks, still chuckling.

I give him the basic rundown of the night, leaving out Carter, the dress, and even the reason for my being at an event with the head curator of the museum, because Jason doesn't know me as a girl who wrestles herself into designer duds and goes to places frequented by those in the upper echelons of society.

"So I think they're expecting a pitch from me in a month or so."

"Just tell them you can't. Seriously, if they didn't come to us directly, they won't care one way or the other if we don't pitch. Our solutions probably aren't what they have in mind."

"Hey." I jerk into a sitting position on my couch. "Our solutions are amazing."

"They aren't sophisticated."

"Yes, they are."

"Em. What were you working on earlier this week?"

I roll my eyes because I know exactly what he's referring to. "I was figuring out how to make dancing bottles of ketchup not fall off the edge of a table when people use an interactive menu."

"Mmhmm. Classy."

I roll my eyes. "You're the one who accepted the commission."

"Not-classy money spends the same as the classy stuff."

"Yeah, well, my family expects me to at least pitch this museum project."

He snorts out a laugh. "Why? You aren't in design or sales or even project management."

I stay silent. While Jason knows I have a, shall we say, tumultuous relationship with my family, he doesn't know the details. We've been best friends for eight years and he's never once met my sister. In fact, Amy sometimes claims I've made him up.

I don't know how to admit my family's misconception of my impossible promotion without telling Jason everything I've never wanted to share. "It's important to my family. My mother sort of called in a favor."

He sighs. "You know I'd do anything for you, Em, but we can't. Even our long shot pitches got picked up this year. No one has the bandwidth to add another project to their plate without working a serious amount of overtime."

He's right. I know he's right. Even my own workload is tight.

We keep the call connected as we log on to *Wizard's World 3*, but I'm clearly distracted. When I accidentally build a well over a stream of underground lava and burn an entire section of corn crops to ash, I make the excuse of being tired and tell him I'll see him Sunday.

As I crawl into bed, only half-heartedly trying to detangle the mess of covers I'd abandoned that morning, I debate ways to break the truth to my family without disappointing them.

There isn't one. I don't have to land the bid, but I can't allow Mr. Leonard to tell my mother I never showed.

Somewhere in the vicinity of two AM the only option becomes clear.

Jason can't ask anyone to put in the overtime to do this project, but he won't stop me from doing it myself.

I need to become a designer.

I work on the presentation in my spare time over the next three weeks. When Jason figures out what I'm doing, he comes to my apartment specifically to yell at me.

He also brought me a pizza, though, and didn't expressly forbid me from doing it.

Working on it makes me think of my interactions with Carter, though. The way he saw people and art as different objects and how he phrased the importance of art make their way into my proposal.

So does my frustration with the many museums I had to suffer through as a child. When I consider I could save some other poor soul from that, it makes me want to suggest a really good solution.

I reassure Amy several times that one of the pantsuits she already brought me is perfect for the occasion. Mostly I don't have a spare two days to prep my apartment for a familial invasion.

As I step into the meeting room at the museum, I start to think that I've given Carter too much space in my brain, because I'm imagining him sitting in the back left corner of the room in the second row of tables, facing the podium and presentation screen.

I nearly stumble sideways on the shoes Amy insisted were the lowest heels available as I meet Carter's gaze.

The man giving me a narrow-eyed frown isn't a figment of my imagination.

No matter how much I told myself that all that mattered with this proposal was showing up, part of me has held on to the slim possibility that I could actually impress my family with it.

I don't think that's going to be happening because sitting amongst the decision makers who could allow that to happen is a man who already knows I'm a fraud.

## CARTER

Ten minutes ago, I'd been fixing myself a cup of coffee and telling myself I could make it through one more presentation. Now, my coffee is growing cold, and my mind isn't thinking of ways to steer the board to one of the less invasive proposals because Emma is here.

Encountering her once was a coincidence, twice was a gift, and the third time in as many months could be nothing short of a miracle.

Emerald Trinket, according to the info sheet on the table in front of me. Emma suits her better.

I flip through the brief and a frown pulls at my face even as a side of me wants to smile. Of course she wouldn't blend in with the other presentations I've endured this week. Unfortunately, she isn't standing out in a good way.

Objectively, she's giving the worst presentation. Her ideas are somewhat disjointed and I'm getting lost in technical specs that none of us would ever need to know. While her concept for the museum's new self-guided tour system is one of the most unique and interesting brought before the board, it's also the most intrusive when it comes to technology.

I want to hate it.

I *do* hate it.

But I remain fascinated by the intriguing bundle of contradictions she continues to be. If I hadn't met her at the gallery and seen her body language for myself and heard her own confession of her feelings about art, I would think she was a passionate aesthete.

Since I know differently, I have to assume it's the technology inspiring her enthusiasm instead of the art.

She has no qualms about encouraging people to pull out their phones while strolling the museum, providing reasons for them to look at a screen instead of study a canvas, and feeding them ideas and information instead of guiding them down avenues of emotional discovery.

I glance around at the board members. Do they find this idea appealing? My voice isn't a vote, but they respect it. Some of these people have known me since I was a child lurking in the galleries. As a consultant, I represent the people who toiled over the art exhibited on the museum's walls.

In good conscious, I can't let this become how those toils are experienced.

Emma's final slide portrays a smiling family with headphones in their ears, holding their phones pointed at a famous painting. It's not a painting from this museum, though another piece from the same artist hangs in the section of gallery chosen to test the prototypes. A cartoon version of Van Gogh is supposedly telling the family about the painting, which is ridiculous because he didn't paint the thing.

They might as well be watching a video online.

Some of the board members look interested, though. Probably because it's fresh and modern and might appeal to teens and twenty-somethings.

It makes my skin crawl.

But if I trash it, if I convince the board not to include it as one of the three proposals that will receive a grant to produce a prototype, there's a good chance this will be the last time I see Emma. Of all the chance meetings I've been granted, this is the first time I have the ability to prolong the connection.

I shuffle a few papers on the desk in front of me, pretending I'm looking at the spec sheet she provided us at the beginning of her presentation. What I really pull out, though, is my sketchbook.

After almost two months of knowing Emma, even in a limited capacity, more than two dozen pages have been covered with at least a partial drawing of some contradictory woman. There's a girl lounging in the library while scrolling on her phone, a woman staring up at the sky and letting the rain hit her face while everyone around her huddles under umbrellas, and a teenager lit by a flashlight and sitting in her bed in a cabin full of bunk beds while others sleep in the shadows.

I don't know how many of the drawings will eventually become paintings, but the plethora of options reminds me of when I first started out. I strolled the streets of New York's Upper West Side, wondering which high-rise apartments might one day have my art hanging on the wall.

If I trash her proposal, I might never see her again, and I'll have to survive on whatever ideas she's already inspired. On the other hand, if I suggest she remain in the running, I will be toying with her career for my own personal gain and possibly prevent a better idea from being fully realized.

A smattering of polite appreciations brings my attention back to the presentation and the woman now packing up her laptop.

"Thank you for your time. We look forward to hearing from you." Her eyes seem to purposefully flit away from my corner, as if she's pretending I'm not in the room.

The moment she exits, an intense desire to follow her pulls me half out of my seat, providing the solution to my ethical dilemma.

I stand to my full height and gather my papers and sketchbook into my leather satchel.

"Are you leaving, Carter? We thought we'd take a preliminary poll on which projects we should move forward with." Grace, the chairperson of the museum board, holds up the packet of information sheets for the different proposals.

"I believe my input is better saved for the final decision." I nod to the papers in her hand. "This narrowing of choices is more a matter of vision for the museum's direction than artistic respect and inclusion."

I'd originally intended to do the opposite and limit the three choices to ones I could live with, but I can no longer trust my ability to be objective. I can't decide between prolonging my exposure to Emma or ensuring she doesn't infiltrate the museum with screens and lights.

So I will leave it in God's hands.

If that means I get to leave this room and try to catch Emma before she leaves, all the better. I'll get one more interaction in addition to a clear conscience.

I sling my satchel strap over my shoulder and give the rest of the board a respectful nod as I head to the door.

Emma is in the testing gallery, sitting on one of the benches that run down the middle of the room when it isn't set up for an event. Her finger glides all over the screen of her phone. Is she playing a game?

I step closer and see she's sending a text message but instead of thumbing it out like a normal person, she's dragging her finger rapidly around to the letters of the various words and somehow sentences are forming.

The view is almost enough to send me back into that boardroom. It's agonizing to see her bent over her phone instead of ruminating over the potential feelings and lives and personalities of the various dancers in the Edgar Degas painting in front of her.

I sit next to her and slide my satchel to the floor between my feet, considering the painted dancers while I wait for her to look up. At this moment I feel connected to the ballerina collapsed on a bench and leaning her head against a wall. The strokes aren't defined enough to allow me to see whether she is exhausted, exasperated, or in despair, but it doesn't matter. I feel elements of all those emotions right now.

She finishes her text and presses a button to turn off the screen before pressing the phone between her hands and turning to me. "I wondered if I'd see you today, but I didn't think it would be in there."

I can't help a small grin. "The surprise is mutual."

"That's your practically volunteer position?"

Does she still not know who I am? If not, I'm not going to be the one to tell her. "I'm a consultant."

"So you don't have a say in whether or not I get accepted?"

"I don't have a vote, no." I narrow my eyes at her phrasing. Just as a painter's chosen lighting changes the depicted scene, so can single words change the meaning of a sentence. "And they're deciding on whether or not to accept your proposal, not you."

One of her shoulders lifts and falls. "Semantics."

"This means a lot to you?"

She presses her lips together before blowing a long sigh out between them. "More than I thought it would."

"Why?"

She frowns at me. "It's my job. I want to be good at it."

"But you're going to have to look at something you hate all day."

A large wince scrunches up her face. "Please tell me you didn't impart that nugget of insider knowledge to the rest of them."

I can't help but laugh. "No, I didn't."

"Thank you." She slides the phone into the pocket of her bag, a large nylon backpack with rubber and plastic pieces lending added structure and decoration. After slapping her hands atop her thighs, she shifts as if about to push herself into a standing position.

"I'm curious." I prop my elbows on my knees and lean forward, hoping she'll see how truly curious I am. "Why would someone who hates art want to spend months of her life working on a project for an art museum?"

She doesn't answer right away. Does she even know why she did it? Was it mere obligation? Something assigned to her by work? If so, she's a better actor than I'd thought. Her passion for the idea had been evident, possibly even strong enough to get the board to overlook the poor presentation.

Finally, she nods to a group of people on the other side of the room. "Them."

It's a family, or perhaps a small school group. Two adults are animatedly discussing the painting before them with hand gestures and quiet tones. Three young teenagers surround them. One girl is looking at the painting across the room with wide eyes and a thoughtful expression, another is trying to copy the positions of the softly depicted people, while the third is standing with her arms crossed, a blank expression on her face as she stares at seemingly nothing.

"You think she hates art?" I ask.

"In about fifteen years she will."

"Or she could learn to appreciate it."

Emma shakes her head. "Not unless someone gives her a reason to."

"Are you that someone?" It's a novel idea, really, that someone would want to save others from disliking something they themselves detest.

She puffs out a determined sigh as she shifts her position to better face me. Once again, Emma doesn't take the turn I expect. "My family likes to go to the theater."

My breath stalls in my lungs. Is she about to tell me she doesn't like the theater either? Does hating all art really pertain to *all* art? "And you don't care for it?"

"Not most of it, no. But I have learned a way to enjoy some shows."

I shift sideways on the bench, bending one knee and bringing it up to the polished wood surface so I can fully face her. In this moment, I have to admit that she is the most fascinating exhibit in the room. "Which is your favorite?"

"*Frozen.*" There is not an ounce of hesitation in her statement.

"The one about the ice queen?" I try to keep my voice neutral, but there is an element of incredulity I can't quite hide.

She nods. "I like seeing how they change the sets and the special effects. There's a magnetic floor and on-stage costume changes. The mechanics of the puppetry is amazing."

Is my growing sense of horror showing on my face? I can hear it in the flatness of my voice as I say, "You like the mechanics."

"Yes. When I went to see *Phantom of the Opera,* I considered how to make the chandelier fall and the mirror wall turn and such, but those are fairly easy to comprehend." She gives a shrug, and a proud little smile touches her lips. "Still, it made the evening better."

I swallow. Hard. This is worse than I feared. I should have stayed in that room, but beyond the door I can see Grace, Carl, and the other board members starting to file out. It's too late to go back. "So, your idea for a self-guided tour is to show people . . ."

"The other elements of the painting. Did they use brushes or those pastel crayons? Is there a reason the artist used that particular size of canvas?"

"That would steal away the magic." I shift so that I'm facing the painting once more. "Are you honestly telling me that knowing Degas used oils for this particular canvas makes the ballerinas more relatable to you?"

"No." She, too, turns to face the painting. "But it makes me less bored looking at it. It makes me wonder. Do oils take longer to dry than whatever the other types of paint are? Water-based, I'm assuming."

I shake my head, pick up my bag, and stand. "You, Emma Trinket, are a conundrum."

She stands as well, throwing the strap of her backpack over one shoulder, catching the lapel of her pantsuit's jacket and bunching one side of it under her arm. Her lip is stuck between her teeth as she looks toward the room the board recently exited. "I know you aren't voting, but you saw all the presentations. Do you think they'll pick mine?"

I want to say something hopeful and comforting, but I'm still reeling from the full understanding of what she thinks enhances the viewing of a painting. "I hope not."

She blinks at me. "Well. I always thought I appreciated honesty in a man, but that was a little blunt."

I shake my head as I walk past her toward the exit. "Unless you learn to appreciate what's actually on the canvas, whatever you create will obscure the experience, not enhance it."

She falls into step beside me. "What makes you think I don't?"

"You hate art."

"People who hate art go to museums."

"And people who hate fish go to seafood restaurants. That's why they put chicken tenders on the menu, but it's still a fish on the sign."

She stumbles. "That's an odd analogy."

"But an apt one." Seafood is one of my least favorite foods. I know where to locate the chicken on the menu at any seafood restaurant, and it is never in a prime location. "You can't tailor the tour for non-art lovers. They need to find their own reasons for coming."

I look back at the Degas painting. Even though I've chosen to play with the nuance of detail in my hyperrealism, I appreciate the soft lines of the art, the way the indistinct edges leave room for interpretation.

That I might have selfishly done these works a disservice by not speaking up about knowing Emma is not the right designer for the job makes my stomach tighten and my chest ache. My only consolation is that even if the board chooses her, there will be two other options to consider.

Part of me wants to dig the sketchbook out of my bag and drop it in the trash can on my way through the lobby, but I won't. Those sketches were inspired from encounters that were meant to be. If I'd been where I was supposed to be, this conversation would never have happened.

After forcing this meeting, anything I else I draw about her will be tainted. Yet the ideas keep flowing and my fingers itch for a pencil.

Whether she knows it or not, she's given me a gift of a fresh perspective on my work. Even if I evidently need to keep her at a bit of a distance to hold on to that gift, it's possible I can return the favor.

"I get it. Charity galas and fancy dinners are dreadfully boring to me, but I go. I'm going to one this weekend, as a matter of fact. It's a necessary evil for my career, but I make it work by being selective about the causes. I can be bored for an evening if it means more children gain access to eyeglasses and hearing aids. It's up to me and not the event organizer to make it palatable."

I can't look at Emma without getting a sense that she's desperately searching for something. Validation? A purpose? Belonging? Whatever it is, I won't sacrifice the way this art impacts future museum visitors for her to find it.

I take two steps and then turn around. "It was nice to meet you, Emma. I hope you find what you're looking for."

7

*EMMA*

"Did you pay them off? Offer to reprogram their home automation systems? Promise to name your first-born child Monet?" Jason swivels his monitor so I can see the slides from my presentation to the museum board. "Because there is no way anyone saw this presentation and legitimately said, 'That's what I want.'"

I slide my backpack off my shoulder and drop it to the floor before sinking into the large armchair in front of Jason's desk. A cheek-hurting grin is trying to break out, but I have to make sure I'm hearing him correctly first. "They said yes? We got the funding for the prototype?"

Jason sits back in his large ergonomic executive desk chair and runs a hand over his face. "Yes. I got the email this morning. You have to tell me how you did it."

I slide my feet from my Crocs and push up on the arms of the chair so I can pull my feet in and sit crisscross applesauce. My black leggings stretch to accommodate but I take a moment to adjust the way my phone is sitting in the pocket along the outside of my thigh.

They said yes. My design got approved. I can't believe it.

There is no holding back my squeal of excitement and my arms pump in the air to accentuate my joy. Somewhere along the way—possibly in the late hours of the evening when I was imagining what my experience might have been like if I'd had something like this when I'd been dragged through a museum—this project had begun to matter to me.

"Try to remember this is a place of business." Jason's tone is dry but he, too, is grinning.

"Try to remember you're my best friend before you're my boss and celebrate this win."

He rolls his eyes and gives a half-hearted "woo" as one hand flaps in the air above his head. "Seriously." He points at the screen. "Is this what you presented or is there an updated set of slides on your computer?"

I frown at the screen. "What's wrong with the slides?"

He clicks back a few slides in the deck. "You gave them the minimum specs for a phone that can handle our augmented reality software."

"That's important to know." I shove my hands into the pocket of my pullover hoodie. "This needs to work with phones that are several years old. We can't rely on everyone having top-of-the-line new tech in their pockets."

"That's why we tell clients this." He hits a few keys and pulls up a presentation from the design team for a pitch to a car show from a few months ago. There are several models of older phones on the screen with a banner that reads *Compatible with most common phones.*

Waving my hand at the screen, I say, "That is not very specific."

"That is all the customer cares about."

I huddle deeper into my hoodie. Would it be bad form to pull up the hood and tighten the strings? They chose the project, so how bad could it really be? "Is it really that rough?"

"As your boss, let me say I'm not concerned about losing my best developer to the design team." Jason's face softens, and he leans forward to put his elbows on the desk. "As your friend, I have to ask, what possessed you to insist on this? You're too young to have a midlife crisis and too good at what you do to have imposter syndrome or whatever else makes people think they can't do their job."

"First off, imposter syndrome doesn't consider actual qualifications, affects more than half of the professional respondents in most studies, and occurs more frequently in women."

Jason smirks as he picks up a pen to twirl through his fingers. "Did you hear that on a podcast?"

"That's not the point."

"Why are you doing this, Ems? You've been on edge ever since you brought this to me, insisting you could make it work."

I slide deeper into the chair. "This is why you called me in today, isn't it?"

Jason hates online meetings and makes me come into the office if our conversation is going to take more than five minutes. Letting me know my project is moving forward could have been done via email.

"You didn't even pick out your own living room furniture. You had my mother do it."

"Your mother is an interior designer."

He rolls his eyes. "Only so she can get into the wholesale warehouses and get discounts for herself and her friends when they go shopping."

I stop fidgeting and tilt my head to inspect Jason and gauge how serious he is. "Really? But she has a business card and everything."

"Her client list could double as her Christmas card list."

"Huh. That's actually rather ingenious."

"And not the point."

I weave my fingers together inside the cozy hoodie pocket. "What is the point?" I nod at the screen. "Because you said we couldn't spare anyone right now and I have a lot of work to do."

"We *can't* spare anyone. Every designer, tester, and programmer—including you—is fully booked. At least with this funding, I can afford to pay you a bonus for the overtime you're insisting on."

"I can keep up with my responsibilities." Despite a few late nights, I'd been surprised at how few additional hours I'd had to add to my workday to work on the museum presentation.

"You canceled the last two game nights."

"The first one was a family obligation, not a work one." That had been the night of Amy's party, the night this entire museum business had started, the night I'd left my encounter with Carter a little sad that he hadn't asked for my number. As opposed to our parting at the museum earlier this week, where I was certain he was going to call the board and ensure I never saw the inside of the building again.

"Yet that's the night you landed this museum pitch."

"You're always saying half of business success is networking."

"For me and the sales team, yes." He clicks through to another slide that indicates ways augmented reality solutions could tap into the emotional center of the brain, thereby increasing the chances of a patron having a resonating response to the artwork.

I wince as I take in the slide. Did Carter recognize his own words? Probably not, seeing as I accompanied them with a picture of a person on their phone layered over a gallery wall. It looks like she's turned her back on the paintings.

"And where did this come from?" Jason waves a hand at the screen. "It doesn't sound like you."

"I can be emotional." I slump back in the chair. "If I wasn't, I wouldn't have foolishly taken on this project."

His eyebrows wing upward at my use of the word *foolishly*. "We can turn this down, you know. They'll move on to their next choice without a thought."

I know how much Jason has been wanting to get into this market. I know that's why he didn't push back too hard when I told him I was going to do it anyway.

When he pulls up the screen showing everyone's workload and project assignments, I also know he's trying to figure out a way to let me off the hook, but still keep the job.

I can't let him take it from me. Not just because it isn't fair to anyone else on the team, but because I need to prove something to my family and maybe to myself as well.

I wave a hand at the screen. "I'm supposed to be emotional about art. That's the point." I have to tread carefully here, since all Jason knows about my family is that they exist. For the most part, my work life, friend life, and family life are very nicely compartmentalized. Yes, Jason has a foot in both the friend and work boxes, but that's the only two feet he has. He can't be allowed to step into the family one, or the boundaries will break.

He's going to keep poking until he gets something, though, so I blurt out, "There was a chicken."

"A chicken."

"In an abstract frying pan."

"What?"

"I went to an art gallery a couple of months ago. It was very inspiring."

"I'm so confused."

I grab the arms of the chair and wriggle and jump until it scoots closer to the desk, and I can reach the wireless keyboard and remote. A click here and a search there and the gallery page featuring the works of Richie Reynolds is on the screen. I scroll down until I find the image of a brown chicken beneath swaths of black paint.

Jason squints at the screen. "That's supposed to be a frying pan?" He reaches for the mouse and starts taking in all the other mind-boggling combinations. "Why in the world did you voluntarily go look at these things?"

"My sister is dating the artist." My nose scrunches into a wince, and I pretend to examine my fingernails to disguise it. The last thing this conversation needs is more family interference.

I'm not sure what I thought going back to that night would convey, but if it was a hope that Richie's art would sufficiently distract Jason, that idea dies as he returns to twirling his pen and considering me like a fly on the wall.

This is what happens when you meet a man at a college gaming event, discover you have all the things in common, try to date only to find neither of you can drive the relationship out of the friend zone, and settle into living life practically joined at the hip with the exception of hiding him from your family and vice versa.

Okay, yes, that is an incredibly specific series of events, but that is the sequence that led to the situation I'm in now.

"Fine." Jason flicks his pen toward the ceramic mug on his desk that holds a highlighter, two pencils, and a replica wand from Harry Potter. It bounces off the rim and lands on the surface of the desk. "You tell me why you're emotionally tied to this project, and I'll tell you why that means we convince Samantha or Paavak to come in on the prototype design."

When I don't say anything, he shoves the mouse and the keyboard to the side, flattens his forearms on the desk, and leans in until he's looking me in the eye. "What's going on, Ems?"

Jason has no idea what my family is like, what I'm like with my family. How do I tell him that I just want them to respect what I do?

Well, I suppose I could just tell him that I want them to respect what I do.

"I want my family to respect what I do."

I just said that sentence multiple times in my head. It was the perfect sentence to encapsulate my current problems. Why, then, does it sound like utter nonsense when I say it out loud?

"That's nonsense." Jason points to the now-blank monitor. "Do they know how many times I've had to give you a raise to keep other companies from head-hunting you?"

"No." I frown. "And you never do that."

"I would if you had any idea how much they'd pay you."

"Oh, I have an idea. It's almost double. But the benefits don't include having my favorite snacks stocked in the break room even though I'm not required to come into the office."

He smiles. "Those are friendship benefits. Not work ones."

"Same difference." I shrug. "I was your first employee, Jason. I'm not abandoning you just because we've grown large enough for the big dogs to take notice."

"All the more reason for me not to let you tank your career by being something you aren't."

"I can design, you know. I had to do all my senior projects in college."

He lifts his eyebrows. He knows my designs got tweaked by other people because half of the time he'd been the one to fix them. "You never talk about your family. I know you've got a sister and they live across town, but other than that, I got the idea you were somewhat estranged."

"Estranged isn't quite the word." I blow a breath out and pull my phone from my pocket. "Actually, it's not the word at all."

I pull up my photos and start showing him pictures of me with Amy, Mom, and Aunt Jade. With every swipe, his confusion grows more and more apparent.

"This is you?" He points at the phone.

"Yes."

"But you're not . . . I mean . . ." He turns the phone so I can see a photo of Amy and myself from Christmas. "What are you wearing?"

I frown, trying to remember what Amy called it. "A cow?"

"Do you mean a cowl? That's the neckline of that shirt, which, I don't know if you realized this or not, shimmers."

I snatch the phone back. "How do you know that?"

"How do you not?" He sits back and points a finger at me. "You're the one wearing it."

"Good thing, because you'd look even sillier in it." I'd hated that shirt. It did indeed shimmer. Also the fabric stuck to my skin, and I was constantly having to battle the extra folds around my neck to keep them lying right.

I look at the picture again. My shirt is green. Amy's is similar but in red. We're standing in front of Mom's gold-and-silver-decorated Christmas tree and showing off the earrings Mom got us.

"I was referring," Jason says, "to what's in your ears. Are they pierced?"

I look up and blink. "Yes?"

He stares back at me for several moments. "Tell me again how you just happened to get this museum opportunity?"

I sigh. "I was at a party."

Normally, the silent treatment doesn't work on me. I can sit and let a conversation die awkwardly with the best of them. But something about the way Jason is looking at me, as if he doesn't know me, makes me open my mouth and start spewing out words.

"Amy was celebrating the launch of her fashion line. The museum guy was there. My mother compared me to a seamstress. They all think I got a promotion, and they finagled me into the presentation to impress you."

Slowly, Jason reaches for my phone, takes my hand, and places my thumb on the sensor to unlock it. He busies himself with something on the screen before sliding the phone back to me.

He's blocked out my calendar for lunch on Sunday.

"Four hours?"

"It's going to take at least that long to unpack any of those statements. Not to mention those pictures." He stands. "I, however, have another meeting in five minutes."

He taps a few times on his own phone. "I forwarded you their acceptance email. I know you know I want this, but . . ." His dark eyes meet mine, and then he sighs and pulls off the baseball cap sitting backward on his head so he can run a hand through his hair. "Are you sure you can do this, Ems?"

I nod because I have to believe I can. "Like you said, I've been doing this for years. Some of that design knowledge has to have rubbed off, right?"

He slaps the hat back onto his head, bill facing forward this time. "All right. You can keep it." He stabs a finger at me. "But log your extra hours. I'll find a way to give you a bonus out of the prototype grant money. And if it becomes too much, let me know. We'll . . . figure something out."

After one more considering look, he leaves the room.

I remain in his office and pull out my phone.

When I open the email, my stomach clenches. They approved my proposal for the grant because mine was one of two pitches with a visual component. Since art museums are largely visual, they liked the idea and want to see if it takes too much from the art in the prototype.

By no means is this a slam dunk of a project. Their words are vague, their concerns unspecific, but between the lines I hear Carter's voice. The board may not realize it or want to vocalize it, but they have the same concerns.

I shove my phone in my pocket and scoop up my backpack. I might as well work at my desk for the rest of the day. It doesn't see a lot of action, but it's nice to have it when I need it.

Samantha's cubicle is three past mine. I could go talk to her. I could pick her brain and get design ideas. If I do that, though, I won't be able to say this is my design anymore.

I drop my bag on the desk and my backside into the chair. One push of my foot sends me spinning in circles. Just because asking Samantha won't work doesn't mean I can't ask someone else, someone outside the company. Amy designs clothing, but she'd want to know why I needed design help and I'd have to confess I don't know what I'm doing.

The only person who actually knows what is going on with this project is Carter. He cares about the outcome. Is there a chance he'd be willing to help me? Maybe.

Is there a chance I'm just looking for another reason to spend time with a good-looking guy who is also an interesting conversationalist? Possibly.

Unfortunately, I have no way of getting ahold of him. So far, we've simply bumped into each other by luck.

I scroll through my contacts as I spin my chair, hoping for inspiration to strike. My mind can't move past Carter, though, and I don't know which events will put me in his orbit.

A sudden thought occurs to me, and I plant my foot on the desk to stop my spin. He said he was attending a charity event this weekend. One for children who need eyeglasses and hearing aids.

Before I can stop myself, I open my texts and click on Amy's name.

*EMMA*

The moment I hit send, my stomach clenches. Am I really doing this? Is it worth it? Too late now. My phone vibrates.

> AMY
> Who are you and what have you done with my twin?

I roll my eyes, and before I can respond, another message comes through.

> AMY
> Blink twice if you've been kidnapped!

> ME
> You can't see me. How would you know if I'm blinking or not?

> AMY
> Twin telepathy. I'd feel it.

ME
By that theory, couldn't you just sense that I'm not
kidnapped?

AMY
Theoretically, but you are volunteering—nay, you
are ASKING—to attend a formal event that does
not fit with your work research. That is abnormal
behavior worthy of concern.

AMY
What's the code word?

When we were kids, Amy struggled with the idea of non-identical twins and was convinced that our true twins had been snatched from the hospital and there was another set of sisters out there, just like us. She made me come up with a code word so she wouldn't be confused by the other me.

Since we were five at the time, the code word is ridiculous, but Amy refuses to let me change it. I sigh as I type the text. At least I don't have to say it out loud.

ME
Purple polka-dotted pineapples.

AMY
I can probably get you in, if . . .

All the possible horrible prices I may have to pay for this favor flood my brain. Listening to her new boyfriend extol the virtues of all his paintings? A sacrificial offering of my favorite yoga pants? A new website for her clothing line?

Actually, that last one wouldn't be too bad. As long as I don't have to maintain it.

Unable to take the suspense, I message her again.

ME
If what?

AMY
You tell me why you want it.

I'd rather be her on-call IT support for a month.

For some reason, Amy thinks because I can write a shell script, I can tell her why her printer isn't working. I usually can, but that's beside the point.

What I absolutely cannot do is tell her there is a man involved in this request. Even though the connection is professional, she'll try to make it more. Yes, Carter is good-looking and a little funny and attentive enough to realize things I'd rather he not and decisive but gentle when sharing his opinions and oh my goodness, I need to get a grip.

I do not want to date Carter. The fact that he has chosen to attend tonight's gala is proof we wouldn't be a good fit, no matter how boring he thinks they are. One day, God willing, I will encounter a similar man who is far more practical and not caught up in the art world and its chaotic creativity.

ME
I need to meet with a work colleague.

AMY
<<gif of a big red X flashing over a game board>>

AMY
Try again.

ME
It's true!

AMY
What sort of work colleague would rather talk to you at a gala event instead of via video chat? You even tried to get me to use that weird cartoon chat program.

ME
They're called avatars and I was testing a program for work.

AMY
Whatever. Aunt Jade says I can give you her ticket, but you have to make it worth my while.

ME
You can pick my dress?

AMY
As if you wouldn't need me to do that anyway.

ME
Didn't you put one in my closet?

There's an outfit for every other uncomfortable occasion in there.

AMY
Nothing in your *Look Book* is suitable for a formal gala. At best, you can swing a semi-formal lun-cheon.

If she knew I spend entire days in plaid pajama pants, she'd really lose her mind.

ME
What will it take to get me that ticket?

AMY
The name of the work colleague.

It's such a seemingly small thing to give her, and yet . . . I can't.

AMY
Emma?????

What if she knows him? My hand tightens on the phone. What if she's dated him? Richie is an anomaly. Most of the men Amy dates don't hang around long enough to meet the family, but that doesn't mean I want to compete with her.

Which I wouldn't be because I do not want to date Carter.

AMY
OH MY GOSH, WHO IS IT?????

I've really done it now. If I'd told her at the beginning, I could insist it wasn't a big deal. Withholding the information implies that the information is personal and important.

I need a time machine.

> **AMY**
> If you don't tell me, Emma, I'm calling Mom and telling her you want her to invite a guy to the next family dinner so you can meet him.

That threat gets my fingers flying.

> **ME**
> Don't you dare!

> **AMY**
> NAME

I sigh and indulge in several bangs of my head against the back of my chair.

> **ME**
> Carter Anderson

I expect the response to be immediate, but nothing comes. I check to make sure the text sent and then close and reopen the text thread. Nothing.

The sudden vibration in my hand as an incoming-call request lights up the screen almost has me jumping out of my skin. I dart into a nearby conference room and shut the door as I answer the call.

"Amy?"

Silence. I check the screen and the call timer is ticking away. I switch to speaker and try again in case I've left the phone connected to my Bluetooth earbuds.

"Amy?"

The sudden squeal that echoes through the room has me dropping the phone, thankful it was on speaker and not pressed to my ear.

"Carter Anderson?" Amy's voice is almost breathless. "Where did you meet him? It was at Richie's showing, wasn't it? I totally forgive you for ditching early now. Oh my gosh, you and Carter? You know he's a painter, right? As in, artist? As in, one of those evil, creative people?"

"I don't think creative people are evil." I sigh.

"Mm-hmm, I bet you don't, not if you've been spending time with Carter Anderson."

Why does she keep saying his full name like that? "I'm designing a solution for the McGrary Museum, remember? Carter is a consultant."

"Carter, huh?" She laughs delightedly. "Oh, Emma, I do not blame you for wanting to have a reason to see him in a non-work setting. Let him see how sweet and sparkly you are, maybe want to connect outside of work, hmm?"

"I . . ." As much as I want to correct her, I can't. What other reason do I have aside from the truth? Admitting to her that I'm a fraud of a designer, and I need to convince Carter to show me what he was talking about so I don't fall on my face after my boss let me keep this project, even though he probably shouldn't have, is not an option.

Since I'm unwilling to outright lie, at least not again, my only other option is to allow my sister to have whatever assumption she wishes.

I clear my throat. "So, can you get me in?"

"Of course. I'd bring hoop skirts back into style and sneak you in if I had to. Fortunately . . ." Her voice trails off and the scrape of hangers fills the silence. "Perfect. We have at least three dresses in inventory right now that will do the trick."

"What trick?" I don't need a trick. I just need a ticket.

"Keeping the attention of Carter Anderson, of course. When I am finished with you, the only work thoughts in his head will be how badly he wants to paint your portrait."

"Amy, no." The last time Amy tried to dress me to catch a man's eye, I had to practically chain myself to the dressing room wall to convince her I wasn't going anywhere in a skin-tight shirt with a V deep enough one of those reality ballroom dancing show guys could wear it.

"The gala starts at seven and Richie has a car picking us up at six-thirty, so you need to be at the boutique . . ." She holds the word out as she thinks through the math. "Ten minutes ago."

I glance at my watch. "It's not even three."

"Your dress needs to be fitted, your hair needs to be done, and your makeup needs to be perfect. Not to mention, I have to get myself ready as well. Just get yourself over here. I'm prepping a dressing room now."

The call disconnects and I'm left staring at a black screen. The reflection of my face shows every bit of trepidation on display.

I take a few minutes to walk around the conference room table. Shaking out my arms helps some, at least enough that I no longer worry my fingers are going to fall asleep.

There's not another option, though. If I want to impress everyone with this project, I'm going to need Carter. To talk to Carter, I need to go to the gala. To go to the gala, I need Amy.

And if I need Amy, I'll have to sacrifice myself to make it all happen.

Fortunately, my apartment isn't much out of the way. I'll have to stop by there and change. Amy has no idea these leggings exist, and both my sanity and my comfy closet need me to keep it that way.

Most of my friends think the plethora of black-tie charity galas and silent auctions are a gimmick for romance novels or movies, but that is not the case. I know this because my family fills their social calendars with such events on a very regular basis. Granted, they are more likely to be $1,000 per table events instead of $1,000 per plate, but living in the northern suburbs of Atlanta means there are no end of philanthropic reasons to don your favorite evening gown.

I turn down the opportunity to join them whenever the invitation is extended, as I am not in possession of an evening gown, favorite or otherwise.

At least, I wasn't until tonight.

Now I own a swath of fabric that makes me look like I went parachuting and forgot to unwrap myself from the emerald-green chute when I walked away from the landing. Granted, it is a very artfully draped parachute. My right arm is lost in a long sleeve that flops around with three times as much fabric as needed. My left shoulder is bare, but a wide loop of fabric circles my left elbow.

Amy tried to call it a second sleeve.

We arrived at the hotel ten minutes ago, but I stepped into the restroom instead of following Amy to the table. This is the first moment I've had to breathe since I arrived at the boutique. I never even got a chance to see what Amy had done with my hair and makeup before she was herding me into the car.

If I'm as objective as humanly possible, the image in the bathroom mirror is of a pretty woman. I don't know if loose clothing is in style or if Amy was trying to avoid a repeat of the tight shirt catastrophe, but the only part of my body this dress snugs up against is my waist, and that thin strip of elastic is lost under the fabric billowing down from the top.

Before this dress, I didn't know it was possible to simultaneously feel completely exposed and suffocated by fabric. I have to simply trust that the massive amounts of yardage are covering everything they should because I can't feel any of it.

Maybe that's a good thing? I didn't particularly care for the feeling of the fabric when I pulled it off the hanger. Maybe it's better that my skin can only sense the ominous presence instead of actually enduring it.

Am I really going to do this? I am never this impulsive. Well, *never* is a strong word. I am rarely this impulsive. Okay, if I'm going to be honest with anyone, it should be myself. I do not impulsively plunge into any social experience or relationship.

A new food comes before me? It can always be spit out if swallowing is truly not an option.

A new movie or television series comes out? Hate watching is almost as much fun as enjoying the show.

A new video game releases? Seriously, what's the worst that could happen?

The same cannot be said of people. People are scary. I require forethought and practice if I want to sound intelligent in a confrontation or whatever this conversation with Carter is going to be.

If I even get a chance to talk to Carter. The way my evening is going, Amy is going to have to come collect me from in front of this mirror, and unless the man accidentally strolls into the wrong restroom, I will not have asked my question.

My purse holds no notecards. There is not a carefully curated plan for what I'm going to say.

Do I want to go into that ballroom unprepared?

Yes. Yes, I do.

Because there isn't another option.

Mentally channeling the little engine that could, I grip my small bag tighter and leave the restroom. Everyone is in their seats when I enter the ballroom. Servers scurry around with plates of salad and baskets of bread.

I carefully slide between the tables, hoping my skirt isn't sweeping up random pieces of silverware or dropped clutch purses. I know our table number, but not how the room is laid out.

I keep moving, scanning the tables for familiar faces.

I find Carter's table before Amy's. My feet stumble to a halt when our gazes connect, but fortunately the skirt merely swooshes around in response instead of trapping my legs in satiny cocoons.

A server touches my arm. "Pardon me, miss."

I jump two steps forward, nearly tripping on the previously accommodating skirt. "Of course," I mutter as I keep walking between the tables. I find Amy a few moments later and sink gratefully into the seat beside her.

The breath I blow out is decidedly shaky. No one is walking around right now, so I have to make it through dinner before I have any chance of speaking to Carter. If he's one of those people who ducks out during dessert, I'll have dressed up for nothing.

There are speeches. Every now and then, I glance over to his table to assure myself he's still here.

Each time, he meets my gaze with a curious lift of an eyebrow. Is he merely sensing when I will turn or is he staring at me the whole time?

Finally, the formal portion of the evening is over, and the mingling and dancing can commence. How should I approach him? Should I just go to his table? Meander around until I find him so I can make the encounter look accidental?

The debate is settled for me as Amy kicks me under the table before looking over my shoulder with wide eyes and an even wider smile.

I turn to find Carter Anderson. His hand is outstretched, and he wears a challenging smirk on his face. "Might I have this dance?"

9

**CARTER**

There's a phenomenon where if a person thinks about red cars, then they'll see all the red cars.

Is Emma Trinket a red car? Has she been on the periphery of my life for months, or maybe even years, and I've simply never noticed her? Or is she truly a sudden new fixture in all the different areas of my life?

Next thing I know, she's going to be behind me in the grocery store checkout line or sitting at the other end of my regular row in church.

I snuck glances at her all through dinner, my brain spinning with the question of whether or not our both of us being here is an accident.

Now I have a chance to find out.

Assuming she agrees to dance. Right now, she seems to prefer staring at my hand like it's going to bite her.

The blonde from the other night smacks Emma on the leg, muttering, "This is what you came for, remember?" Then she turns a wide smile in my direction. "She would love to."

The woman pops up from her seat and moves to stand behind Richie. His nod to the formality of the night is a sport coat over a turtleneck. It's a stark contrast to the woman's dress, which seems to be made of a million panels of pink cotton candy all held in place by a wish and a prayer.

"Richie and I were just about to go dance ourselves, weren't we, darling?"

Richie gazes up at the ceiling. "The only thing that matters is what we are doing now. Our intentions are nothing but flimsy—"

"Exactly." Two spots of color that match the frothy dress appear on the woman's cheeks. "Which is why we should already be on the dance floor."

She drags Richie away from the table. I'm certain he's still talking about intentions being dust or dreams or some other drivel, but I don't care. The woman confirmed what I'd already suspected, that Emma came tonight seeking me out.

The question that remains is why.

"Right. Dancing. Yes." Emma slides her hand in mine, and my fingers curl reflexively around hers.

Long ago, I learned the only way to have an uninterrupted conversation with a woman at these events was while dancing. Yet as we cross the room, I can't decide what I want to say.

There are enough couples scattered around the floor to keep me from feeling like I'm on display as I turn to face my partner, but not so many that we'll risk bumping into each other.

I place my right hand at her waist and extend my left, but at that same moment she places both hands around my neck as if we're a couple of teenagers attending the prom. Her clutch is still grasped in her hand and smacks me on the back of my head.

As subtly as possible, I pull one hand from my neck and clasp it in my left hand, tucking it in close to our bodies the way the couples around us are doing.

Her other hand slides over my shoulder, making the clutch scrape against my neck. She looks from the bag to the table and then sort of props the thing on my shoulder and presses her hand on top of it.

I maneuver us to the side of the floor and stop dancing to pry the bag from my lapel. "May I?"

She nods while giving the bag a small frown.

A squeamish sensation winds up my arm as I slide my finger gently under the flap to disconnect the strong magnet holding the bag closed. Opening a woman's purse, no matter how noble the reason, feels like some form of violation of privacy.

The bag isn't large, but as I expected, there is a loop tucked in one side. I try to ease it out without looking at anything else, but it's impossible to miss the large mobile phone taking up most of the space.

Squeezed in around the device is a lipstick, a crumpled bill—likely a twenty—and two cards that I assume are her ID and a credit card. I close the bag, resisting the urge to shake my head over the size of her phone. I've seen children with tablets that weren't much bigger.

I slide the loop onto her wrist, noting the presence of the chunky smartwatch under the long sleeve. I wave my hand over the bag as if I were revealing a work of art. "Voilà."

Her lips turn into a small, self-deprecating smile as she tilts her head and extends her arm with the now-dangling clutch bag. "Well. Isn't that convenient?"

I merely lift my eyes and give a slight nod before silently inviting her back into a dancing position.

Which Emma is on the dance floor with me tonight? Is she the out-of-place woman I met at the gallery, the confident woman from the presentation, or some completely new configuration?

I focus on the feel of the music for several bars, waiting for Emma to bring up whatever it is she came here to say, but she stays silent.

If she's not going to take the opportunity, I will. "How is it I've never met you before?"

Her eyebrows lift. "I don't get out much. I mean, I do, but I tend to go to the same places over and over. Considering the number of people in the greater metropolitan area, our meeting is actually more of a statistical improbability than our never seeing each other."

"And yet, here we are. Four times in less than two months. I can't seem to get away from you, Emma Trinket."

She winces. "Did you want to?"

Is there a way to answer that question that wouldn't be considered either flirting or rude?

Before I can formulate a response, she continues, "Tonight isn't by chance."

"Oh?" I hadn't expected her to admit that so easily.

She takes a deep breath in and seems to brace herself for her next question. Tension stretches palpably through her fingers, yet she continues to sway with me in a graceful rhythm.

After letting out a sigh, she says, "You seemed to have some strong feelings about the augmented reality tour guide system."

"I have strong feelings about the benefits of art and how much our technology already distracts us."

She glances down at our feet, then away. The confident woman who presented at the museum is nowhere to be found now, and I miss her a little. It's probably better that she be careful and unsure, though. As nicely as she fits in my arms, asking her on a date is a bad idea if I'm going to speak on the final prototypes.

"The museum seems to share some of your concerns."

I frown. "But your project is on the list."

"Yes." She draws the word out and tilts her head to the side before wincing. "But their approval came with hesitations."

A coil of tension releases at her confession. If they share my concerns, I likely won't have to worry about seeing people waving phones about in front of paintings, and since they pushed her project through anyway, my voicing those concerns wouldn't have mattered. I can continue to utilize her as a muse without feeling guilty.

Her blue eyes shift to meet my gaze directly. "I truly think an augmented reality design will greatly enhance a museum visitor's experience."

I lift my eyebrows. "You already have the prototype grant, and I have no vote in the final decision."

"We both know your opinion matters. Otherwise, you wouldn't have been in the room." Her chin lifts a fraction of an inch. "They've obviously heard your views before. You removed yourself after my presentation, but the wording of the email was very similar."

"The final presentation is weeks away."

"Just over twelve weeks, if we're counting."

The almost timid creature from a few moments ago intrigued me, but this woman, who tries to take the lead in the dance every time she finds the courage to meet my gaze, fascinates me. I find myself wanting to push her just to see how straight her spine can get.

"Everything I said at the museum still stands. Why are you the right person for the job?"

She sighs. "I can respect something without loving it. Like a journalist. They can report on events they don't approve of or enjoy."

If a guide were nothing more than a cold reporting of facts, visitors could just pick up a nonfiction book in the gift shop. Art needs to be more than that. It's a window into someone else's life in a way that facts can never be. Putting up curtains and safety bars and even instructions for opening the window block some of the experience.

How can I make her see that?

I guide—or perhaps strong-arm is the better term now that she is no longer pliant—us to the edge of the dance floor and step off the temporary parquet. Her hand is still clasped in mine, and I tug her behind me. "Come with me."

"I don't seem to have a choice," she mutters.

I lead her into a large room off to the side of the main ballroom. Tables and stands circle the room, displaying the items included in tonight's silent auction. A few people are milling about, but most have already perused the selection and are now monitoring the auction itself on their smartphones.

In the middle of the long wall, in one of the most prominent positions, is a framed painting on a large easel. I guide her through the room until we're standing in front of it.

It's a landscape painting from the perspective of a bug perched atop a mushroom. The grasses are tall in the front and the nearby trees seem skewed while the mountains in the distance appear almost normal.

"What do you think when you look at this?"

She glances at me, eyes flicking about as she takes in my face. Is she trying to decide what I want to hear? I keep my expression as blank as possible.

Finally, she turns to the painting and blows out a breath. "It's incredible. It's a very *Alice in Wonderland* sort of thing, like when she drinks the potion and gets small or however it went. I enjoyed that old live action television series as a kid. It was some of the first special effects I remember seeing."

I wait, silently indicating that I want something more.

She slips her hand from mine, and I'm surprised to feel the loss even though I'd forgotten I was holding on to her. Her fingers twine together, and she holds her hands close to her middle as she steps as close as the draped red cording allows.

"It's impressive," she says with a nod. "I wouldn't be surprised if I reached out to it and my hand got wet. The skill is incredible. Do you know how it's done?"

I'm answering before I can stop myself. "With paint?"

Her glare inspires a laugh I can barely contain, and I fake a cough to hide it.

She points at a blank section of the wall. "That is also covered in paint and yet no one is dropping thousands of dollars to have it in their home."

"Tens of thousands."

Her face scrunches up. "What?"

I nod at the painting and a slight heat tinges the ends of my ears. Why did I say that? The point of this conversation is not how much the painting is going to sell for. "Never mind."

She pulls out her phone and points it at the QR code on the small plaque in front of the painting. The blue and white screen of the auction app appears, and her eyes widen before she darkens the screen and tucks it back into her purse.

"Wow," she whispers before taking a small step back.

Not liking the current trajectory of this conversation, I go back to her earlier question. "Oils. It's done with oil paints. Some sections are worked wet on wet and then others are left to dry before glazes and small details are brought in."

The distraction works as she allows her eyes to travel across the canvas again. "Fascinating. How long does it take?"

"This one?" I dig back through my mind for the right records. "It was about two hundred hours. Over the space of several weeks, of course."

Her assessing gaze turns to me. What is she putting together in her mind? I don't care if she knows who I am now, but it's not what I want her thinking about.

"The painting, Emma." I move behind her so that she can't examine me anymore. "What does it make you think?"

The edges of her frown are barely visible from my new vantage point, but her disgruntlement is clear in her voice. "I just told you the crafts-manship is exquisite."

How do I get her to see? I gently take her elbow and guide her to another painting on display. This one is a modern work, all colors and lines. A vague idea of a face can be seen in one corner and the piece is entitled *Stargazer*.

I say nothing as she dutifully stands in front of it.

Finally, she emits a defeated sigh. "I'm sorry. I don't know what you want from me."

I step beside her and our shoulders brush as we face the painting. "Art is not about technique. It matters not how much time, sweat, or skill goes into the work if it doesn't evoke an emotion in the viewer."

"So every piece of art is meant to make me feel like I did when looking at the bridal skeleton?"

I laugh. "No. Not every piece moves every person, but every piece deserves a chance." I turn to face her, wanting to see her expression as I ask, "When was the last time you've had a reaction as pleasant as that one was bad?"

"Never." Her mouth presses into a tight line as she faces me. "Which makes me a neutral party and therefore perfect to create a good experience for the museum."

I wish she didn't have a point, but she does. That she wants to make it all about facts, though, spurs me to continue what seems to be a pointless conversation.

"Art is not merely academic."

She snorts a small laugh. "It isn't academic at all. Not by itself, anyway. That's what the guide is for. There's nothing to learn when viewing art on its own."

"That's why your design will fail. It's cold."

For someone who seems so out of touch with her emotions, she certainly feels a lot of them. And each and every one plays out across her face in subtle ways. A pucker of an eyebrow, a pressing of lips, a tightening around the eyes.

How can someone who obviously feels so much not ever feel anything when looking at art?

My fingers itch for a sketchpad. My schedule will be thrown off once more by an encounter with Emma as I pull the ideas from my head before managing to find sleep.

The past couple of years, I've fallen into perspective paintings like the field on the other side of the room. I've done a teacher from a child's point of view, a piano player as seen from between the keys, a mail carrier from inside the mailbox. They aren't the philosophical statements that made my career, but they've kept me in the game.

Without her knowing it, Emma has given me the incredible gift of inspiration. Perhaps I can give her one back by opening her mind to the idea that one doesn't have to live the moment to feel the experience. It can be conveyed in other ways.

I take her back to the landscape. "When you look at this, do you not get the idea of what it's like to be smaller than the world around you?"

"Is that what you thought when you painted it?"

I blink and look at her. "Did you Google me?"

She waves her purse in the air. "Your name is on the auction listing." The clutch drops to dangle by the wrist strap once more as she points to the painting. "Are you telling me you painted this with the idea of showing how small we are compared to the world and didn't just ask yourself how cool it would be to see the world from the perspective of a mouse?"

It had been a cricket, but she was far too close to the reality for me to admit it. This wasn't an inspired painting. It might be worth six figures, but it means almost nothing to me.

She'd been at least somewhat captured by my piece hanging in the museum. I'd painted it almost four years ago. I wish I could show her some of my earliest works.

Even if I'm not currently painting with that lost passion, I still know what it is. I know how it can flow through art and how even the uninspired artist can create something someone else can find meaning in.

"Art isn't about conveying facts. That's what books are for. Even portraits from the days before cameras weren't about depicting the exact truth but rather capturing the essence of the person being painted."

"And you think if I don't understand that, my design has less chance of being chosen."

"It won't be chosen." I swallow hard and push ahead. She deserves the truth, even if it means I never see her again. "I won't let it."

She nods, a thoughtful look replacing the myriad of emotions that have been dancing across her features. "I need a teacher."

Would she never stop surprising me with her responses? "A what?"

"A teacher." She waves a hand at the painting. "Someone to teach me how to love art, how to find all these emotions that are supposedly hiding beneath the surface."

"That's not exactly a class at the community college."

"No, but I know the perfect person to teach me."

"Oh? Who?"

Her face turns my way and her lips are twisted into a shape that can only be called a smirk. "You."

**10**

*EMMA*

S ometimes I come up with fabulous plans that involve days, if not weeks, of planning and forethought, only to have them completely fail because of a last-minute wrench in the works.

Other times, I throw a complete spitball into the wind, and it miraculously turns into a home run.

This is one of those other times.

Also, I have never played baseball.

I'd gone to the gala to get Carter's help, but I'd been thinking along the lines of a book suggestion or an offer to send me detailed feedback on my presentation. My audacious claim that he should tutor me in art appreciation wasn't even a complete thought when it came spilling out of my mouth. I was just as surprised as he was.

I was even more surprised when he agreed.

Now I'm jumping every time my phone buzzes because he said he'd text with the details of my first lesson once he decided what it would be. It's wreaking havoc with my productivity.

Which is why I'm sitting at my desk, clutching a cup of coffee, and trying to sort through my task list at eight o'clock on a Saturday morning. Normally, I'd still be in my pajamas.

Okay, I am wearing pajamas right now, but they're clean pajamas that I put on after I showered. I actually never—okay, rarely—sleep in these. They're more like what Amy would call loungewear.

Given that these particular fleece pajama pants are covered in tiny cartoon donkeys, Amy would probably call them trash, but that's beside the point.

After two days of disappointing notifications, I am proud of the fact that I don't jump and spill my coffee when my watch vibrates to signal an incoming text.

I turn my wrist as I lean forward to place the coffee on the desk and only spill a couple of drops when I see that it is, in fact, from him.

Only the first three words are visible on my watch, so I snatch up my phone and press my thumb on the screen to unlock it.

CARTER
Are you free tonight?

I take a deep breath and set the phone down so I can shake out my suddenly trembling hands. Why am I so nervous? This isn't a date. It's barely even a work function.

With my composure at least temporarily regained, I pick the phone back up.

I type *No, I'm very expensive* and then quickly delete it. Official or not, I should try to be professional. I try *Yep, I sure am* but delete that as well because, well, just because. Finally, I just type *Yes* and hit send.

CARTER
First lesson tonight, then. Do you know where Marcel's Diner is in Appleton?

I close the texting app and reopen it to make sure I read that right. Marcel's is a diner just off the square in a small town about thirty minutes north of me. That puts it very far away from any of Atlanta's cultural venues.

ME
Yes. I've been there.

CARTER
Can you be there by 5:30?

ME
I can. Is Marcel's a hot bed of artistic inspiration?

CARTER
No, I just happen to like their food. Art lesson comes after.

ME
Where are we going?

CARTER
It's a surprise. If you have time to prepare, your reactions won't be natural and open.

Logical, yes, but not helpful.

ME
What's the dress code?

CARTER
I'm sure what you normally wear will be fine.

I glance down at my cartoon-covered pajama pants and blow a stray strand of hair away from my face. I must have missed it when I threw the rest of it up in a haphazard bun.

ME
Humor me.

CARTER
Whatever you would wear for a casual night out with friends will work. I've never seen you in anything that wasn't appropriately elegant.

I drop the phone like its lithium battery is threatening to ignite. Whatever giddy little sparks were dancing around at the idea of deliberately going out with Carter fizzle and fade as they get smothered by reality.

We don't know each other much but he knows me less than I know him unless he, too, has been putting on a complete front every time I've seen him and both of us are nothing but a pair of frauds.

Based on the internet searches I did when I got home from the gala, that's not the case.

There isn't a lot about Carter on the World Wide Web, but what exists is pretty interesting. Ironically, most of the available information is cold, emotionless facts. Very little commentary exists about him, although there are plenty of blogs and articles and even a college survey course discussing his works.

After graduating college with an art degree, he went to New York for some sort of artist-in-residence program, where he refined his painting skills while earning money doing illustrations for children's books. He also spent some time as a barista.

In an epic case of right place, right time, right person, he had a painting purchased by a Broadway producer. The painting hung in the man's house and was then used on the set of a musical that had a short but highly successful run.

That seems to be all anyone knows about him until he connected with the gallery that still handles his work. He had a twenty-piece showing and all of them went for at least five figures.

After that, there's nothing but occasional appearances at fundraisers and art functions such as gallery openings and museum galas. He teaches classes twice a year at two different artist retreat schools and has paintings hanging in many modern art museums as well as private collections.

He was less intimidating when I thought he was a local artist the museum had brought in to fill the consultant position. I suppose that is what he is, but it's rather like saying Bill Gates is the technical consultant for your website.

New York is a four-hour plane ride away and he's not taking me anywhere particularly high brow if we're meeting in Appleton for dinner, so I'm not sure what to expect.

Another text message notification buzzes through my pondering and I pick up my phone.

> AMY
> New sushi place alert! I hear the chef trained in
> Tokyo. Wanna do lunch?

I don't see the appeal of sushi, but Amy and Aunt Jade love it so I've learned what to order. California rolls and deep-fried salmon rolls taste pretty much the same wherever I go, so a new place doesn't get me hyped up.

ME
Can't. Sorry. Gotta work through lunch.

AMY
Look at you, working on a Saturday. Just can't say no
when the inspiration hits, huh? You'll learn how to
wrangle it.

AMY
Eating and working is not good for the digestion,
though.

I've worked plenty of Saturday mornings since Jason doesn't care
when we put our hours in as long as we track them and hit our deadlines.
I have no idea how late I'll be out tonight, though, and I'm already feeling
behind.

Also, I don't want to have to wrap myself in uncomfortable clothing
twice in one day.

ME
I'm already having to limit my hours. I have plans
tonight.

AMY
<<eye roll emoji>> Are you and your "friend" Jason
going to the movies or something?

My family, Amy in particular, bounces back and forth between thinking Jason doesn't exist to being convinced he's my secret boyfriend.

They've never met since I keep my lives as separate as possible, but I can't always avoid mentioning him.

> **ME**
> No. I'm having dinner in Appleton.

> **AMY**
> Who with?

Not this again. I can't tell Amy the real reason I'm meeting with Carter.

For one, while Amy knows I find art boring, she doesn't realize it's a somewhat active hatred, and two, she'll be insistent that the entire encounter is a date.

And it isn't. It absolutely isn't. No matter how good he looks in the casual picture of him at one of the artist retreats that graces a blog I haven't quite brought myself to take off my computer screen.

In an act of defiance, I minimize the window. Closing it would be better but, you know. Baby steps.

> **AMY**
> Emma … WHO are you going with?

> **ME**
> It's just a work thing. Research for the museum design.

That should distract her. She and Mother are so excited that they can now call me a designer, even though I've been extremely vague when answering their questions.

Mostly because I don't have any answers for half of them, but also because I don't want them to think there will be another design project after this one.

> AMY
> The last time you were evasive about a work meet-
> ing, it turned out to be with Carter Anderson.

I swallow and fake a laugh, even though she isn't here to hear it.

> ME
> Ha! Yeah. No.

I have no idea what I'm saying or even implying. It's an answer that can be taken in one of a dozen different ways. I don't honestly care which one Amy chooses as long as I don't have to tell her I'm meeting Carter tonight.

> AMY
> Yeah, it's Carter again? Or no, it's not Carter?

Once again, I'm caught between lying to my sister or suffering the results of the truth.

> ME
> Yeah.

Maybe she'll assume I'm agreeing with the last question? Wouldn't that be the case by the actual rules of grammar?

I brace myself for an onslaught of questions, excited gifs, and thrilled exclamations.

But nothing comes.

My phone is blessedly silent.

I slump down and indulge in a celebratory wiggle before reconfiguring the moving panels that make up my adjustable office chair. The website I bought it from called it an "ergonomic meditation chair." I just consider it a life saver as I can sit in it cross-legged, backward, or even sideways and still see my computer screen.

The section of code I'm refining this morning is almost cleaned up when my phone dings.

Then dings again.

And again.

By the time I finish what I was typing and pick up the device, there are six messages from Amy.

AMY
You've changed your calendar to private. I can't see anything.

AMY
What time is the date?

AMY
Where is he taking you?

AMY
More importantly, what are you wearing?

AMY
I can bring over this new skirt we got at the bou-

tique yesterday.

AMY
Or there's a design I've been toying with. I think
you'd fit in the sample. I can bring them over.

I glance around my home office and at the section of living room I
can see through my front door. Amy cannot come over here. My family
descends upon my apartment exactly once per year and it takes me an
entire weekend to prepare for it. I don't have time to get the place ready
for them today.

ME
It's not a date.

ME
I have plenty of clothing in my closet that you
personally put there.

ME
I'll even wear something from the date night section of the Look Book if it will make you happy.

If I can find the pieces. Did I stick them in the closet in my office or did
I store them in my suitcase? Probably the office closet. Otherwise, they
would be too wrinkled when I put them back in my regular closet during
my annual apartment prep.

AMY
What time?

ME
It's 9:22, weirdo. You have a device with a clock in
your hand. There's a timestamp next to your name.

AMY
<<gif of one cat bopping another on the head>>

AMY
What time is the date?

ME
It's not a date.

AMY
Fine. What time is this completely emotionless and
boring work meeting?

ME
5:30.

AMY
You're meeting him there, right? Just because he's
a celebrity doesn't mean you should give him your
home address right away.

ME
How famous do you have to be before you become
a celebrity?

AMY

If people you don't know talk about you on social media, you're a celebrity.

ME
Wow. The world is full of a lot of celebrities, then.

AMY
When are you leaving?

ME
5:00.

I wait, but no more messages come in, so I set my phone aside and get back to work.

As planned, I work through lunch. By my calculations, I'll need to stop work around four in order to find an outfit and get ready. That means I've got time to run one more set of test data through this new code.

The scenarios are just finalizing on my screen when my phone chirps. I don't have many apps set to make noise, so I immediately pick up the device.

It's my apartment complex access app telling me that I have a guest at the gate. Clicking the access request button, I see Amy's smiling face hanging out the driver's side of her car.

Oh. My. Goodness. What am I going to do?

I have to let her in. She knows I'm home. She knows I'd never leave her out there. She's my sister, for crying out loud.

My heart is pounding out of my chest as I hit the button to accept her and hear the beep of the gate-opening warning before the app closes.

My apartment complex is big and windy, and I deliberately chose a unit that is as far from the main entrance as one can get. That means I have about five minutes before Amy is parking her car and climbing the steps. She'll probably have bags to unload as well, so that gives me at most eight minutes.

Eight minutes to change all the things I normally take a weekend to do.

I tear out of my home office, nearly taking my shoulder off as I knock into the door frame. The living room will just have to stay. There isn't time to get the framed art prints down from my closet and cover all the video game and movie posters surrounding my television. The game consoles will have to stay as well.

Decor is not the priority right now.

My closet is.

I run into my room, almost take myself out as I step on the corner of the sheet I threw off the bed while getting up this morning, and fall into the large walk-in closet.

When I snatch the enormous army surplus duffel from the top of the closet, a tumble of shoe boxes also rains down on my head. I leave them and their contents on the floor as I brace my leg on one of the shelves so I can hold the duffel bag open.

College hoodies, leggings, and jeans so worn they've lost color but are now fashionably torn at the knees get ripped from their shelves and hangers and thrown into the bag. A basket of folded T-shirts gets upended over the duffel next.

Two pairs of sneakers and some hiking boots I can't recall ever wearing get tossed on top of the crumpled clothing as I drag the duffel out of the closet.

I try to shove it under the bed before remembering I bought a platform bed three years ago because I wanted the storage.

The sudden pounding knock on my apartment door nearly makes me scream. I yank the comforter off my bed because it's somehow still in place, even though the top sheet is on the floor, and toss it over the duffel.

My chest is heaving with exertion as I throw open the door with a fake smile on my face. Instead of my sister, though, I see nothing but the wall on the other side of the breezeway.

"Take those bags in. I'm grabbing more from the car." Amy's voice drifts over from the stairs she's already heading back down.

Sure enough, three bags sit at my feet. One is full of colorful fabrics I can only assume are clothes, another is a tumble of cords and hair tools, and the third is her travel makeup case.

I hook my foot around the three bags and drag them inside before resuming my scramble. On my way into the home office, I smack my other shoulder into the door frame. At least I will have matching bruises now.

I fling open the closet and wrap my arms around a chunk of the clothing my family brought over for my birthday and muscle it off the hanging rod. My neck aches as I twist my head to see around the bundle of clothes as I run to my room.

Half the hangers miss in my attempt to sling the mass onto the hanging rod of my closet and the clothes fall to the floor.

I'll fix that in a minute, but first I have to move the duffel bag to the office.

The front door opens as I fling the comforter away from the duffel. I'll never be able to get it across the apartment without Amy seeing it.

"I am so thirsty. Do you have any of those flavored seltzers in the fridge?"

"Usually," I call out, trying not to sound breathless. "Have a look and help yourself."

That gives me a little time. I grab the extension cord from my bedside lamp and yank it from the wall, sending the lamp toppling onto the bed.

After tying one end of the cord around the bedside table leg, I tie the other around the duffel's strap. I push open the window, making the screen topple to the grass below, and lug the duffel over to tip it over the sash.

The table isn't remotely heavy enough to hold the now-dangling army duffel, and it slides up the wall until it's acting like a grappling hook. My book and journal hit the floor and last night's thankfully closed bottle of partially drank water rolls toward the door.

A single glance around my room and closet reveals that, for a very smart person, I am incredibly stupid.

My panic has done nothing but draw a neon sign around the parts of my life I never wanted Amy or anyone else in my family to know about.

Amy steps slowly into the room, eyes so wide they seem to take up half her face. A can of water is clutched tightly in one hand and a large hanging bag is held in place over her shoulder by the other.

Her gaze flits from the floor to my bed, to the window, to the disaster beyond the closet door, and finally to me.

Silence weighs everything down for several moments until finally she says, "What are you wearing?"

**11**

*EMMA*

"U m." I glance down at myself to confirm that I am indeed still wearing what I put on after that morning's shower. "Pajamas?"

Behind me, the table gives an ominous creak and I wince as I wave a hand toward the window. "I should . . . probably get that. You know, before the table breaks."

"Yes." She takes a sip of her water. "Because that would be the greatest of tragedies at this moment."

"Right." I take a deep breath and turn to the duffel because that, at least, is something I know what to do with.

Hauling the duffel back in the window is far more difficult than tipping it out was and by the time I drop the thing on top of the comforter now gracing a large section of floor, I'm starting to sweat.

I wince as one hiking boot and an old shirt emblazoned with Link from *Zelda* tumble out the top opening of the bag.

"This explains why your clothes look practically new when we clean out your closet every year." She looks around. "Did you redecorate? Where are the throw pillows and the sea glass candle holders?"

"Ah ..." My gaze drops to the bed and the narrow drawers beneath it that hold all the decorative gifts my family has given me over the years that I only set out when they're coming over.

"The art prints from the living room under there, too?"

"No." My voice is dry and croaky. "Top of the office closet."

Her nod is small and slow as she steps farther into the room, carefully missing the bedding now repurposed as a throw rug. She steps into the closet and hooks the hangers from the garment bag over the rail.

With the care and efficiency of the professional she is, she gathers the dropped clothes and begins to place them back on hangers.

"I do wear them." I move to stand at the closet door. Would it be bad to grab a few hangers and put away the clothes from the duffel bag? Probably.

"When? Family functions?" She holds up a dress that makes my skin itch just looking at it. "Has anyone ever seen this outside of me and Mom?"

"Aunt Jade. She was at that dinner." I knew the dinner she was talking about because I'd spent every torturous moment wanting to change clothes. I'd actually pushed the top of the dress down and slapped on a hoodie for the ride home that night.

"Hmm." She straightens a few more garments.

"I wore that suit to present to the museum board. You weren't at that." I point to the suit hanging at the end of the rail. "I got the approval to move ahead with my prototype, er, design."

"Congratulations." She pinches the fabric of a pair of yoga pants that I missed earlier and rubs it between her fingers. "What did you plan on wearing for tonight's date?"

"It's not a date."

Her gaze flits around the closet and then looks over my shoulder. "You'll forgive me if I don't exactly trust your judgment on social encounters at the moment."

"My lack of throw pillows does not translate to an unawareness of social cues."

"Does an abundance of squishy stuffed animals?"

I frown because I really don't want to defend my animal pillow collection taking up the entirety of the chair in the corner. "It's not a date."

"It could be. You're just not seeing the potential."

The look on her face says she's talking about more than my night out with Carter. Something in me shrivels into a ball and retreats to the corner to whimper underneath the stuffed animals.

All my life, it's been me and Amy against any and every obstacle. Mother. School. Boys. Customer service reps. No matter what, I always knew Amy was on my side and I was on hers.

Not anymore.

I'm not sure where I stand with Amy right now, but we certainly aren't shoulder to shoulder.

As a hopeful gesture of peace, I grab the three-ring binder full of clothing and accessories suggestions and flip to the date night section. I pick the first one that doesn't make me cringe.

"I was thinking this one." I turn the book to show her a cheetah-print skirt that hits mid-calf paired with a snug black sweater.

She blinks at me and then the book. "He's taking you somewhere in Appleton and you want to wear leopard print and stilettos?"

"Probably not the stilettos. I fall over in those." I swallow and confess, "I usually switch them out for those round-toed flats or the little, tiny heels."

We both look down at the mess of shoes scattered on the floor.

"So you do have the ballet flats I brought you?" Amy asks.

"I have everything you brought me. I'm not going to haul it away or anything."

"No, you let me do that."

I want to tell her she's got the wrong idea, that it's not fair for her to catch me off guard like this, but the truth is, I feel like I owe her every dig she wants to get in. She could probably tell me grass is orange right now and I wouldn't correct her.

She unzips the garment bag and pulls out a slinky green jumpsuit. It looks like a casual version of the evening gown she put me in a few days ago. At least, casual for her. Which means dressy and uncomfortable for me.

"I think you should wear this."

"Okay." I can always change into something more appropriate after she leaves. Maybe even jeans? I mean, I am going to a diner in Appleton. I could wear my jeans.

"And you will make me a promise not to change out of it until you come home." She stabs me in the chest with her perfectly manicured finger.

I rub at the spot as I step back. "How did you know—"

"Twin telepathy."

I snort. "That's baloney or you'd have known about the clothes already."

Really. I hope I learn how to shut my mouth before I go see Carter tonight.

Amy pulls the jumpsuit from the hanger. "You will promise to wear this on your date tonight or I take that duffel with me and you'll never see it again."

Just the idea that I would lose all my leggings and jeans and oversized hoodies is enough to make me ill. The room spins around and a few dark spots float across Amy's face.

In the next moment, I'm lunging for the duffel, trying to upend the thing that is half as big as I am and dump the contents on the floor.

Amy's arms wrap around me, and we both topple sideways into a pile of clothes and bedding. She tries to wrestle the duffel from me, but I'm not going to make it easy for her to take my clothes.

"What are you doing?" she shrieks in my ear.

"Saving my clothes." I grunt as I push another cluster of clothing out of the bag. "I can't afford to replace everything if you toss it in a dumpster."

She stops wrestling and flops onto her back to stare at the ceiling.

I flop down beside her, the half-full duffel draped across my legs.

She plucks a hooded sweatshirt up from the floor and looks it over. "Did you have a giant boyfriend in high school?"

"What? No." Was Amy trying to give me mental whiplash?

She waves the sweatshirt in the air. "Emma. This is a men's extra-extra-large."

"I know."

"You wear a size eight."

"Sometimes I get a ten."

Her head falls to the side until she's looking me in the eye. "Do you really wear this out in public?"

I shrug one shoulder. "Not often. To the grocery store sometimes. Mostly it's around the house. It's like a blanket that doesn't trip you up."

Her mouth opens, but no sound comes out. Her teeth snap shut as she turns back to the shirt. Suddenly, she springs into a sitting position, turning so she can face me. "This is a cry for help."

"No." I sit up and take the sweatshirt from her. "This is my shirt. You were never supposed to see it."

Her gaze doesn't stop moving over the pile of clothing around us. When she reaches out and grabs the duffel to pour the rest of it onto the floor, the normal roll of emotions returns to her face.

And I don't like it.

She's realizing how old some of these things are and she's hurt and confused.

This time it's her realizing we aren't standing on the same side.

"I'll wear the jumpsuit," I whisper, because what else can I do? "But you have to tell me what I'm going to do when I go to the bathroom. I can't go to dinner and not drink anything."

She blinks at me for several long moments. A shudder passes through her body, and the smile she gives me is weak. "You sort of roll up the top and lay it in the pants."

And then proceed to sit around in a public bathroom stall practically nude? Lovely. I give her my own weak smile. "Can't wait."

For the next hour, we don't say anything about my apartment or the clothes all over the floor. I see her cataloging the differences, taking note of everything I hide and all the items I put out just to make them happy.

What has always seemed like a perfectly brilliant plan suddenly feels childish, but I can't change anything now.

I sit while she curls my hair, even though nothing has ever stayed, and I'll have board-straight locks running down each side of my face before I make it to the diner.

The makeup takes far too long for how natural it appears when she's done, but I don't complain about that either.

Finally, she stands in front of me, arms crossed, examining me with narrowed eyes. "You're ready for your date."

"It's not a date."

"Yes, it is."

"How do you figure?"

She holds up a finger. "Will there be dinner?"

"Yes."

Another finger extends from her hand. "With an activity after?"

"I assume so." Otherwise this will be a very strange lesson.

"Is he paying?" A third finger joins the first two.

"Um, I don't know?"

"Did he make the arrangements?" The look on her face is one I might give Jason when he tries to tell me he didn't mess up the code, but his is the name on the last upload that refuses to compile.

In other words, like I'm a total idiot.

I clear my throat. "Yes."

"Then unless stipulated otherwise, he's probably paying."

Should I be writing this down? Because these feel like rules other people need to know if I'm going to live by them.

"We already established you're driving yourself, but that still leaves a lot of wiggle room for the end of the evening. Especially if you leave your car at the square and he drives to the next destination."

"I . . . don't know . . ."

"Doesn't matter." She wiggles her fingers in my face. "There's dinner and an outing that he's arranging and paying for and the possibility of riding in his car. It's a date."

"Food and transportation? That's a twisted definition, Amy." And also a possible hint that she doesn't actually date as much as she wants me to think she does. I mean, by her definition, if a nice man offers me a token for the city metro because I've lost mine and I offer him a piece of gum, we'd be on a date.

"Trust me. Carter Anderson is from my world. I would have said *our* world, but clearly you've only been visiting mine, not living in it."

Never let it be said that a sister doesn't know how to throw a sucker punch, even if it's a verbal one.

I frown at her but don't say anything because a part of me fears she might be right. Growing up, I didn't feel like I ever really belonged. It wasn't until college that I learned a new way of approaching life. Does that mean I don't know how to relate to people like Carter?

The idea doesn't sit right. Even our more contentious conversations seemed to flow well. Plus, he wasn't born into the tuxedo-wearing, gala-attending sort of crowd. According to the article I read, he grew up in a normal middle-class suburb and attended a normal middle-class public school.

Of course, how a person grew up doesn't define the adult they become. My private-school-self is living proof of that.

And if I keep allowing my brain to circle like this, I'll never leave my apartment.

I stand and look at myself in the mirror, only to freeze in horror. "I can't wear this."

"Why not?" Amy stands shoulder to shoulder with me. "You look amazing."

Objectively, yes, I suppose I do. The green is a nice color on me, and the cut of the jumpsuit makes me look very womanly without plunging to my navel. "I look like I'm going on a date."

"You are. And this"—she waves a hand at my reflection—"is what people who date Carter Anderson wear."

"Do you know him, then?"

"Not personally, no. The first time I met him was at Richie's exhibition."

"So he has a reputation?"

"Not that I know of. I mean, I've heard of the man. He donates two large paintings a year that always sell for over $100,000 and he sells his other work through a place in New York."

"I can learn that from an internet search."

"Well, here's what you can't get from your precious internet. I know dozens of women who would trade shoes with you in a heartbeat tonight, so you'd better take advantage of your opportunity."

Everything about this feels wrong. The jumpsuit, hair, and makeup practically scream *This is not about work*. I promised Amy I wouldn't change out of the jumpsuit, but maybe I could cover it up? A black hoodie, a ponytail, and a makeup remover wipe should do the trick.

"Now. Where's your bag?"

"Um." I have a feeling if I bring out the brown cross-body sling bag I use when I can't shove everything into my pockets, whatever weird unspoken truce we have going on will shatter. "I haven't packed one yet."

"I know the perfect one." She walks into my closet and stumbles to a halt when she realizes the array of bags she's given me over the years aren't in their neat little hanging organizer in the corner of my closet.

She spins and looks at me, golden eyebrows raised. "Where?"

"Office," I mutter.

I trudge after her as she crosses my apartment. What will she think of the space? Most people find my chair with all its changeable panels to be a little weird, but there's also the papasan chair, the plethora of fuzzy blankets, and the wall-mounted monitor set up with a wireless mouse and keyboard that can be used from anywhere in the room.

She takes it all in but says nothing as she crosses to the still-open closet and quickly retrieves a medium-sized black bag.

I sigh in relief that it's at least big enough to hold my wallet and phone. I may have to take my car key off its ring, but that isn't much of a hardship since I bought one of those quick-release kinds.

A glance at my watch reveals I need to be leaving soon, so I stick my hand out for the bag. "That will look perfect."

We return to my room, and I pack the purse while she collects the other items she brought over with her. The entire time, she keeps up a running commentary of what to do and not do on a date.

I snag two travel packets of acetaminophen and shove them into the side of the bag because there's a good chance I'll have a pounding headache when the tension of this afternoon finally releases.

"Oh, I almost forgot." She rummages in her bag and pulls out a small square and extends it to me. "I know you haven't dated in like five years, so anything you have is going to be expired."

I accept the square automatically, but drop it like it's on fire when I see what it is. No matter how many times I've tried to tell Amy how I feel about sex and marriage, she insists it's all to save face because I'm not dating anyone. She's wrong. "I don't need that."

She rolls her eyes and picks it up. "You aren't going out with a nerd." With a grin, she picks up my bag and shoves the square inside. "Just in case."

"Or not." I take a moment to dig the packet out, make sure I haven't just deprived myself of pain reliever, and drop the square on the bed one more time. I can throw it away when I get home.

I give my purse one last look and then push my sister toward the door. "Time to go."

One of her arms is laden with her makeup and hair tools, so I prop my purse in her other hand while I disconnect my keys. My apartment has a smart latch, so I leave the carabiner that normally holds my car key behind along with the lip balm holder, thumb drive, flashlight, digital business card, and Minion puffball.

Amy and I part ways at the bottom of the stairs, and she watches me all the way to my car as if daring me to return to my apartment and change. If I have to circle the block and come back, I'll be late meeting Carter for sure.

I grin as I open my car door and give Amy a wave. A bundle of black fabric—a cardigan I borrowed from Stephanie while at the office last week and forgot to take off when I left—lies crumpled in the back seat and a hair claw with only two broken teeth is clamped to my rearview mirror.

I may be able to salvage tonight's meeting after all.

**CARTER**

"You look like you're heading to an interview. Art not paying enough these days? You need a little boost?"

I shake my head at the old man in the rocking chair that blocks a third of the sidewalk every time he rolls back in it. "The paint's giving me a roof and food, Grandpa." I hold open one side of my sport coat as if showing off my fancy clothes. "I am going to the play at the community theater tonight."

Two men sit in ladder-back chairs on either side of a table near the rocking chair. Their heads are bent over a checkers game. One of them looks up and gives me a nod. "Good show. Got the Brackett kid directing it."

The Brackett "kid" used to babysit me when I was little and has four children of her own now, but I don't correct him.

"You taking a lady friend?" Grandpa lifts his chin and narrows his eyes as if trying to read my mind. It's a skill I'd been totally convinced he had when I was five and trying to pretend I hadn't snuck a cookie from the cooling rack.

As an adult, I realize that he is just an exceptionally observant man. Fortunately, the store he and his retired friends like to hang out in front of does not have a view of the diner or the theater, because I do not want to explain to my grandfather or anyone else what my relationship with Emma is.

Mostly because I haven't the faintest idea.

"I'm going with a work colleague."

Grandpa snorts. "Work colleague? You sit around your living room poking at canvas boards all day. How do you have a colleague?"

I laugh because Grandpa was my biggest supporter when I declared an intention to pursue art. For years, he sent me fifty dollars a week to make sure I was getting enough to eat. He only stopped four years ago when I revealed I'd been saving the money for a while and used it to send him and Grandma on a Mediterranean cruise.

I don't know if he finally believes I'm successful or is terrified I'll make him get on another international plane flight.

"She's working with the museum."

Grandpa's eyes light up and he hits his friend on the arm, making Neal send two checkers flying. "Hear that? It is a lady friend."

I pick up the checkers and hand them back to Neal. "We're not dating."

Grandpa frowns. "Why not?"

The answer should be *because I don't think of her that way*, but I can't quite bring myself to say that. Is it a big step from intrigued to infatuated?

Do I want it to be?

"I'm just helping her with a project."

"That's how I met my Cecily." Carl points at me before sliding a checker across the board.

Neal snorts. "She got a flat tire."

Carl pats himself on the chest. "And I stopped to change it for her."

I shake my head as I tell the men goodbye and keep walking. It's been a long time since I strolled through the center of Appleton. When I make the forty-five-minute drive these days, I usually go straight to my grandparents' house. As a teenager, though, I spent hours in the tiny downtown.

As I make my way back to the diner and where I parked my car, I take a break from memory lane and peek at my watch. Still half an hour until I'm due to meet Emma. Is she the type to arrive early? I hope she isn't late. The show starts at seven.

With nothing to do and too many thoughts in my head, I enter the diner, asking for a booth in the back corner. The server brings me a glass of iced tea and while I settle in to wait for Emma, I pull my sketchbook out of my leather satchel.

I started this book three months before I met Emma and had laboriously managed to create twelve sketches. Since meeting her I've added thirty-two, plus a scattering of doodles in various corners.

Those earlier efforts are quickly flipped past as I move to the newer ones. Several of them aren't anywhere near complete. Over the years I've learned how to spot an idea that won't quite translate to canvas and abandon it.

The ones that are fleshed out, though, make my heart pound. None of the subjects look like Emma, but they all feel like her. Contradictions. A hidden story beneath the surface that I want to slowly uncover.

What is it about her that makes me think I'm missing something? It's like I'm looking at her through a warped fun house mirror.

Is it because she works for a tech company? Because she didn't pretend to like the art? Maybe it's the way she never seems quite comfortable in her clothes even though they're high end and fit her perfectly.

I flip through the sketches, trying to decide which ones to paint in my first set. The questions continue to swarm with every picture until a tight, aching buzz forms at the base of my skull.

At five-thirty, I put the sketchbook away and watch the door.

When she walks in five minutes later, I want to pull the book back out or maybe just take a picture of the moment. I don't normally paint real scenes from photographs, but the one before me is too incongruous to pass up.

I wave and she gives me a small smile before making her way through the diner.

Green, flowy trouser legs made from a satiny, shiny material brush against the metal legs of the simple diner chairs she passes. They're a little fancier than this location would normally dictate, but I expected nothing less based on the other clothes I've seen her wear.

What baffles me, though, is the chunky cable-knit black cardigan she has wrapped around her torso. It's a little large for her and the sleeves have been rolled at the cuff. The sides form a V as they join at the first button and a sliver of the same green fabric as the pants is visible. The sweater hangs in a straight box to the top of her thighs.

Aside from the fact that I'm not sure a blind man would put those two items of clothing together, it's nearly eighty degrees outside. Even with the air conditioning on in the diner, I was considering shedding my sport coat.

"Hi." She comes to a stop next to the booth.

I push aside my bafflement and scramble to my feet. "You made it. Good."

Once she's settled into one side of the booth, I slide onto the other bench. With the pants out of view, she should present a single look now, but she doesn't. Her makeup is delicate perfection, but her hair is twisted up into one of those giant clips that makes the strands spout off one side of her head.

She pulls a menu from the rack on the side of the table. "Have you been here before? Do you have a recommendation?"

"Ah, yes." I pull a menu for myself even though my order is always one of three things. "Most anything is good, but I would stay away from the burgers."

Her eyebrows angle up as her mouth quirks into a small grin. "Not good, huh?"

"They're basically a slice of meatloaf that's been seared in a frying pan."

"Oh." She looks down at the menu. "That actually sounds good."

"You'd think. It's dry as dust, though."

"Ah."

We lapse into silence until the server comes by and takes our orders. Pork chop and assorted vegetables for me, chicken and dumplings for her.

"So." She tries to push the sleeves of her sweater up but there's too much fabric and they fall back to her wrists. "How do you plan to teach me art appreciation? I think that was a class in college."

I roll my eyes. "Likely a series of paintings on slides you had to memorize and regurgitate for a test."

She shrugs. "Probably. My university wasn't really known for the arts."

"Fortunately for you, mine was."

"Right, yes." She lists off a few statistics about my alma mater and then shyly ducks her head. "Sorry. I looked you up online."

"Then you have me at a disadvantage because unless I miss my guess, you don't have a Wikipedia page." I still remember the first time a friend showed me that page. It was completely disconcerting to see people I didn't know working to collect information about me in a single space.

"That would be a no." Her laugh this time is more genuine than nervous. I like it. "I have an Instagram page, but I don't post on it very much. And it's private, so you wouldn't have been able to see it anyway."

"If you had a Wikipedia page, what would be on it?"

Her nose wrinkles in thought and she idly stirs her water with her straw. "All the boring stuff, I suppose."

She launches into a recitation of facts such as where she went to high school and college, how she started working part time during her senior year, and that she drives a hybrid car.

It's what slips out in between the facts that pulls me in, though.

She works for her best friend and did the part-time job as a trial run because she didn't want to risk the friendship if they couldn't work together.

Right after college she adopted a hamster and named it Gigabyte, but she was so devastated when it died that she's never gotten another pet—not even a fish.

The mentions of her family are fleeting and always accompanied by an odd expression I can't pin down.

"And that's pretty much me. No Who to Watch lists or anything like that."

The server brings our plates out and I sit back as she arranges them on the table. Emma smiles at the young girl. "Thanks."

After a few moments of shifting flatware and repositioning our drink cups, I return my attention to the woman across the table.

She's shoving at her sleeves again and two spots of pink are brightening her cheeks. Why on earth is she still wearing that sweater?

"Seeing as very few people make Who to Watch lists and yet many still lead interesting lives, I don't think they make a good yardstick for the merit of someone's story."

She tilts her head as she chews, considering me as she swallows and then takes a drink of water. "I suppose not." She shrugs. "All those facts don't really matter though, do they?"

"On the contrary. Art is a relationship. What you bring to the viewing is as important as what the artist brings to the creation."

"And yet, no one is paying me ten thousand dollars to look at it."

"True. After dinner, we'll be crossing the square and attending a show at the community theater."

She shifts in her seat and pokes a fork at me. "Did you know that the most expensive Broadway show ever produced was quite the failure?"

I pause with my fork partway stabbed into a piece of broccoli. I thought she didn't like art? "It was?"

"Yep. *Spider-Man: Turn Off the Dark*. Ever heard of it?"

"Ah, no." Why has she? "How do you know that?"

"From a podcast."

"I was once a guest on an art podcast. Trying to describe brushwork without any visual aid was so frustrating, I've never done another one."

I'd meant to use this time to prep her for how to watch the play and appreciate the simplicity of no fancy special effects or slick sets. Instead, the conversation flows from one topic to another until our plates are being cleared and it's time to leave the diner.

When was the last time I was this comfortable on a date? Not that this is a date. Not once in the planning or consideration of this evening did I consider it a date. I deliberately considered it *not* a date.

I blink and shake my head, reminding myself of the pounding pain that's been lurking just underneath my consciousness. I rub my hand across my neck and the back of my head.

"You've been doing that a lot."

I look over at Emma as she picks up her purse from the bench seat and sets it on the table. "I have?"

She nods. "Headache or habit?"

"Headache."

As she opens her purse, she nods again. Her eyes meet mine and she gives me a lopsided smile. "There's no reason for both of us to have a miserable evening."

She pulls a small square out of her purse and passes it across the table. "Here."

I take it, look at it, and forget all about the pain in my head. In fact, I forget everything I know because I haven't the faintest idea what to do now.

The woman has just handed me a condom.

"Ah, I don't think . . . that is . . . I'm not sure what you thought when I asked you . . ."

I may have fleetingly compared this evening to a date, but I didn't expect her to assume it was one. Even if this was a date, we're in the middle of a diner. Not to mention this doesn't particularly fit with what I thought I knew about Emma and definitely doesn't fit with what I would expect on a date. Her brows pull together in confusion and her gaze drops to my hand.

I've read in books where it says people lose all the color in their face, and of course there are paintings where people's skin has gone pale enough to be practically see-through, but I've never witnessed the phenomenon in real life.

There is no question about it, though.

Emma Trinket has gone completely white. I can even see the faint trace of veins in her temple.

"I'm gonna kill her," she whispers before she snatches the packet from my hand and shoves it into the pocket of her cardigan.

She then jerks as if it burned her, yanks the square from the pocket, and shoves it into the purse. After a bit of rummaging around, she pulls out another square foil packet, but this one contains the familiar logo of a pain medication company.

Silently, she places it on the table and pushes it across with one finger.

I take the packet and swallow the pills one by one, taking extra care with each because the show across the booth from me right now is better than the play could ever be.

In what seems to be the purest, most genuine moment I've spent with Emma, she has dropped her head to the seat back and is muttering about her sister while flapping the front of the cardigan so that air whooshes across her face.

I set my glass aside and her head pops up. The bright pink overheated splotches have returned, and her eyes are wide enough to see edges of white all the way around her blue irises.

"I'm so sorry."

Do I say it's okay? Mumble *No problem*? Apparently, she doesn't need me to say anything because she keeps talking.

"It's not mine."

Is that supposed to make it better?

"My sister thinks I need to date more."

I cough. "It's a unique approach that would certainly land a lot of guys, but I'm not one of them."

She folds her arms on the table and drops her head on top of them.

Clearly, she is far more traumatized by this moment than I am. I've turned down propositions before and, other than finding them uncomfortably distasteful in the moment, I don't give them much thought.

Somehow, I don't feel like I've actually been offered what was implied just now.

"Emma?"

"There's food."

Is she crying? Did I hear her mumbled words correctly? "What?"

She raises her head and presses her fingers to her eyes. There are no tears running down her face, but it doesn't look like it would take much to make it happen. "There's food and surprise plans and something about cars and she thinks that means this is a date."

"She being your sister?"

"Yes." More fluffing of the cardigan. "Is it hot in here?"

"Only if you are wearing the equivalent of three sheared sheep."

More color hits her cheeks as she groans. "I don't suppose it could actually get worse."

I haven't the faintest idea what she means until she undoes the buttons and pulls the cardigan off with a deep sigh of relief.

I don't know if it's a vulnerability caused by the ridiculousness of the moment or the connection made from an hour of easy conversation, but whatever the cause, I'm very glad I'm sitting down.

Because Emma Trinket is absolutely stunning.

**13**

*EMMA*

It's official. My life is falling apart. Is there a tech company in Appleton that needs a computer programmer? Because it's very possible embarrassment is going to fuse me to this bench seat and I will have to build a life right here in this corner booth.

I'll even order the dry meatloaf burgers as penance.

I run my hands over my face one more time before remembering that Amy did my makeup. Is it smeared all over now? Do I look like a raccoon?

My elbows thunk onto the table with my face still propped in my hands. "I'm so sorry."

He clears his throat. "You said that already."

I slide my hands to my temples so that I can look him in the eye and express my sincerity. He looks like . . . actually I can't tell what he looks like. His eyes are tight, almost squinty, but his mouth is just a little bit open, the way someone does when they're too congested and have to breathe through their mouth.

"I mean it. The first chance I get, I'm sending my sister fifteen angry gifs and then blocking her number until noon tomorrow." I may even send thirty if I can line them up fast enough. I'll have plenty of time since I'm sure my evening hours are now freed up.

His face smooths into an expressionless blank for a moment and then he starts to chuckle. "Why noon?"

"Because Amy will invite my mother to brunch in order to gain access to her phone." I slump back in the booth. "And I can't block my mother."

"No, you can't do that." He considers me, a small curve to his lips. Finally, he nods toward my side of the booth. "Why the sweater?"

I did not think my face could fill with any more heat, yet somehow a fresh flood of flames burns from my neck to my eyes. If it isn't obvious, how am I supposed to explain it? "Ah . . . it was in my car."

His eyebrow lifts. "Were you cold?"

Now the man is just being deliberately obtuse, and I give him a look that should let him know I'm on to him. "Did you go outside this afternoon?"

He spreads his hands wide in a claim of innocence, laughter still lighting up his eyes. "I don't think this is the right time to be making assumptions."

I groan and scrunch up my face. "No assumptions would be good."

"So why the sweater?"

It's my turn to throw my arms wide, but my gesture is more of a presentation. "This is a date outfit."

His gaze flicks down over the part of my torso he can see before he quickly looks away and clears his throat. "Yes, it is."

I wave the arm of the sweater at him. "Therefore, sweater."

If I'd been asked twenty minutes ago if I thought my dinner companion was being guarded, I'd have said no. Our conversation had rolled along easily, and he'd seemed comfortable.

The way he's looking at me now is different, easier, relaxed in a way I hadn't realized he could be.

He leans forward over the table. "Let's make it one."

"I . . . what." It's not a question. It should be a question. I should be making him repeat himself and, if I did indeed hear him correctly, explain himself.

Instead, I think my brain has malfunctioned and is shutting down.

I can only hope it decides to reboot itself.

He grins. Dimples, teeth, the whole bit. This is not helping my brain come back online.

"I said, let's make it a date."

"But you're teaching me about art."

He sits back and shrugs. "Why can't we do both?"

Why . . . why . . . why . . . Part of me knows there's a very good reason why, but I'm having difficulty finding it. "Be . . . cause."

"Very convincing."

I blurt out the only reason I can formulate into words. "You didn't ask me on a date."

"True." He shakes his head. "At the time, I had no intention of asking you to consider turning it into one either, but it's been a long time since I found someone both intriguing and pretty. It seems a shame to waste that."

"That's the embarrassment talking."

"It is?"

I nod. "The brain processes embarrassment like any other sudden crisis and can send adrenaline pumping through your body. Depending on how your body processes adrenaline, that might make you think you, er, find me more appealing than you do."

His eyebrows shoot up. "Is that so?"

Those hormones are surging through my body right now, causing more blood to rush to my cheeks. I take a deep breath and plunge ahead with a nod. "I heard it on a podcast."

He considers me until I'm about to grab my sweater and run for the hills. Then he speaks. "In that case, why don't we keep to the original plan and go over to the theater?"

"The original plan is good." I can revert back to the original plan. Not to mention, once we're in the theater, I'll have a valid reason not to look at him for at least two hours.

"Let's go, then."

He picks up the check and walks toward the register at the front of the diner. I should catch up to him, offer to pay half or leave the tip or something, but I don't. Instead, I take my time following him, taking slow deep breaths as I pass him and step out onto the sidewalk.

I pull out my phone as I wait to the side of the entrance.

First, I queue up a series of angry gifs that include everything from Michael Scott declaring her a traitor to a little girl clocking her younger sister with a stuffed dog to a cat attacking a man's face.

Then I send them. One after the other. I open up the menu to block her but change my mind at the last minute and simply mute her contact. She is still my sister, after all.

I flip over to my text chain with Jason, but my finger hovers over the keypad. We've been friends for years and told each other so many things, including dating horror stories, but I haven't even told him I'm meeting Carter tonight.

And this is not a dating horror story.

Because it's not a date.

Even though Carter offered to make it one.

I look over my shoulder. He's smiling at the server as he signs the credit card receipt. Did I just make a huge mistake?

No. No, I didn't. Tomorrow all the adrenaline will be gone, and he'll thank me, and I'll still have the resource I need for my project.

Instead of texting Jason, I open a text to my friend Trina.

Only I don't know what to say to her either.

Frustrated, I darken my phone and open my purse to shove it back inside. The traitorous square packet stares up at me. I dig it out, shove the phone inside, and march toward a nearby trash can with every intention of disposing of the thing so it can't cause any more problems.

Carter exits the diner at that moment, and I jerk to a halt to keep from bumping into him.

The packet slips from my fingers, slides down the leg of my pantsuit, and lands on my shoe. Carter doesn't seem to notice, so I kick the packet in the direction of a nearby bush.

I'm a litterer now.

Seriously. How did this become my life?

We cross the little town square and enter the theater. The lobby is small. One end has a concession stand selling lemonade poured from pitchers into plastic cups, and the other has doors to the bathroom and is papered with signed posters from previous shows.

Directly in front of us is a wall proclaiming the current show, *Little Shop of Horrors*, and pictures of the cast. On either side of the display are curtains that I assume lead into the actual theater.

"I've never seen this show."

Carter grins. "You'll love it. There's a man-eating plant."

Why would that make me love the show? Unless it eats the spectators. I wouldn't mind having someone else bring an end to this evening before I make a bigger fool of myself by falling asleep in the theater.

The last time I did that, Amy poked me with the needle from her emergency sewing repair kit.

"Do you want any lemonade?"

Do I? I haven't yet dared to try going to the bathroom with the jumpsuit, though I need to brave the adventure before the show starts. If I skip the lemonade, I can make it home before needing to do it again.

"I think I'm good, but you can help yourself. I'm just going to . . ." I point awkwardly toward the bathroom doors and scoot away.

A glance in the mirror as I enter reveals that the jumpsuit is still looking as fabulous as it did when Amy put it on me, aside from a few extra wrinkles from being trapped beneath the cardigan. I give myself a twist so I can see if the back looks equally undamaged. It does. If I can master putting everything back in place after using the facilities, I may have to consider this one-piece clothing idea some more.

Sure enough, I leave the restroom looking just as put-together as when I went in. Do they make these things in cotton? Maybe with a stretch fabric? It's like a dress you don't have to worry how you sit in.

Carter is waiting for me with the tickets in hand.

Tickets he paid for.

Amy's voice tries to creep into my head again and I drown it out by giving Carter a giant—and terrifying if his reaction is anything to go by—smile. "Ready."

"Okay, then."

We give an older man in an army veteran's cap the tickets and slide past the curtain into the theater. It's small. Maybe two hundred seats, tops. A large center section of chairs is flanked by the two aisles behind each curtain. Smaller rows of seats line the outside walls.

I've never been in a theater this small. We take only a few steps before finding our seats in one of the side sections of the theater about halfway down the aisle.

The program is a folded 8-1/2 x 11 sheet of paper that went a little sideways when it passed through the copier. A teenage girl dressed in all black comes around the curtain and down the front steps of the stage. She talks to several people as she walks toward the lobby.

Once we're seated, I turn to Carter. "All right. What is the objective here?"

"To have fun?" He pulls out his phone and turns it off before sliding it back into his leather satchel.

He doesn't just make sure everything is still silent. He turns it all the way off.

I stare at his satchel.

"Emma?"

"What?" My gaze jerks up to find him grinning at me again. He's been doing that a lot since the incident in the diner. "Oh. Right. Have fun."

I settle deeper in my seat and examine the curtain. It's a little faded but still a nice red color. One section of tasseled trim is a little different from the rest.

Exactly how does the instruction to have fun help me here?

Spinning my upper body to face him and trying to look stern, I ask, "Did you study art?"

"Didn't you look at my Wikipedia? I have a college degree in it."

"And how many of those teachers handed you a brush and said, 'Paint well'?"

He pretends to think for a moment, but I can tell he's still laughing at me inside. "None. I had to buy my own brushes."

I roll my eyes but appreciate the joke. "My point is, you're a terrible teacher."

He holds up a finger and waves it as if I've got everything wrong. "You asked me the objective, not how I intended to achieve it."

I open my mouth to argue, but I can't because the dratted man is right. "Very well. How do you expect me to achieve the objective?"

"Look around you. This is theater in its simplest form. There are no fancy special effects—"

"I thought you said there was a man-eating plant."

He holds up his program. "We'll be lucky if it's not a refrigerator box wrapped in fabric with a slit cut in it."

The man makes a good point.

"All you have to do, all you really can do, is focus on the story."

"And that will make me enjoy it?"

He shrugs. "It might."

I've no reason to think his methods are a bunch of baloney, and yet, I do. My confusion must show on my face because he reaches into his satchel and pulls out a pencil.

After flipping the program over to the mostly blank back side, he starts to sketch. In moments, a collection of people playing soccer emerges on the page, but they aren't detailed, lifelike people. They're round heads and disjointed lines that don't seem like they should make any sort of recognizable shape, but they do.

"When you study people and movement and perspective, you learn how to draw them in the most basic way. Without hair or clothing or any other detail."

He hands me the paper and slides his pencil back into the satchel. "If you try to start with the details, they become nothing but a distraction. It doesn't matter if I draw perfect skin texture if the proportions of the leg are off."

I nod toward the stage. "So why theater?"

"The story's more obvious than with a painting."

Is he saying the obscure meaning behind a painting is too complex for me to understand, or is he unsure of his ability to explain it?

Probably neither, but the moment still feels heavy and charged with something I can't quite explain. It makes me want to fidget in my seat.

It's almost a welcome distraction when a couple asks to slide past us to reach the seats closer to the wall.

The weird tension in the air persists even after we sit back down, so I break it the only way I know how. I hold up the drawing. "Do you think you could sign this? It'd be kinda fun to be able to say I have a Carter Anderson original in my apartment."

By the end of the play, I don't need Amy's voice in my head. I'm doing an excellent job of putting my own mind in a blender. It might have something to do with the way Carter slumped down in his chair and leaned onto our shared armrest so I could speak directly into his ear as I asked questions and made observations about the play.

He would toss me wry grins or lean over to whisper into my ear as we took in the story that was interesting in a rather disturbing way. He'd been right about the man-eating plant, though. For the first act it had been played by a kid standing in a flowerpot and wearing a giant flower on his head.

As he walks me to my car, I can't help but wonder how this night would end if we had turned it into a date. I might as well admit, at least to myself, that I want to see Carter again.

"So. What next?"

He slides his hands into his pockets and looks around the town that is all but locked up tight. The only thing open is an ice cream parlor receiving a steady stream of people from the emptying theater.

"I was thinking we return to our homes. If the agenda is anything else, it won't be happening around here."

The heated cheeks I'd managed to avoid in the darkened theater return with a vengeance. "I meant as a lesson."

"I know." He grins and bends down to look me in the eye. "But you're cute when you're flustered."

He stays where he is, leaning into me, eyes traveling over my face under the scattering of streetlights around the tiny parking lot. What is he seeing? I didn't stop by the bathroom after the play, so I haven't checked myself in the mirror.

Finally, he straightens. "I'll let you know."

I nod because my tongue has rolled up like the towns' sidewalks. I climb into my car and give him a wave as I drive off.

I pop in one earbud and start my favorite theological podcast. By the time I walk into my apartment, all worries of possibly smudged make-up or future date-like non-dates have been forgotten, or at least pushed aside, as I wrap my mind around the implications of the historical considerations around the woman at the well.

In an effort to keep my equilibrium, I turn on my phone's speaker while I take a shower and climb into bed.

A therapist would probably have a grand old time discussing my coping mechanisms, but until I make that appointment, any thought I'm not yet ready to consider will find itself drowned by the onslaught of continued education.

## CARTER

I wrap my hands around my mug of coffee and stare at the only line I've written in my journal this morning.

*Emma was right.*

In the light of day, I'm glad she didn't accept my out-of-character spur-of-the-moment suggestion to turn the other night into a date.

Not that I didn't have fun with her or think she looked beautiful or wonder what it would have been like to kiss her goodnight at her car. I did all those things.

But I also have to keep working with her.

I can't recuse myself from the final discussion at the museum. They asked me to be a voice for the artists and I've already shirked that duty once because of Emma.

Still, I want to see her. I want to hear more of her observations. Never would I have thought to wonder if the parents took the child who'd played an early version of the plant home during intermission, so he wouldn't see what his character became at the end.

Since we saw the kid in the lobby after the show stuffing his face with popcorn and watching a cartoon on his tablet, I'm going to assume he's doing okay either way.

Despite the musings, I'm in my studio by my normal time. I prep three canvases for color studies, but when I go to select some sketches, I run into the same problem I've had since meeting Emma.

I have too many ideas and I don't know which to do first. It's been so long since I experienced such a flood of inspiration that I don't know how to handle it anymore.

Thirty minutes later, I scoop up the sketchbook and head for the door. If I'm struggling with a buzz like I felt when I first started out, I might as well return to the solutions from that time as well.

Frank is helping a customer when I enter the gallery, so I stroll around looking at the art while I wait. Some of Richie's paintings remain, but they are no longer gathered together in the front section of the gallery.

I wander around, taking note of which items have been on the walls for a while. Some of the pieces will stay because Frank just likes them, others because he has a good relationship with the artist, and a few because they might be of interest to his regulars that only come by a couple of times a year when their travels bring them to town.

Frank finds me staring at a cubist-style painting of a person at a desk in an office. "Looking for a new piece? That's not your usual taste."

I shake my head. There is, of course, quite a bit of art hanging in my home, but each piece was carefully chosen because of how much I like it, and I've no intention of taking any of them down anytime soon. Still, I nod at the painting. "Who do you think's going to buy that piece?"

Frank turns to consider the painting before looking at me with his eyebrows raised. "I don't know. Bob? Sue? Ricardo? Anyone on my client list that might want this piece has long since been contacted."

Yet it's still here. "What type of person would buy it?"

He turns to study the picture with me. "I always saw it going into a workplace. Maybe a reception area or even a corner office somewhere. It doesn't really scream home office, but ..." Frank shrugs.

Would this type of game work with Emma? Should I take her to a museum or a gallery and ask her what type of person she could see buying the work or where she could see it hanging? It might give her a reason to connect with the piece in a different way.

"You got a piece in the car you need me to ship?"

"What?" It takes me a moment to grasp the question Frank asked. "Oh. No. Nothing yet."

"Didn't think so. We just sent some pieces a couple weeks ago." Frank nods toward the door to the office section of the gallery. "Want a tea? Coffee? Truth serum?"

I pause in the act of reaching for the door. "Truth serum?"

"I don't know, man, you're the one looming around all mysterious and not talking. I deal with artistic eccentricities better than most, but this isn't your usual bag of tricks."

"I'm not eccentric." I roll my eyes as I open the door and walk through it.

"You keep telling yourself that."

The office area isn't as quiet as it was that night with Emma, but it's more the buzz of electronics and potential than actual people. Other than Frank and me, the only other person is his office manager, sitting at her desk near the reception area, typing an email.

We both get a cup of coffee from the machine and retreat to Frank's office. I take one of the chairs in front of his desk and he takes the other.

"To what do I owe the pleasure?" he asks.

"You're pushy today. Trying to get rid of me?"

"Trying to get back to work."

I forget sometimes that other people have hours in which they confine their jobs. While I have hours in which I normally work, my schedule is flexible if the need arises.

Like today. Right now, I should be painting. But since I don't know what to paint, I'm here.

I set the coffee on the desk, several inches from the edge, and pull out my sketchbook.

Frank's eyes light up as he, too, sets his coffee down well out of the possible range of being knocked onto the drawings. "Please tell me you're here to get help with a selection and not because you can't draw anything but stick figures anymore."

My grin escapes before I can even think of pranking my friend. "Selection."

He sticks out his hand and wiggles his fingers in a *come here* sort of gesture. I hand the book over.

It doesn't take him long to flip past the first few drawings. They're old, partially completed perspective ideas.

The moment he gets to the new stuff is obvious because everything in him, even his breathing, slows. With near reverence, he turns the pages until he gets to the blank ones. He closes the book and stabs the cover with his index finger. "You have no idea how happy I am to see this."

I retrieve the book and start flipping through the pages again myself, trying to give them a critical eye. "Why? It's not like you get a commission off my shipments."

"Because it means you're living again."

I look up to meet Frank's serious, pointed gaze. "I wasn't aware I was dead."

"There are a lot of kinds of dead. Only one involves a funeral."

"Presumably not the one I've been suffering from."

He shrugs. "You're still here, so . . . guess not."

Standing, he takes our coffees and puts them on a small table on the other side of the room before taking the book from me and opening it flat on the desk surface. Then he presses his palms to the desk and looks at the book.

"You live through your art. Always have. Those first years I could even tell by the illustrations you did for those books. If things were going well, you used rounder shapes and brighter colors. During the bad times, there were sharp corners and heavy shadows."

I wince. "It's a wonder I kept a job with that kind of inconsistency."

"Probably not recognizable to the untrained eye." Frank shrugs. "I'm not untrained."

"That's why I'm here. Which should I paint?"

He drops into the chair behind his desk and folds his hands over his stomach. "Which do you want to paint?"

"If I knew that, I wouldn't be here."

"Look." Frank flips to the first drawing in the notebook. A piano. Not even from a very interesting angle. "See this?"

I think it's a rhetorical question since I'm staring right at it, but when he doesn't speak again, I give a hesitant, "Yes."

"It's flat. When your work's flat, you're flat and you've been living flat for a while. Ghosting through life even at church. Just going through the motions."

"A non-funeral sort of dead?"

He points at me. "Bingo."

I sit back in my chair. He's not wrong. I thought something along those lines that first night I started spitting out sketches after meeting Emma.

To have him see the same things is more than a little disturbing.

"Well, I'm not flat now."

"No, you are not." Frank flips to one of my uncompleted sketches. "This has the potential to be your best work in years, maybe ever. What inspired it?"

I open my mouth to tell him about Emma, but nothing comes out. Not because I want to hide her, but because he would ask questions I don't know the answer to.

Or worse, questions I do know the answers to but don't want to admit.

"I've been people watching," I say.

"People are interesting." The slow way he says it indicates he knows I'm lying. "Person watching is good too."

No way am I going to acknowledge that one.

We get to business, discussing the merits and salability of the different ideas, finally narrowing it down to four for me to put in my work rotation.

As I close the book and slide it back into my bag, Frank stands. "A word of advice?"

"Can I stop you?"

He gives it thought. "Nope." He grins. "When you get to prepping those canvases, if one of those other ideas calls to you, answer. There's not a bad trick in the stack. I haven't seen you produce a book like that since you first got started. Whatever's brought the spark back into your life, I'll be praying you figure out how to keep it."

I pick up Emma for our second lesson. It's hard not to call it a second date, no matter how much I remind myself it's not.

Last night, after I caught myself thinking of it as a date for the fifth time, I sat down and tried to come up with someone to ask out on a real date. If I had a real date to think about, I wouldn't keep trying to make this into one.

Frank's words have haunted me until I have to admit their truth. My life has been flat, which means my relationships have been flat, which means there's not a single girl of my acquaintance that I want to take to dinner.

Yet I'm picking up Emma and taking her downtown to the Lowell Museum of Fine Art, an excursion that will require us to spend far more time together than a simple little meal.

The first twenty minutes of the ride are silent as we slip into thicker and thicker traffic until we're slowly creeping along toward our downtown exit.

"Do you get to come down here often?" I cringe inwardly as I ask the question. I sound like I think I'm doing her a favor.

"Not anymore. I went to college down here, though." She points out the window to the Georgia Tech dorms lining the interstate. "Right there."

"Not an easy school."

"No, but I enjoyed it."

Another layer of Emma Trinket. Was she a nerdy brainiac? Was everything cold numbers and calculations? Was that why art didn't make sense to her? "What did you study?"

"Computer science, with a focus on models and simulations."

Yep. Definitely sounded nerdy. "Models and simulations?"

She laughs. "I know what you're thinking, but it's not the same."

I take an exit and guide the car toward the museum. "What am I thinking?"

"That simulations are virtual art."

"Well, aren't they?" I grin at her. Part of me is curious about her answer because it really seems like they should be connected. Most of me just likes the idea of seeing her get passionate about something.

"No, it's more about creating a virtual version of a real thing."

"That's what I do."

Her mouth opens and shuts before she sits back in her seat, arms crossed. "Well, it must be different, otherwise we wouldn't be doing this trip today."

And wouldn't that be a shame.

We pull into the museum's parking garage and a few minutes later, we're standing before a painting.

"Okay." Emma straightens her shoulders and looks at the painting, steadily moving her eyes from one side to the other and from the top to the bottom. "Tell me about it."

"No, no, the objective here is for you to tell me about it."

She frowns at me. "But you wouldn't let me get a guidebook."

Using one finger, I gently push her face back toward the painting. "This isn't about the guidebook. It's about the art. What do you see?"

She looks at it and if I had to guess, she's really trying to give the picture her full consideration.

Her shoulders lift as she takes a deep breath. "I see a sad woman."

"Well, that's a start. The painting is called *La Mélancolie.*"

"So she's a sad French woman."

I resist the urge to laugh. "What do you feel when you look at her?"

After a few moments, Emma decisively answers, "Bored."

I stand behind her and look at the painting over her shoulder. Almost immediately a sense of pity for the poor woman engulfs me. She looks like she's lost absolutely everything in life. "Do you have trouble with empathy?"

She turns around, eyebrows high, clearly shocked at my question.

I can't say that I blame her.

"For real people? I don't think so. For fictitious paintings where the artist isn't even still alive? Yes."

"Fine. We'll look at it differently."

She gives me a nod of consideration.

"What type of person do you see buying this painting?"

Her answer this time is immediate. "A sad one."

"Why?"

"Because in my experience, some sad people like to surround themselves with things that make the sad feel normal. Like sad movies and sad music. I assume sad art would be the same."

I have never considered it like that, but I suppose it's true.

As I guide her toward the next painting, we continue talking. "Is the same true for happy people? Happy movies, happy music?"

She tilts her head as she thinks, and it makes her hair slide across her shoulder. Not that I should be noticing her hair. Or talking about anything other than art.

But Frank did say to keep whatever had caused that spark around, so maybe I should rethink my stance.

My skill for finding excuses to do what I already want to do is growing daily.

I redirect her attention to the art. "This is one of my favorite paintings."

"Really?" She looks from me to the painting and back again. "But it's so . . . not detailed."

"It's expressionist."

"If you say so."

I grin and tell her the basics of art movements throughout history. This actually seems to interest her, but it isn't the point of this lesson.

"Look at this. Tell me what you see."

"I'm assuming you want something other than a pool table, chairs, and several random people."

"We'll just focus on the random people for now."

She squints at the painting. "I think most of them should be at home and not in a pool hall. And no, before you ask, I don't feel the need to make sure they get there safely."

I laugh. "You aren't far off. This was a café known for being a hang-out for less reputable people. People who might be better off sleeping at a table in a café instead of at home."

"See, these are things I would know if you'd let me get the guidebook."

We fall silent as I look at the painting. It's been a while since I came down here to see it.

"You really like this painting, don't you?" she asks quietly.

I break my concentration and turn to see her standing a few feet away, observing me instead of the art. How long have I been standing here?

I nod. "It's one of those paintings that tells a story. It makes you wonder. You itch to go behind the curtain, to know if that man is going to help the drunk at the table or steal his wallet. Is that a couple at the table in the back or another person sleeping?"

"You know, they probably sell prints of this in the gift shop."

"It's not the same." I shake my head and point at the painting. "A print won't have the colors and textures. It will never get the same depth of color. See, stand here."

I position her in front of me, hands on her shoulders. "Doesn't the light appear to be moving? Can't you see it shining through the room?"

"Um, no."

My sigh ruffles her hair, and the scent of her shampoo distracts me from the painting. I cough lightly and step away. "Anyway. What sort of person do you think would purchase a painting like this?"

"You, apparently."

I'm saved from answering by a three-tone alarm from my phone.

She stares at my phone as I pull it from my pocket. "You have the sound on?"

"Only for certain notifications."

I put in my code and open the phone. Sure enough, there's an error notification from the environmental control system at my home. I go into the app, but it's not an error I recognize, nor one that I appear able to fix. All I can tell is that it has to do with the humidity in my studio.

"My apologies, but I have to cut this short."

She almost jumps toward the exit. "As delighted as I am to be leaving the art museum early, is something wrong?"

"Maybe." I frown. "There's a system in my home that controls the humidity in my studio."

"I can see where that would be important."

We return to the car, and I put both of our homes in the map system. Unfortunately, there's a wreck causing enough traffic to make taking Emma home first add almost an hour to my trip.

She reaches over and hits the X next to her address. "Let's go take care of your system first. I can always call a friend or get an Uber if I need to."

"Are you sure?"

"Absolutely."

Grateful, I set off and soon we're zipping back up the interstate we recently crawled down.

"Did you know that studies have shown actually knowing about the art does not have an impact on your enjoyment of it?"

I send a quick glance in Emma's direction. "What?"

"Art experts and novices tend to rank the emotional impact of art similarly, even though the novices don't have any idea which paintings are theoretically better done."

"Did you look that up for tonight or something?"

"I heard it on a podcast." She frowns and angles her body to face mine in the car. "Do you think that means there's something wrong with me because I would rank the emotional impact as nothing?"

"I still maintain you're just experiencing the wrong art or looking at the wrong aspects."

She sighs and faces forward again. "If you say so. You are, after all, the expert here."

And yet somehow, I feel like a complete novice.

15

**EMMA**

I hadn't given a great deal of thought to where Carter lived, but if I'd had to guess, I would have gone in the complete opposite direction of the way we were now traveling. We cut between Eastborne and Benson and continue north. The roads narrow to two lanes. Neighborhoods, sidewalks, and streetlights give way to single-family homes with large plots of land with an abundance of trees.

Finally, Carter turns into a driveway. We're not much more than fifteen or twenty minutes from my area of town when there aren't giant wrecks happening, but it feels like hours. The drive curves as it cuts through a band of trees and the space opens up into a large, barely tended field of grass and wildflowers on the edge of a body of water.

I'm not an expert on farms or anything, but the large, barn-shaped structure standing in the middle of the field looks way too nice to house animals or tractors. Add to that the fact that there are no other structures around that are large enough to be a house, and I have to assume the man lives in a barn.

Color me stunned.

He presses a button on the dash as he pulls up to the side of the house and a nearly hidden garage door slides up. After he pulls the car in and parks, he looks at me, appearing more awkward than I've ever seen him.

"Ah, would you like to come in?"

"As opposed to sitting in your car in a dark garage?" The question is out before I can stop it. I can normally keep snarky comments like that inside around my family and I'd intended to do the same around Carter, but it slipped out.

Instead of looking upset or confused, though, he grins and pushes open his door. "Good point."

He rounds the hood of the car, but the door to the house is also on this side of the room, so it's not a clear indication that he intends to open my door. It's a move I normally associate with being on a date, but some consider it regular gentlemanly behavior. I know I opened my own door when we got to the museum, but he'd opened it for me when we went to leave, so perhaps he would rather I wait.

This is an absolutely ridiculous debate swimming around in my head, and it has one very obvious solution. I grip the handle and attempt to open the door, only to smack it straight into Carter. The sudden cessation of my shove propels me face-first into the window, which causes the door to ram into Carter again.

To his credit, he says nothing but "Oof" before wrapping one hand around the edge of the door and guiding it the rest of the way open.

"Sorry," I mumble as I get out of the car and check to ensure my skirt is obeying gravity.

"Not a problem."

There's another awkward shuffle as he seems to consider taking my hand or offering his arm or gesturing toward the house or possibly even shoving me inside, but eventually he just moves to the door and sticks his key in the lock.

Inside, my mind continues to boggle as I look around the entrance area. It's as neat and organized as I expected, but it's also . . . homey. A large painting that consists of swirling lines of chunky paint hangs over a wooden upholstered bench with shoes lined up neatly beneath. A spiral staircase is sculptural as well as functional.

Carter goes to the bench and removes his brown leather shoes and replaces them with a set of suede slip-ons. They're more substantial than slippers, but far more worn in than anything else I've seen him wear.

It would be rude not to take my shoes off as well, but I don't have a pair of comfortable house shoes to switch to. Some people are very weird about bare feet. Still, when in Rome . . .

Not wanting to make him stand around and stare at me like I've been staring at him, I use one arm to prop myself against the wall and lift one foot and then the other so I can loosen the t-straps of my low-heeled pumps After that they are easy to step out of.

The floor is colder than I expected and my toes curl in on themselves. When was the last time I painted my toenails? A month ago? Three weeks? I don't look down to check.

Carter does.

Granted, he's probably not trying to determine the state of my nail polish, but he's definitely looking down at my feet.

"Ah, thank you." He takes a step toward me, hesitates, then leans down to scoop up the shoes from where I stepped out of them near the wall. "I'll just . . . put these over here."

He slides the shoes underneath the bench before pulling a set of house slippers out of a small basket on the floor. "Here."

"Thank you." My eyes widen as I accept the slippers and rescue my feet from the chilled floor. My aunt doesn't even have a basket of guest slippers at her door and she's the most fastidious person I know.

I follow him through a hall with doors opening into an office, a bedroom, and a bathroom. Everything is excruciatingly neat, but with a comfortable, homey feel. Where are the angles and modern lines of Amy's apartment or the pristine don't-touch-it-or-you'll-die elegance of my mother's house? Carter's decor, at least in this area of his house, is almost cozy.

Carter leads me through the door at the other end of the hallway. Two steps past the portal, I stumble to a halt and cannot keep my mouth from dropping open. It's not the cute little gasping space that girls on television make when their crush isn't working his shift at the ice cream parlor. No, this is full-on Lifetime movie wife discovers husband staying out late for non-work reasons mouth agape in shock.

This is his studio? It's two stories high and goes the full width of this end of the house. The last of the evening sunlight floods the room through the massive windows filling the tall wall. Beyond the glass lies a stunning view of the fields and water.

A small seating area consisting of a couch, two chairs, and a coffee table in the same exquisitely cozy vibe as the rest of the house sits to one side. Behind that, a set of stairs leads up to the second level of the rest of the house.

I don't spare a glance for that upper level though I can see it's lined with a banister instead of a solid wall. Instead, I can't stop looking at the other end of the room.

His work area.

A large desk filled with drawers sits near the window with a cart of organized cups of pens and pencils beside it. The wall beneath the upper level is covered with racks upon racks of hanging paint tubes arranged in rainbow order. A sink is next, followed by another wall rack holding bins of brushes, rags, and some other odd things I'm assuming are for creating painted masterpieces.

The tall, non-windowed wall has been divided with the top looking like something out of an art supply store. Canvases of various sizes, panels in different materials, rolls of paper and cloth.

And then beneath . . .

In a trance I cross the room to look at the canvases in different states of completion. Having seen some of Carter's completed works, I know these will all eventually look so real it will be impossible to believe the subject isn't actually right in front of you. At the moment, though, they're random blocks of colors, only a few of which can actually be identified as the basic shapes of people or furniture.

"Is this how all your paintings start?"

"Mm-hmm."

Carter's answer is matter of fact and distracted as he looks from his phone to a few corners of the room and then disappears back down the hall.

I trail after him slowly, continually stealing glances over my shoulder at the works in progress. One is nothing but a mix of browns and tans, another has some circles and lines in deep brown or black. The next one in the line has some blocks of color, but the last one is nearly blank.

He's not in the hallway when I finally make it there, so I poke my head in the rooms until I find him in the home office, tapping at a box on the wall.

As I get closer, I can make out the control panel for what appears to be a fairly extensive environmental control system. With all the canvases and the drying paintings, I can see where it would be important to maintain the air quality and temperature.

I can't quite tell what he's trying to make it do, but it's obvious he isn't finding success.

Channeling my favorite animated should-be-considered-a-princess, I clasp my hands in front of me, dig one toe into the ground, and say, "Whatcha doin'?"

"Nothing, it would seem." He sighs and presses the home icon again.

A series of options appear on the left side of the screen. He presses one with water droplets beside a percentage signal. A connection error appears on the screen.

"Do you have another way of accessing the system? Maybe through the computer?"

"Yeah." He shakes his head and gives me a lopsided grin. "It gets confusing, though. It took me a while to learn how to use this." He waves a hand toward the console.

"How about I take a look at your computer while you tell me how the brown blobs in there are going to become a hamburger so real I want to eat the canvas?"

He grins. "None of them are going to be hamburgers."

"Not the point. Computer?"

"All yours." He waves a hand toward the desk, where a laptop sits squarely in front of the chair. The whole office is as neat and organized as the studio but looks even more so because there aren't dried paint splatters on the floor or any tools on display aside from the laptop.

How does anyone work like this? At this moment, I imagine there are no less than twelve pens sitting on various surfaces in my office, three dozen spec printouts thumbtacked to the corkboard, and twice as many Post-it notes stuck to the wall. Then there are the blankets, spare cables, USB drives, and who even knows what else.

He opens a drawer, removes a small notepad and pen, sets them on the table by the laptop, and opens the computer. After he's typed in the password and clicked the icon to pull up the environmental system, he steps away, gesturing to the chair.

"Okay, then." I start clicking through menus, familiarizing myself with the options. "Start talking."

"About my painting process?"

"Yep." I find the log and read through the error messages, copying the most recent one so I can paste it into a search engine.

"Well, I prep the canvases and set the undertones. That's most of what's been done out there."

I look up at him, eyes wide. "Like skin."

"I, what?"

"Well, with makeup, it matters what the undertone of your skin is." I wave a hand in the air. "Magenta amber doesn't look good on everyone."

He frowns. "What sort of color is magenta amber? Those don't go together at all."

"Have you seen makeup names? Magenta amber would be completely rational, but as it so happens, I'm making it up. Anyway, Amy and I can wear the same blush, but it looks completely different."

"Well, then, yes, it's exactly like that."

I file the information away as an interesting tidbit, then turn back to the computer.

While I scroll through search results, he talks about sketching out the key points of figures to ensure everything is laid out correctly on the canvas before blocking out tiles of color to create basic shapes, using colors that work with the base to create deeper tones and an overall balance.

After that I don't understand what he's talking about because the vocabulary isn't familiar, but I also can't picture it.

I check a couple of blogs and think the most time-honored method in IT support will do the trick.

If it doesn't, he's going to have to call a technician.

He falters in the middle of a sentence as I walk past him and return to the studio.

"What are you—"

"So, what's that going to be?" I point to the canvas that's farther along than the others based on his description of the process as I start searching the room for the humidity sensor. Based on the name in the system and the need for a power source, I'm guessing . . . aha! A small white box is plugged into the wall near a collection of lights with their cords wrapped neatly around the poles.

"A face. Can't you see the eyes and the mouth?"

I move to the box and disconnect the power supply. "Are you painting realistic zombies now? Because I don't know if you noticed, but that thing is gray."

"What are you doing?"

"Counting to ten."

He keeps staring at me, so I grin and add, "Rebooting."

"Oh."

I nod toward the painting, eyebrows raised.

"Ah, no, that's not a zombie. Once the hair and other elements are put in place, it will look exactly like a realistic skin tone."

It's my turn to stare at him.

"No, really." He crosses to the painting and pulls something from behind the canvas. "See?"

He holds up a smaller canvas with blobs of color, some of which look similarly shaped to the ones on the big canvas. It's impossible to tell what the final picture will be since there are not details, but the area in the middle does indeed look like a healthy, olive skin color.

I plug the power cord back into the sensor, then point between the two paintings. "Those are not the same."

"Oh, but they are." He grabs a rag and drapes the ends over the canvas, hiding some of the color blocks.

Sure enough, it looks gray.

I look around the room, at the field and water outside, and the sunset starting to crease the sky. What color are they really? "My eyes are round little liars."

His laughter fills the studio as beeps sounds from down the hall. He leaves the room.

I look at the sensor, trying to see if it's come back online, but the LED indicator lights have been completely obscured.

"You fixed it." Carter returns with his phone in his hand, the app pulled up and turned toward me to show an error-free control panel.

"What can I say? You make gray look tan, and I know how to turn things off and on again." I tuck the sensor back into its corner.

"Thank you."

"It's the least I can do for the tutoring you're attempting to give me." I scrunch up my nose. "I don't think it's working, by the way."

He looks from me to the canvases, even as he guides me back toward the hall and our outside-going shoes. "Are you busy tomorrow?"

It's Saturday so my greatest plans involve eating cereal for lunch and beating the next level of my video game before tackling the necessary evil that is cleaning. Chances are I will never get out of my pajamas. "Why? Are you going to make me get fancy and peruse more paintings? If so, I'm bringing sheets of posterboard because I want to know which ones are lying to me."

"It isn't a lie if you see it correctly."

"Maybe. But it's still a trick. People with shaved heads don't look gray."

"Ah, no, they don't. And while, yes, I was thinking of having our next lesson, we wouldn't be looking at paintings."

"Theater? Statues? Oh, please don't make me go to the opera."

He shakes his head. "No. This time you're going to be the one making the art."

**CARTER**

I'm sure there are many a journal entry that start with the words *it seemed like a good idea at the time* and mine tomorrow will likely be one of them. But in the light of this morning, it still seems like the best plan.

Why didn't I think of it sooner? The easiest way to appreciate a chef's talent is to attempt to cook for yourself. Art should be much the same.

If I'm very fortunate, the effort will make her see that asking people to look at art through their phone screens is an insulting idea.

I glance at my watch. She's due to arrive in fifteen minutes. Is she the sort of person who's early, on time, or late?

My last-minute run-through of the house straightening pillows and emptying trash cans baffles me. For one, she'll have no reason to go anywhere except my studio and possibly the downstairs bathroom. The state of my kitchen and living room don't matter.

And yet, I'm prepping them as if this is a date.

There's that d-word again.

My studio is usually a near-sacred space for me, but I hadn't minded having her in it last night, and not just because she was saving me a customer support phone call that, apparently, would have been rather embarrassing. The idea that she'll be in my studio again should cause me concern, but it doesn't. Even having Frank in my space makes me nervous.

Is it because she doesn't know what she's looking at? She isn't judging my unfinished works because she doesn't know how and wouldn't care if she did. If I decide to scrap a painting, she'll never know.

Everything is ready so I take the bag I've been emptying trash into out to the outside trash can.

And laugh.

There's a little silver hatchback, and the driver is staring at my house as if it might explode and she'll need to make a quick getaway.

I close the trash can and walk over to her car. As I get closer, the low hum of an electric engine meets my ears. So she really is thinking about driving away. I give the window a light tap.

Her face jerks toward me, but the expression doesn't change. Two long braids frame her wide eyes. The relaxed hairstyle fits her.

The window lowers. "Hi."

"Hello." I point to the house. "Want to come inside?"

She glances at the dash. "I'm five minutes early."

I spread my hands wide. "We can wait out here if you'd like."

"You don't need the five minutes to . . . get ready or whatever?"

"Ah, no." My face pulls together in confusion. "You were here, what, twelve hours ago? What do you think I've done in that amount of time that requires a lot of cleaning?"

"I once spent a total of nine hours in a hotel room. Seven of those were spent sleeping. And yet, somehow, my stuff was everywhere when I went to pack up the next morning."

This strange detail about a moment in her life fits my interactions with her, even if it doesn't sound like the type of person who would wear designer pantsuits and attend benefit galas.

Partly because most of the women I know who do such things wouldn't be able to fit their night and morning beauty routines into two hours, not to mention the packing and, it would seem, unpacking. Not that I have a lot, or really any, first-hand knowledge of beauty routines, but I've heard other men talk about waiting on their wives, sisters, and girlfriends.

I give the door handle a tug and it swings open. "I promise it's okay if you come inside now."

"Okay." She turns off the car and slides out, straightening her silk T-shirt.

It's the most casual I've seen her, which is good since we'll be painting. I glance down at the jeans and quickly jerk my eyes to the sky as she leans back into the car to grab her purse.

Her jeans fit really well.

I step back so she has room to situate her bag and close the door. I was expecting a small purse, but she's brought a nylon backpack like I carried in high school.

We go inside and I trade my outdoor shoes for my indoor ones. Just like last night, she removes her shoes without a word. Instead of retrieving the slippers from the basket, though, she opens her backpack and pulls out a pair of lime green Crocs.

"I know they look a little rough, but I cleaned them last night. Ran them through the dishwasher, actually, before realizing that's not a recommended method. Are they okay?" She holds up the shoes for inspection. "I can wear the slippers if you'd rather."

The look she gives the basket is a flash of utter disgust, and I struggle not to laugh. It's interesting that she put the forethought into bringing shoes but not into checking the best way to wash them. "Those are fine."

"Great." She puts the Crocs on and grabs up her book bag. "Let's do this, then."

I take her back to the office first, since she's already been there once. "You can leave your stuff in here."

"In here?" She looks around. "Aren't we painting?"

And this is another reason I don't let people into my studio. I like my studio clean. Very clean. Nothing goes into it that isn't strictly necessary. The fact that furniture and large items have to be taken up the stairs in my studio is one of my only dislikes about this house. I needed a new dining table last year and I almost didn't buy one because of that.

I clear my throat. "Yes, um, I don't like distractions."

"I know you're amazingly talented, but I don't think I'll be creating any masterpieces in there today."

"All art is a masterpiece. The value is in the meaning to the beholder."

She drops her backpack on the desk. "You know, Richie Reynolds would have said that much more poetically."

My eyebrows lift. "You spend a lot of time with Richie?"

"No, but my sister does and she's currently mad at me. I can't decide if she's trying to prove she's better than me or deliberately torture me, but she's been sending me updates of his views on things lately." She slips her phone out of her back pocket and opens it to a texting thread. "This morning they had brunch at my favorite breakfast place and 'food cooked in the oil of adoration must be sprinkled with the salt of privacy to be enjoyed.'"

Even though it's rude, I can't help but glance at her phone screen, certain she's quoted that wrong.

She turns the device so I can see the thread and, sure enough, that's exactly what it says.

Again, I tell myself not to look at anything else, but she did voluntarily show it to me, so my gaze quickly takes in the rest of the screen.

Most of the messages are from her sister and definitely of the taunting variety that include several other bits of Richie's egotistical nonsense. The only message from Emma to Amy is partially visible at the top of the screen and reads, *"you're understanding things these days, the apology thrown back a forty-second time ceases to be genuinely extended."*

She pulls the phone back and darkens the screen before sliding it back into her pocket.

"Uh, the phone too." Heat crawls up my neck. This was an absolutely terrible idea. Actually, teaching her to paint is a fabulous idea, but doing it here in my own studio was a bad choice.

"What about it?"

"Can you leave it in here, too?"

Her gaze flits to the laptop and the wall-mounted environment panel.

"So the covered LEDs weren't a light-pollution thing, huh?"

I sigh. "No."

Slowly, as if she can't remember the last time she did it, she sets her phone on the desk, then blows every thought from my mind as she wordlessly slips off her watch and places it on the desk as well. She takes a step away and shudders. "This feels so weird."

Some of the tension over my plan fades away at her easy acceptance. I lead her toward the door. "Are all tech people so attached to their phones?"

"Are all artists weirdly eccentric?"

I stop to think about it and have to admit that once again Frank was right, I'm eccentric, and yes, every artist I know is in possession of at least a few quirks.

Once in the studio, I take her over to where I've prepared a small canvas and secured it on the easel.

She takes some time to inspect it, looking at the back, running a finger along the edge. I try to remember it doesn't matter if she gets oils from her skin on the canvas, but I can't say I'm teaching her and allow her to form bad habits.

"Normally you wouldn't want to touch the canvas."

"That makes sense, but . . ." She rubs her fingers together and leans in to look at the surface. "Is there something on it already?"

"Gesso. Keeps the paint from affecting the fibers of the canvas."

I start to teach her about layers and how we'll work them onto the canvas, but we don't get far before she begins asking questions.

I don't remember the last time—if ever—that I tried to teach an absolute beginner how to paint, but I know it didn't go like this. Painting students are usually anxious to do just that—paint. Teaching them to carefully prep their canvas and palette and take the time to build the bottom, less exciting layers properly can be like trying to hold back a dog who's seen a squirrel.

Emma has yet to ask when she can apply brush to canvas. Oh, she has plenty of questions about the brushes, but they have more to do with what they are made of, how different ones are used, how often do I have to replace them. She asks about the easel and marvels over the magnetic palette knife holder on the side of the table I use to hold my tools while I'm working.

I realize that for her, at least, I've started too close to the beginning and while she wanders the studio asking about everything from why I have a stock of different mediums to paint on to why I have linseed oil stored by my paint rack, I prepare a palette and apply the first base layer of paint to the canvas so she can focus on painting things she knows.

It's not what I intended to paint with her, but I think, given the circumstances, it's the better choice.

Finally, I call her back to the easel. "You do remember why you're here, don't you?"

She strolls back over, eyes wide, as she takes in the canvas and paints. "You did all that while I was asking you questions?"

"Yes. Now. Let's make a mountain."

"Okay." She gives a decisive nod and picks up a skinny paintbrush.

I can't help but smile. "No."

She exchanges it for a wide, flat brush.

I shake my head.

We go through this process three more times before I hand her a palette knife.

She looks at it, looks at me, and looks like she's considering stabbing me with it. "Are you serious or do you have a hidden camera somewhere to catch you pranking me?"

There actually is a security camera, but it's technically in my living room space and only aimed at my studio. I don't mention it.

"Do you want me to make one first?"

She turns the knife so the handle is pointed toward me, but she doesn't extend it. Instead, she looks from the palette to the canvas and bites her lip. Then she sighs and pushes the knife forward. "Yes. But only because it's ridiculous to try something without instruction just because you think you know what you're doing."

"That sounds like the voice of experience."

"You have to lean forward when you roller skate."

It shouldn't make sense and yet somehow it does, and I can't help but laugh as I take the knife and load it with paint. When was the last time I laughed this much?

I show her how to slide the paint on, then give her the knife to try. Her mountain peak is decidedly paler as she pushes too much of the paint down the canvas, but it isn't bad. That part is hard to mess up unless you stab the knife into the canvas.

Adding snow works about the same way, though this time she pulls the knife away from the canvas in an attempt to keep from using too much pressure.

When we paint the lower portion of the distant mountain, it's a repeat of yesterday's color conversation.

She points at the palette. "That is yellow paint."

"Yes."

"And brown paint."

"Actually, it's umber."

"Whatever. Do you know what it isn't?"

I smile, knowing where this is going. "What?"

"Green. It's not green." She points at the painting. "That looks green and I know you're going to tell me it's like the gray skin thing, but we put this over white. It should look yellow or orange or something. But it's green."

"Or at least appears that way."

"You painted this blue sky while I was walking around. Did you actually use pink?"

"Nope." I point to the partially spread dollop of blue paint. "Just blue."

"Ugh. Fine. Show me how to paint a happy little tree."

I pause in the act of reaching for a brush to do just that. "You know who Bob Ross is?"

"Everyone knows who Bob Ross is." She gives me a sideways look. "My church's youth group occasionally does a Bob Ross night. It's kinda cute, actually."

My church youth group does Bob Ross nights, too. It must be a thing, which makes me pretty happy.

"When I need a dose of humility, I pull up an old Bob Ross video."

She takes the paintbrush I offer her. "I know he's great and all, but I'm pretty sure all his rivers look like paint, not something you could wash your hands in."

"And yet, I still can't keep up with the man."

I show her how to paint an evergreen tree with long, droopy limbs but her attempts at the needles keep spreading, turning her limb into more of a splotch.

After I demonstrate again and she's still creating bushes in the sky, I set the palette down and move behind her. My left hand can't hold a brush for anything more than cleaning, so I have to stand behind her and bring my right hand around hers to change the way she's holding the brush.

I guide her hand through a few branches, then slowly pull my hand back so she's doing the work without me. As my fingers leave the handle and brush against the skin on the back of her hand, I become all too aware of how we're standing.

That doesn't mean I rectify the situation. I can tell myself it's because I don't want to scare her or startle her when she's just getting the hang of painting, but I know when to call myself a liar.

"Good job." My voice is deeper and thicker than I thought it would be and her hand tightens on the brush until the knuckles turn white.

"Thanks." Her voice whispers across my neck and I look down.

She's watching me instead of the painting. There are still several inches between our lips but that's only because I'm a foot taller than she is.

Her shoulders are firmly against my chest and her head is tipped back, the temple brushing my shoulder.

I want to close the space.

That alone scares me into moving. I step back and shove my hands into the back pockets of my pants.

"Right. So." She sets the brush down and rubs her hands along her thighs, looking everywhere but at me. "Should we clean up, or—"

"I'll get it." I need her gone but kicking her out would be rude.

Fortunately, she's of the same mind because she's already moving back toward my home office. "I'll just . . . get my things, then."

As she clears the doorway, my brain kicks back in gear and I follow to walk her out like a gentleman. She's already collected her backpack and is moving toward the door. "Thank you." She kicks out of her Crocs and slides her feet into leather loafers. "The lesson. So much sense. Great teacher."

Good to know I'm not the only one feeling off-kilter.

Actually, no. That's not good to know. It would be much easier to tell myself this was a strange, one-off occurrence if she hadn't felt anything.

She pushes out the door, still mumbling incomplete sentences, and all but runs to her car.

I wave her off, trying to look normal, but when I go back inside, I spend several minutes staring at a pair of abandoned lime green Crocs.

**17**

*EMMA*

"I agree, she's totally dating him."

If we weren't walking down the hall of a church, I just might push my two closest friends in front of a moving bicycle.

I'd told Jason about yesterday's painting debacle while we got coffee before our life group class. After class, he shared it with our friend Trina, although he added plenty of his own embellishments and observations.

Such as his opinion that Carter and I are dating and just don't know it.

I'm never introducing Jason to Amy.

"We're not dating." I give in to the urge to shoulder bump my best friend. "And you shouldn't be making this more difficult. He's helping me make this project better. For free, I might add."

"Well, yeah," Trina says, flipping her dark curls over her shoulder, "because that's what boyfriends do."

Why do I hang out with these people?

"Speaking of the project," Jason says, "are you sure it's going well? I know I said we didn't have the bandwidth for it, but we can do some juggling if we need to."

I do not want to admit that I'm in over my head. There are still over two months before the prototype presentation. I can get a handle on everything.

Fortunately, this conversation I can bypass. "Nope. We agreed. No office talk when we aren't little worker drones."

"Why doesn't that rule go the other way as well?" Jason grumbles.

"Because you never stop being people." Trina links our arms at the elbows as we enter the large main lobby that runs the length of the front of the church. "Besides, I want to hear more about this Carter Anderson fellow. What's he look like? Handsome?"

I am not answering that. Very well, I'm answering it because not answering will only make her poke deeper, but I'm not answering honestly. "He's okay. Brown hair. Hazel eyes. Tall."

"So you're practically twins," Jason quips.

Ew. No.

"I dunno. He's a guy." I wave my arms in front of me like a magician trying to make a person appear out of thin air.

I look up, as if inspiration is going to float down from the skylights above the wide staircase that leads to the worship center balcony.

And I freeze.

It would seem I actually am a magician because Carter Anderson is walking down the stairs of my church, talking to a slightly older man who also looks vaguely familiar, but I can't place.

Not that it matters because . . . Carter Anderson.

I shove past Jason, duck into the nearest alcove, and press my back to the wall beside an information poster about mission volunteer opportunities while my heart threatens to turn me into a jackhammer.

Jason and Trina come after me, both looking worried and alarmed. Jason has his phone out, ready to call for help.

At least I managed to distract them from the Carter conversation, although that reprieve is going to be temporary because apparently the man goes to my church.

Has he always gone here? How did I not know? Not that I know everyone who goes to church here. It's a large church. Two services each Sunday plus livestream to the internet. Nearly four thousand active members. Obviously, I don't know everyone, but how did I not know him?

Trina presses a hand to my forehead. "She's clammy."

Great. Does that mean I'm sweating? Clammy means it feels wet, right? I don't have time to Google it.

"Do you need me to call for a medic? There's usually at least one on the Sunday security team." Jason moves toward the lobby.

I yank him back into the alcove. It's a needless move because Carter isn't going to recognize Jason or vice versa, but my rational thoughts aren't forming quickly right now.

Jason slides the phone into his pocket and crosses his arms. "What is going on?"

Trina looks between us. "You don't think she's sick?"

"No, she's not sick. She's panicking."

"Why?" Trina sticks her head out. "Is your mom here?"

That's laughable. While Amy will at least talk to me about faith—at least she did before she got mad at me—Mom likes to pretend I just sleep in extra hard on Sundays.

Still, I shake my head. I don't know if it's to answer her or try to shake some sense into myself.

Okay. First things first, I need to get Jason and Trina out of this alcove because it is not big enough for the three of us. It's meant to hold one of those stand-up retractable banners or a table of pamphlets or something, not three grown people.

"I'm fine. You guys go. Save me a seat."

"Yeah, right," Jason says. "Who's out there?"

"Lots of people. It's a big church." At least my brain is coming back online.

"Mm-hmm. With lots of space for people to walk. So why are we hiding?"

I roll my eyes. "I don't know why *you're* hiding."

"Good point." He turns to Trina. "Let's step back out and talk to her from the lobby."

Because no one will be at all curious about why they're talking to a wall. "You'll look ridiculous," I mumble.

"Only until someone comes up and sees you. Then you'll be the one looking ridiculous."

Trina gives Jason a look of admiration. "You handle her amazingly well."

"Years of practice." Jason folds his arms. "One more time, who's out there or I go start introducing myself to people."

He would, too. Jason may have decided to run his own tech company, but he grew up in North Benson, with his parents hobnobbing around as much as my family does now. If he hadn't left that behind, he probably would have run into me with my family a time or two. He got taught the skills, though, and can work his way through a crowded room in ten minutes flat.

If Carter is still out there, Jason will find him.

That's a big if. Surely Carter has had time to get down the stairs and head to wherever he's going. "I just thought I saw someone I know." I wave my hand in dismissal as I push myself off the wall. "Probably because we were talking about him."

I realize my mistake as soon as the words leave my mouth.

Trina is once again peeking around the wall. "Carter Anderson is here? He goes to this church? The plot thickens."

Jason is just grinning.

"What?" I ask warily.

He keeps smiling.

"He's probably gone now."

"Great." Jason throws an arm across my shoulders and guides me back into the lobby. "Let's go to service, then."

What is he doing? We never walk like this. It makes people think we're— "Oh no. Jason, no."

"Oh, yes." He presses a kiss to my temple.

I can practically feel my phone burning with all the messages I'm going to get because there's no way no one saw that.

"Is he still here?" Trina asks in a whisper, her gaze darting around the lobby.

"Yep." My gaze doesn't have to dart because it is completely caught in Carter's.

Jason follows my gaze and walks us in Carter's direction. "I'm a guy and even I know you were lying about his looks."

The daggers Trina is sending my way say she's thinking the same thing. About Carter. Not about being a guy.

As for Carter, I can't read him well enough to say, but I'm guessing he'd like some time in an alcove to process.

I jab my finger into Jason's ribs.

He just pulls me in closer.

Fine. I'll just make this awkward for everyone and not say anything.

Carter has other plans. "Hello, Emma. I should have guessed you attended here after the Bob Ross comment yesterday."

I wish he'd said something then. It would have saved us all the embarrassment because I would have found a sudden desire to volunteer in the nursery.

"I normally attend the early service." He points up the stairs. "I got caught talking to some people this morning."

That would explain why I've never seen him. Along with the fact that we walk right by people we don't know every day without ever thinking about them.

He turns to the man beside him. "Do you remember Frank? He owns the art gallery where Richie exhibited."

So I have seen the man before, just surrounded by very distracting paintings. Keeping silent now would be unforgivably rude instead of simply awkward. "Of course. Good to see you again."

We all fall silent, Carter looking pointedly from me to Jason, Jason grinning like he's having the time of his life, and Frank and Trina both looking torn between fleeing the scene and bursting into laughter.

I vote they both flee and take me with them.

When I can't take it anymore, I say, "This is Jason."

Carter's eyes widen. "Your boss?"

"Yes." Jason extends his hand. "We've known each other far longer than that, though. Went on our first date her sophomore year of college."

The expression on Carter's face is distinctly unhappy, maybe a little angry, and definitely confused.

I don't like it.

"And we went on our last date two weeks later, you jerk." I squat and spin out from under his arm, arching my back to keep his hand from grabbing me as I roll by. I take a step away and glare at his grinning face.

Carter looks between us. "So you aren't . . . together?"

"No." I cross my arms and keep glaring at Jason because that's easier than dying of embarrassment while looking at Carter.

"No, we are not." Jason leans in. "And isn't it interesting that you seem happy about that?" He spins on his heel. "Come on, Trina. Let's find seats."

He set me up. The man strolled me across the lobby with every intention of setting me up.

I really am going to push him in front of a bicycle.

Frank must have made his escape as well because when I find the courage to look back at Carter, it's just him and me standing here as the lobby slowly empties.

He sticks his hands in the pockets of his dress pants. "So . . ."

"So," I parrot.

The man looks just as good as he always does. Slacks. Button-up shirt. Sport coat. It seems to be his usual look.

I am also in my usual Sunday look, which is nothing like what he's ever seen me in. Well, he's seen the jeans because they are the same ones I wore yesterday, but today they're paired with a boxy green shirt that couldn't decide if it wanted to be a T-shirt, a sweater, a tunic, or a beach towel. I personally love it and think it's perfect for church because it's comfortable and doesn't have a cartoon character on it, but it certainly didn't come from Amy's *Look Book*.

I'm also wearing running shoes. The kind that come from an athletic store.

"Is there a real boyfriend waiting in the wings somewhere?"

That is not what I expected him to ask. "No. What about you? Any girlfriends?"

Oh my gosh, why are we asking each other this?

He shakes his head. "None, pretend or otherwise."

"Oh. That's a shame."

"It is? Why?"

Excellent question, Emma. Why *do* you think it would be good if the cutest guy you've ever seen who made you put away your phone for hours yesterday and then helped you have a good enough time that you didn't even think about it had a girlfriend?

"I don't know. Seemed the thing to say."

He grins and relaxes. I didn't even realize he'd been stiff. That's a talent I'd like to learn.

"Your non-boyfriend friend had a good point."

Oh goodness. Is he going where I think he's going? I swallow. "One would think he could get his point across in a better way."

He grins. "Are you going to do anything about it?"

"I was considering pushing him in front of a bicycle."

He jerks his head as if my words actually hit him in the face. Through a laugh he asks, "Why a bicycle?"

"Because it would be unpleasant but probably wouldn't do any real damage."

He considers it and gives me a nod. "Good point. Maybe we can consider doing it after."

"After what?"

"After we go on a date. A real one this time. No theater or galleries or museums."

My heart does the cha-cha with my stomach. "Do you go other places?"

"I do. So what do you say? Want to go to one of those other places with me?"

I should probably take the time to consider the ramifications of this idea. He still goes to galas. He's still part of the museum board. I still need him to help me with work. His sport coat collection rivals my video game one. Yet all I can really give consideration to is standing in front of him while we painted yesterday.

With that in mind, I smile and say, "Yes."

**CARTER**

Dating Emma has several benefits. I laugh. A lot. I think about things other than art because I want her to enjoy our dates. I have conversations that make me think because she doesn't see life the way most people do.

What dating Emma is not at all good for is my work.

Oh, she's still inspiring sketches and ideas, but it doesn't do me any good if those ideas aren't getting transferred to canvas.

A week and a half. In that time, we've gone on three dates. Four if I count the art appreciation lesson I slipped in, though Emma insists we call it work. Sitting together in church this past Sunday could bring the count up to five, if I was looking to sound like a lovesick puppy.

I step back from the canvas I've been working on all morning and a sense of pure satisfaction fills me. Even Emma wouldn't call it mere blobs anymore, though there's a lot of work to do to bring layers and details into the picture.

When I look at the canvas, I see where I'll add fine lines and shadows, where I'll use glaze to change the perceived depth.

Part of me wants to keep going, to start in on the next step of my painting plan, but I'm thirty-one years old and my body needs movement, food, and at least two tall glasses of water.

I'll get another painting session in this afternoon. I should probably not make plans with Emma so I can fit one in this evening as well. The idea makes me frown as I set about cleaning the palette and brushes.

I'm fortunate to be an artist who lives off my art. I can guess the minimum my agent will be able to sell a painting for these days and I know how many I need to paint each year to keep myself living comfortably, free to deny commissions, and saving for a rainy day.

If I don't get back to putting in three sessions a day at least three times a week, I'll have trouble making that quota.

Although what painting sessions I've gotten in this week have been amazing.

I give the easel one more satisfied look before moving upstairs to take a much- needed break.

I pour a glass of water from the filter pitcher in the fridge, then cross the kitchen to retrieve my phone from the charger on the counter.

Before Emma, I'd have expected maybe three text messages to be waiting for me. One from the environmental sensor system with the average humidity from the day before, one from Grandpa letting me know his Wordle score for the day, and one from my mother reminding me to answer my grandfather.

She still feels a little guilty that Dad's job took them to South Carolina, and she isn't around to check on her parents anymore. The last thing she wants is for them to feel abandoned by the rest of the family.

I play Wordle myself so I can send Grandpa my results and assure Mom I've done my grandsonly duty before I click on Emma's name.

Seventeen unread messages. That's a lot, even for her.

It's hard to drink water while grinning, but I manage as I scroll through the texts.

They start as normal.

> EMMA
> Good morning.

> EMMA
> Actually, more like good afternoon by the time you read this.

> EMMA
> I tried to pour my milk into my coffee in a heart shape. It failed.

> EMMA
> <<Picture of a cup of coffee>>

It looks just like a regular cup of coffee. I can't even see where she tried to make a heart.

> ME
> Did you steam the milk first?

I hit send, then scroll back up to where I was. Her response makes my phone vibrate almost immediately, but I just shake my head and keep reading.

She knows I'm responding as I read, so she won't mind waiting.

> EMMA
> Did you know latte art started in the 1980s?

EMMA
I'd have thought it was older than that.

There's a large gap in the timestamps after that until she starts in with
sharing the interesting things she's learning from podcasts.

I'll never understand how that woman can listen to someone talk while
writing out an email and be able to keep up with what's going on in both.

EMMA
Did you know that no one really knows the value of
Van Gogh's *Starry Night* because it's never sold at
auction?

She's added art history podcasts to her rotation. The paintings themselves might not interest her, but history sure seems to.

EMMA
Knock, knock

EMMA
<Deep Carter Voice> Who's there?

EMMA
Yourself

EMMA
<DCV> Yourself who?

EMMA
Your cell phone is buzzing, you'd better check it!

Well, that explains why I have seventeen messages. The daily factoid messages started after our second date. Every interaction is purely Emma, but the tiny bubbles of text on my phone seem more authentic somehow, even if I can't quite picture them being written by the woman I've been picking up.

I scroll through a few more informational tidbits as my phone buzzes two more times.

Growing concerned, I skip the last few and scroll down to check the ones she's sent since I answered her.

> EMMA
> Oh, good, you're on your phone.

> EMMA
> What's taking you so long?

> EMMA
> Oh my gosh, I forgot about the knock, knock joke.

> EMMA
> That was dumb because I really need an answer.

An answer to what? I flip back to the last two messages she sent.

Ah. She has art questions. Or rather, museum ones.

A niggling worry presses against the nape of my neck. I keep forgetting about the prototype and I squirm every time something reminds me of it.

> ME
> I have no idea how far people stand from the paint-
> ings when they look at them. Some people sit on

the benches.

ME
Some people can clear the museum in an hour,
others stay for the whole day. It's not predictable.

As expected, her thanks comes through immediately, and I set the
phone down to make myself some lunch.

If we follow the pattern we've done for the past few days, I'll have
another group of texts after my afternoon session. On the evenings when
we don't have plans, like tonight, I'll send her some messages about how
my day went while I relax in front of the television.

My hand has barely connected with the refrigerator handle when my
phone buzzes again.

Frowning, I pick it up.

EMMA
How long do the guided tours last, then? Wouldn't
that be the average amount of time spent?

ME
Some people hang out at the museum before and
after the guided tour.

Once more, I set my phone down and see about getting lunch.
I don't even make it to the fridge.

EMMA
Do you think the museum would let me watch the
security camera?

ME
No.

EMMA
<<gif of a guy on a couch with a stack of papers
saying "I need answers">>

Gifs are an art form I sort of knew existed before Emma came into my life, but I hadn't seen many of them.

I am on my way to becoming proficient.

ME
I can take you to the museum Saturday. We'll sit and
watch the people.

I set the phone down slowly, like it might turn into a snake if I move too fast.

Sure enough, it buzzes right as it touches the counter.

EMMA
<<gif of a cat laid out on its back sleeping>>

This is ridiculous. She can't possibly be getting any work done. I pluck the wireless headphones from my charging station and put one in my ear. Once all the beeps signaling proper connection are finished, I go into Emma's contact and press *call*.

Then I set the phone firmly on the counter and return to making lunch.

"Ew, gross, you weirdo. What are you doing?"

Of all the things that have made me happiest since I asked Emma out on a date, the best one is how quickly she's let me see the real her. The more we talk, the more the various layers and contradictions I was seeing make sense. The puzzle isn't all put together yet, but it's getting closer, and I only like it more the fuller the picture gets.

"I am making lunch." With my hands full of the ingredients for a club wrap, I close the fridge with my shoulder.

"But you're calling me."

"That is what phones were originally made to do."

"They also originally charged by the minute, but we don't expect that anymore."

I layer my ingredients into my spinach tortilla. "We do, however, expect to use two hands to make lunch and I can't do that if I'm texting you."

"It only takes one hand to put a frozen meal in the microwave."

"Now it's my turn to say ew."

She scoffs. "I do not make the societal rules. Phone calls are for making doctor's appointments and getting ahold of customer service people who aren't answering their email and don't have someone monitoring their social media accounts."

"I'll be sure to let Grandma know that next time she calls."

"Grandmothers don't count."

"These are very complicated rules." I put the ingredients back in the fridge, add a selection of fruit to my plate, refill my water glass, and take everything to the table.

"Whatever." She sighs. "Okay, while I have you on the phone, I have questions."

"Okay."

"Since you don't know about normal people—"

"What even is normal, anyway?"

"—tell me how you go through a museum."

While I eat, I talk her through my museum pattern, because of course I have one.

"Hmm. I think I can scale the camera. Maybe use .5 zoom so the painting leaves enough room on the screen for the tour elements."

I'm glad she's not there to see my wince. "I wouldn't know. I never take my phone out to look at a painting."

"Not even to take a picture of it?"

"There will be a better one online if I want to see it digitally."

"Well, this is at least a place to start. I don't suppose you'll be available to answer questions this afternoon if I have more?"

"I'm not taking my phone into my studio, but if you want to yell them at me, feel free."

There's a pause of silence on the phone that makes me mentally walk back through what I said in case I misphrased it.

"You mean, like, from your office?"

As soon as she says that, I realize what I practically invited. I should hate the idea of anyone being in the house while I work, but just imagining her being here living her life while I live mine makes me happy.

"Sitting in the kitchen or living room would probably be easier. You can just call over the railing since it opens into the studio."

Once again, there's silence over the line. I invited her farther into my house without thinking about it. She hasn't been here since the painting lesson.

Remembering how that turned out has me hoping she both accepts and declines the invitation. Though we've been on somewhere between three and five dates, we've been careful with the touching. Neither of us wants to rush that. I've only even held her hand once.

"Okay." Her voice is small, as if she's checking to see if I meant it.

"Okay." I make sure to convey a confidence I don't know if I feel, but I don't want her to think for one moment she isn't welcome here.

"Okay." I can almost hear the smile in her voice. Text can't ever give me that. "You've got, what, thirty minutes left on your break?"

I glance at the clock. It's more like forty-five minutes, but I don't want to give her time to talk herself out of coming, so I agree.

"I'm packing up my computer now." The faint sound of zippers gives proof of her statement. "I can be there in twenty."

"Drive safe."

"See you soon."

She disconnects the call and I make myself do everything I would normally do during my midday break. I go for a short walk, do a handful of bodyweight exercises, check my work email.

I almost jump when the doorbell rings, but there's no denying the smile on my face as I move to answer the door.

The moment I see her standing on the other side, the final puzzle piece slides into place.

I think I finally know Emma.

I can see this girl making snarky comments and being obsessed with learning. I can see her wishing she didn't need to even own fancy pants, much less go anywhere that required her to pretend to like something she didn't just to be polite. I can see her playing the video games she sometimes mentions and living off easy-prep meals.

"Come on in. You left your shoes here last time." I point to the Crocs I've made a space for under the bench.

"Oh, good, because I didn't think to bring any with me."

As she's exchanging a pair of black Crocs for the lime green ones, I take the time to catalog her appearance.

The large computer backpack is the same one she had the day of the museum presentation. It's almost half the size she is, with a sturdy rubber bottom and handle.

It's the clothes that really make me smile, though.

She's wearing black camo leggings with her phone tucked into a large pocket along the outside of the thigh. A hooded sweatshirt that is at least three sizes too large and emblazoned with her college logo drapes from her shoulders to past her hips. Her hair is wrapped up in a scrunchie and looped into something that isn't a bun but still keeps everything on top of her head.

And she isn't wearing a lick of makeup.

This is what Emma looks like when no one is watching. Or at least when I'm not watching.

That first Sunday I saw her at church, she was wearing what might be considered the publicly appropriate version of this outfit.

Last Sunday she'd been in a long flowy sundress and a cardigan sweater.

I lean against the wall and just look at her, drinking it all in.

She turns to catch me looking, and a small frown puckers between her eyes. "What?"

"Nice outfit," I say softly because I'm willing to bet she thought about her clothes as much as I thought about the invitation.

Sure enough, a look of utter horror crosses her face.

Before she can make a run for the door, I lean in and whisper, "I like it."

"Wait." She swallows. "You're being serious."

"I am. Can't say I'd suggest you wear it to dinner, but here? Just us? Yeah. It's nice." I slide the computer bag from her and gesture to the spiral staircase that will take her into the part of my house I actually consider my home. "Now let me show you where I live."

The smile she gives me is so bright, so warm, I may need to make an adjustment to my environmental maintenance system.

Especially because I think my smile might be just as big.

**19**

## *EMMA*

I dress carefully for my monthly family dinner, making sure to match the *Look Book* outfit exactly so Amy has nothing to complain about. Although she'll probably make a snide comment about my being dressed perfectly as well. I don't think I can win with her right now. The best I can hope for is that she hasn't told Mother what she found at my apartment. If I don't walk into a slaughtering tonight, I'll be grateful.

It takes three tries to find an outfit I can actually wear because my basket of things that need to go to the dry cleaner is full. Between all the social events I was attending with my family and the outings and dates with Carter, I've gone through a lot more of the designer clothes than usual.

The memory of Carter's reaction to my hoodie makes me smile all over again. I seem to be stuck with a permanently goofy grin these days. Jason says it's a creepy thing to see when I come into the office, but he's happy for me as long as I don't start canceling game nights.

Carter and I went out for dinner and mini-golf last night and I'd tested the idea that he really didn't mind how I dressed by wearing what I would have worn if it had been me and Jason or Trina. When I'd answered the door in my jeggings that have a legitimately worn hole in the knee, a black tank top, and an orange zip-up hoodie, he'd just looked me over, smiled his version of a goofy grin, and asked if I was ready to go.

My cheeks are starting to hurt as I relive the moment and I really need to get going or I'll be late.

I slide my feet into the appropriate shoes, compare my reflection to the *Look Book* one more time, and head out the door.

As always, the monthly dinner at Mother's house is a parade of inefficient consumption. I don't mind that the evening starts in the living room, as we're all there for the primary purpose of seeing and talking to each other.

It's the tray of tiny appetizers and the pre-dinner drinks we have to eat while we're in there. There's even a brass and glass cart with the ingredients for everyone's favorite cocktails.

I tried alcohol once in college and absolutely did not like what it did to my head, so I usually just get a glass of Sprite and let everyone pretend the clear, bubbly liquid is whatever they'd like it to be.

Tonight, I splash a little cranberry juice in it, hoping it makes me fit in a little better. After getting so comfortable spending time with Carter, I'm worried I've lost touch with the skills needed to meet my family's behavior expectations.

He asked me out for dinner tonight and I had to tell him no. It was probably a good thing. Is it normal for people to squeeze in this many dates so quickly? I doubt it. Doing so requires both people to either neglect their established friendships or have previously spent most of their time sitting around their houses.

For two people who both spent a lot of time alone in our respective houses, Carter and I manage to share a space rather well.

Mom and Aunt Jade are sitting on either end of a couch, discussing a party one of them attended last night. Since that pretty much means they're gossiping about people I don't know or can't remember well enough to attach the face to the name, I settle in a chair and discreetly pull out my phone.

> **ME**
> <<gif of an animated bunny with the caption *Wish you were here*>>

It's silly to text my sister because at this moment she should be on her way here and none of us text and drive. She'll check her phone before she comes inside, though, and maybe this will help set the tone for the evening.

> **AMY**
> We're almost there.

We? Is she bringing Richie? We're not allowed to bring anyone to family dinner except serious boyfriends. In the last five years, that's only happened twice. Both were Amy's. Inviting Carter dropped through my mind for the space of half a second, but fortunately I came to my senses before the words popped out.

Carter is already muddying the waters of my work/friend/social gathering divisions. I need family to remain solidly in its own box for a little longer.

> **ME**
> I didn't realize you and Richie were that serious.

> **AMY**
> I guess you don't know everything about me, either.

I hate to say it, but she's right. In an effort to keep parts of my life private, I've stopped asking about hers.

Maybe that's how we fix this.

ME
I like to dip french fries into milkshakes.

AMY
I thought peace offerings were supposed to make you like the person more, not find them even weirder.

Amy comes in a few minutes later and Richie is indeed with her. All the ladies, myself included, are dressed in what Amy calls "casual chic." I call it uncomfortable dinner clothes. Richie is in dark skinny jeans and another V-neck T-shirt. Is that an artist thing? To just have one type of outfit and live in it? Because I haven't seen Carter in anything but a button-up and slacks, even when he's working at home.

I slip my phone back into my little clutch purse before I can give in to the urge to ask Carter about it. If I start texting him, I'll start smiling and forget to be sneaky and I'll get caught.

"How's work going?" Mother asks after greeting Amy and Richie.

I almost choke on my Sprite when I realize she's talking to me. Mother never asks about work. Ever. "It's, um, fine. I just finished working on an app that lets you see what a paint color would look like on your walls."

Aunt Jade looks at Mom's cream-colored wall. "Sometimes simple ideas can be so helpful. I imagine that wasn't a very difficult design to put together. It's good to get your feet wet on something small."

I didn't design it. I coded it. And I would not be telling Stephanie that the hours she and the rest of the team spent figuring out where the line was between enough user-controlled customization and too much complication had been thrown away on an "easy" task.

Mother sighs. "It's hard to accept that a simple design is best some-times, isn't it? When Amy showed me her sketch for a jumpsuit, I was unconvinced, but after she showed me her finished test creation, I had to agree with her." Mother frowns at Amy. "Whatever happened to it?"

"I loaned it to an actress to wear as a costume." Amy takes a sip of her drink but doesn't look my way. I'm at least fifty percent sure Mom is asking about the jumpsuit I wore to the theater.

"The depths of simplicity can only be grasped by the complexities of an elevated mind."

If I hadn't been staring at Amy and willing her to look at me, I'd have missed the slow blink that almost became an eye roll.

Perhaps the relationship with the not-quite-sensible philosopher isn't going as well as she's pretending. Has she brought him tonight just to be a buffer between us?

"Shall we move to the dining room?" Mother stands and waves us toward the formal room as if we didn't all pass it on our way to the living room. "I'll get the first course."

She takes the cart into the kitchen so she can replace the beverages with plates of salad, and the rest of us carry our drinks to the dining room. Amy and I usually sit beside each other to the right of Mom's seat at the head of the table. With Richie here, though, I'll be sitting on the left side with Aunt Jade.

Amy waits until I've chosen a seat before arranging it so that Richie is the one directly across from me. I'm starting to feel a little less sorry and a lot more perturbed. No one tells their family everything about their life.

By the end of the salad course, I'm beginning to think Amy might be keeping secrets of her own and they might have to do with Richie not being the best of boyfriends.

"Is everyone ready for their entrees?"

I jump up from my seat. "Amy and I will get them."

Before Mother can protest, I've grabbed the cart and pushed it past the end of the table.

Mother's answering smile is tight. "All right, then. The plates are, um, just being kept warm."

I nod because we all know that. For some reason, at this dinner Mother likes to pretend she has a housekeeper/cook instead of just a weekly maid service. She really picks up everything from a local caterer and the hot dishes are stored in the warming bag she plugs in in the kitchen when she brings the food home.

Amy follows me because it would cause a scene not to, but the moment we close the kitchen door behind us, she's talking. "This doesn't require two people."

"No, but a relationship does." I pull plates from the warming bag and set them on the cart. "Is everything all right?"

She crosses her arms. "Why wouldn't it be?"

"Because the man followed up 'please pass the salt' with 'even the blandest of paintings can be tolerated when the frame is gilded in gold.'"

"That has nothing to do with me."

"It was his response to Aunt Jade asking how your relationship was going."

Amy shifts her weight and glues her gaze to the warming bag behind me. "That's so nosy. Who asks about a couple's relationship at dinner?"

"Who puts salt on their salad?" Actually, the salad had tomatoes and plenty of people put salt on tomatoes, but my question gets Amy to look at me.

"He wasn't talking about *me*. He was talking about how comfortable we've gotten with each other. You're taking your anger that I learned about your secret frumpy life out on him."

"Really?" I think about how comfortable I am around Carter. *Bland* would be the last word I would use to describe that. "I wasn't aware that my anger was over the discovery. I thought it was because you weren't handling it well."

"I'm not having this conversation with you."

"Why? Because I hid my clothes? Because I'm not creative enough to understand your life?" I really want to shove this cart at Amy and stomp out of the house, but I don't. This is family and if any relationships get to be hard in life, I guess it would be the ones you don't get to pick.

"We can't let the food get cold." Amy reaches for the cart and pushes it out of the kitchen.

I spend the rest of dinner imagining flicking food across the table at Richie. My contribution to the conversation is to try to spin it so he has to use normal sentences if he wants to participate.

I'm successful at getting him to tell an actual story about adopting a dog to fill the emotional hole left by his dad. It's a little sweet and a little sad until he admits he stole the puppy from his neighbor when his mother moved them across the country. I can't help but give Amy a wide-eyed stare. She becomes very interested in the remains of her baked chicken.

My fingers itch to pull out my phone and search up the difference between psychopath and sociopath and what the statistical chances are that my sister's in great danger, but I can't do it at the table.

Fortunately for the dog and the neighbor, Richie's mother returned the animal to its rightful home, but I'm not sure Richie learned anything from it because that painful experience is why he does not include dogs in his work.

Or, as Richie put it, "The very shape of a canine is a reminder of the hole left behind by the ripping away of my first chosen love."

"Speaking of chosen love," Mother says, toasting her wine glass in my direction, "how are things going with your love life, Emma?"

"Ah . . ." I avoid looking at Amy.

She isn't avoiding me, though. Out of the corner of my eye, I can see her glaring at me as she stabs a carrot. "I think Emma met someone at Richie's exhibition."

"Oh." Mother preens. "Are you seeing Greg? He's a member of the Plainsridge Country Club."

Yet another reason not to date him. Who names anything Plainsridge? It's like someone was playing the opposite game and said, "Yes, that sounds fancy."

"He's a good man, Greg."

We all turn to Richie, waiting for the normal statement to be followed by one that, well, isn't. Nothing comes. Perhaps his brain gets tired of himself.

Is Amy right? Am I letting our argument, or even my personal taste, make me misread the situation?

Dessert comes out. It's individual dishes of cheesecake dip with an assortment of items to dunk. It's mostly slivers of graham crackers, but there are also pretzels, waffle cookies, and a single chocolate-covered strawberry on each plate.

I slide right back into hating his guts when Richie steals Amy's strawberry with the declaration that they're his favorite.

They happen to be her favorite as well.

Clearly, I need to mend our rift so I can convince her to kick that man to the curb.

## 20

*EMMA*

After spending a morning in meetings, I'm packing up my computer to leave the office. I've been working extra hours on this museum project for a month now, mostly early in the morning and on weekends, and I'm starting to feel the effects.

"Working at your boyfriend's this afternoon?" Jason leans against the side of my cubicle door.

"He's not my boyfriend." I glance at the nearby cubicles, but everyone is either working from home or off at lunch. Good. I don't need anyone hearing this conversation. That's how rumors get started.

"Keep telling yourself that." Jason shakes his head and chuckles.

"Isn't that something that has to be discussed and agreed to?" I open a folder to see if I'm going to need the schematic inside and then tuck it into my backpack just in case.

"One would think. Of course, one would also think only a boyfriend would let you work at his house every afternoon."

"It's not *every* afternoon."

His eyebrows fly up. "Want me to pull up the code depository change logs? It tracks IP addresses, you know."

I narrow my eyes at him. "Yes, but you only see them if you deliberately pull the information."

He holds his hands up. "Just doing my best friend duties."

"Oh really?" I sling the backpack onto my shoulder. "Which duty is that?"

"The one that makes sure your morning code check-out isn't also happening at his house."

Heat tinges my ears even as I know he's right. If the tables were turned, I'd be checking on him to make sure he hadn't been caught up in the moment, too. "Yeah, no, that's, um—" I wave a hand in the air. "We haven't even kissed yet."

Instead of looking relieved, he frowns as he runs a hand over his short, dark beard. "You're not collecting another male best friend, are you?"

Trust my best friend to zero in on the concern I won't admit to myself. "I worry about that, you know. Except this time it would be worse because I definitely do not think of him as just a friend."

Jason looks around and sighs. "Let's take this to my office."

Once the door closes behind me, I drop my bag in one chair while I flop into the other. Jason moves behind his desk but leans against the window instead of taking his own seat.

"All right. Lay it on me."

I feel sorry for girls who have to break down a date's play-by-play with just other girls. A male perspective is certainly helpful.

This conversation feels bigger than our previous relationship dissections, though. More important.

"Working at his house in the afternoons just sort of . . . happened. We'd be texting during lunch, and he'd say I should just work from his place so we could both get something done besides talking on the phone."

"Because rationalizing what we want is a natural human thing. Carry on."

"Well, you'll be happy to know that we no longer pretend it's for the museum project. I just check to see if it's a good day and then go over."

"Do you have a desk there yet?"

"Sort of. I sit on the floor and use his couch."

His eyebrows pull together. "Because you'd rather sit on the floor than have a door in between you."

"There's a very soft, fluffy rug." That had not been there until four days ago, but I'm not going to mention that part. Or should I? It does seem an important indication of whether or not I'm tripping my way down to the friend zone. "Would you buy me a rug if I worked at your place?"

"He bought you the rug?"

"Well, he didn't actually say as much. I also didn't ask. But it wasn't there before."

"And when do you go home?"

"Usually around nine."

He frowns and leans down to nudge his mouse and wake up his computer. After logging on, he makes a few clicks before pointing at the screen. "You've been logging off almost religiously at five-fifteen."

Because that's when Carter comes up from the studio every day. "Yep."

"So those four hours are spent . . ."

"Dinner. Then we've been watching this documentary series about animals."

Jason watches me, obviously thinking. He and I have hung out in each other's homes. We've shared dinner. We've played video games and watched TV.

"Oh my gosh, I'm being friend-zoned." I cover my face with my hands and peek between my fingers. I do not want to just be Carter's friend.

"Not necessarily." Jason drops into his chair and leans back so he can look at the ceiling. "Where do you sit?"

"When?"

"During the documentary, where do you sit?"

"Um, on the couch?"

"Like we do? Do you burrito yourself in a blanket and stab your feet into his stomach?"

I open my fingers wider so I can glare at him. He doesn't notice because he's still staring at the ceiling, so I give up and drop my head back so I, too, can stare at the ceiling. He's got the right idea. This does make the conversation easier.

"No, I don't stick my feet in his stomach. We . . . snuggle."

"Snuggle?"

"Yeah, I sort of curl up on the couch and he puts his arm around me, and we snuggle."

"You kiss yet?"

"No."

"You think about it?"

"Sometimes."

"Catch him thinking about it?"

"I—what?" My head pops up and I look at Jason like he's crazy because he is. "How on earth would I know that?"

"Never mind." Jason shifts to a normal sitting position, though in a slower motion that I just used. "I think it's safe to say he likes you."

I can't stop the smile. "You think?"

He nods. "I think. Just . . . be careful. I know it seems like this is going slow but it's not."

"He's only held my hand twice." I swallow. "But he has started giving me a quick hug when I leave."

"If you're measuring the depth of a relationship by the physical stuff, you need to reevaluate. Locking lips is serious, but it's nothing to locking up emotions. Y'all talk?"

"Of course."

"About what?"

I shrug. "I dunno. Work. Food. What we learned in the sermon. We pause the documentary to talk about that sometimes."

He picks up a pen and starts twirling it between his fingers. "Okay. Here's the deal. He's your boyfriend. You're exclusive, together, committed, whatever the kids are calling it these days."

I roll my eyes. "He's actually two years older than you."

"Which is why he should know to have already taken care of making things official but men in love can be stupid and blind."

I almost choke on my tongue. I thought we were talking about the *B* and *G* words. No one said anything about the *L* word.

Jason rolls on as if he hasn't just dropped a land mine into my considerations. "So what you need to do is inform him that the relationship status has changed. If he doesn't agree, get out of there."

My mouth gapes open and I'm pretty sure I look like a drowning fish, but Jason just grabs his mouse and starts clicking on things.

He lifts his hand to point toward the door. "Now get out. My capacity for emotional conversation has more than overflowed."

Because I can't think of anything to say anyway, I collect my bag and move to my car. I eat lunch on my way to Carter's house and try to box up everything Jason said so I can think about it later.

Much later.

Carter meets me at the door and greets me with a short hug and a kiss to the top of my head. Has he been doing that and I missed it because it goes so fast and feels so natural? Or is that new?

I remove my shoes and slide on my green Crocs. I never know where they are when I go to leave in the evenings. Just like in my own home, I kick them off sometime in the afternoon. Yet every time I arrive, they're tucked under the bench, waiting on me.

Should I read into that or is Carter just being a neat freak? The man does alphabetize his spices.

Before I get to work, I send Amy a get-to-know-you question of the day along with my answer. I've been doing it every day since dinner at Mother's house. Sometimes she answers. Sometimes she doesn't.

I spread out on the couch like I normally do, but I get minimal work done. Jason was decisive in his opinion that I should tell Carter we're official, but I don't know if I can. At least, not tonight. I need to know how I feel about it all first, right?

Carter comes upstairs at five-fifteen, sleeves rolled up, leaving his forearms on display, complete with the dark metal watch he wears on one wrist.

It has to mean something if I find even his forearms attractive, right?

We cook dinner together, which means he does most of the work and we pretend I'm contributing by shoving things into the oven. He's some sort of master with quick, healthy meals, and my body is going to revolt if this all falls apart and I have to return to a steady diet of frozen pizza and air-fried chicken nuggets.

"We finished season one of that documentary last night."

I'm filling the dishwasher when he says this, so I can't see his face. Is he hinting I should leave? Asking if I want to start season two?

Maybe I can convince Jason to step into the dad role. He can call Carter and ask what his intentions are, and I won't have to be the one to start the conversation that might end with me bawling my eyes out so hard I have to pull over as I drive home.

I clear my throat. "Yeah?" I'm a chicken.

"So, I was thinking we might do something else tonight."

Okay, not sending me home but he doesn't sound very confident about this either. I turn, wiping my hands on a kitchen towel. "Like what?"

He looks embarrassed. "I, well, I got a new puzzle."

I have to stop for a moment and process this idea because it's not the direction I would have gone even if I'd been guessing for the next three hours. "A puzzle. You do puzzles?"

He shrugs. "We don't have to, I just thought—"

"Yes." I nod my head vigorously. I do not remember the last time I did a puzzle, but clearly Carter very much wants to do one, so I'm all in.

Oh my. Talk about dangerously invested emotions.

I kick the dishwasher closed and move toward the dining table. His chairs aren't comfortable for longer than the thirty minutes or so we sit in them to eat dinner, but I can't think where else we'd put a puzzle.

Carter looks like a kid as he pulls a box from a cabinet and grabs a knife to break the seals around the edges. This really is a brand-new puzzle.

He's quiet for the first several minutes as we sort pieces into piles and attempt to find all the edge pieces. Despite the fact that we're doing something he clearly enjoys, his mood seems to grow darker as we work.

If I don't find a way to break it, he's going to end up under the table, pouting.

"Anything interesting happen at work today?" It's my best guess since I think he'd have already told me if something was wrong with his parents or grandparents.

He grunts.

Guess I'm on the right track.

"You had a call scheduled with your agent, right?"

He sighs. "Yeah. They put out my pieces from the last few months last week. I send them up as I finish them, but I trust him to know when it's time to put them out."

I nod. "Is it going well?"

"A few have already sold, one for more than I thought it would."

"That's good, right?" I don't know much about art, but I do grasp the basics of business. Getting more money for something is a good thing.

Again, he sighs. "I mean, yeah, but . . ."

"But what?" I link the final section of the top edge in place and fold my arms on top of the table so I can give him my full attention. I need to read him like a girl right now, because there is something he isn't saying and I'm going to have to find it myself.

Unfortunately, this is part of being a stereotypical girl I've never been very good at. People who mean what they say and say what they mean are much more my speed.

He sits back in his chair. "An art critic wrote up a review in the *Times*."

Well, that would be a big deal. He isn't happy about it, though, so I'm guessing it's not good. That or everything got misinterpreted, and Carter's artistic sensibilities are bruised.

Probably the former, based on his attempt to get me to appreciate art.

I lick my lips. "What did he say?"

"That my skill with brushes and paints is evident and I could give a masterclass on mixing glazes."

I am now thoroughly confused. "That sounds good?"

He looks over at me and gives me a small smile before slowly shaking his head.

I brace myself for him to say the things I've always heard. *You don't understand. How can you think that's good? Can't you see the obvious flaw? I suppose some people can simply enjoy without thinking.*

"It's not what he said, it's what he didn't say."

It's like walking down the stairs and expecting one more tread only to come up short because you've made it to solid flooring. He's just going to explain it? "What didn't he say?"

"He didn't say he liked it."

"You're the one who told me all pieces aren't for all people."

His eyebrow quirks as if congratulating me for remembering. "He also didn't say he hated it."

"Ah." I think back to our many art appreciation discussions. "No emotion is bad."

He nods. "He said I was skating by on my name. That my work was technically sound but lacking in impact. If I'd created things like this ten years ago, I'd still be illustrating books."

That seems . . . really personal and harsh for an art critique. I pull out my phone and search for the article. It takes three different search phrasings, but I finally find it. It's not long, so I take the time to read the whole thing twice.

"Um, Carter? He didn't say any of those things. I mean, the part about skill and glazes, yes, but not the rest of it. I mean, he's pretty complimentary. Says he expects they'll all sell quickly."

"Because they're Carter Anderson paintings."

"And Carter Anderson is an amazing artist." I take a deep breath. Having the tough relationship conversation may be past my capabilities, but I can do the girlfriend thing and have the tough-love life conversation. "I think you may be projecting your own insecurities a bit."

He seems to think about this and then groans. "I don't know. Maybe."

"That's an artist thing, right? The concern that you won't live up to your past self?" Amy's mentioned something like that a time or two.

"Yeah, it is." He sits up and pushes a few puzzle pieces around. "The thing is, I really do think he's saying some of that between the lines. Because those paintings aren't as good as my old ones. It's been a tough couple of years."

"Is it going better now?"

He looks at me a long time before nodding. "Yeah. Yeah, it is." He pushes a piece aside. "You know what? I have not taken you out on a date in, what, two weeks?"

I look at his couch. He didn't consider those dates? I certainly did. "I mean, not like a go-out-to-a-restaurant date or something, but I like—"

"Tomorrow night. Let's go downtown. I know a great restaurant. There's a club attached if we feel like night life."

I never thought I would be glad for an excuse to tell Carter no, but I am so glad I have plans tomorrow. "I can't. It's game night."

"Game night?"

"Yeah. I host it at my place every few weeks. Jason, Trina, and a couple other friends come over. We eat pizza and play games." I shrug. "It's fun."

I can't tell what he's thinking as he considers me for a long time. Finally, he picks up a puzzle piece and says, "Oh."

He needs to get out of the house. He needs to meet my friends. I need to stop trying to live life in all its separate boxes.

I take a deep breath and knock down a wall. "Would you like to come join us?"

**21**

**CARTER**

Considering how much time Emma has spent in my house lately, it's strange that I feel nervous about walking into hers.

I want to see it, though. I want to know what she surrounds herself with, what makes her happy. Slowly, she's brought bits of herself into my house. Not things, necessarily, but qualities. Like sitting on the floor, kicking off her shoes, and randomly rolling my spice jars around on the counter when she talks to me while I cook dinner.

Frankly, I'm not certain if I'll be walking into an adult apartment or a modified children's playroom. It isn't that Emma is immature so much as the things she likes to surround herself with are ones I'd normally associate with a young kid.

I climb the stairs to her apartment. I've been to her door, but never past it. When I've picked her up, I've always been too focused on the woman herself to take time to look past her door.

The other reason I'm somewhat anxious about tonight opens the door when I knock. I'm face-to-face with the most important man in her life, and I still don't know how I feel about that.

I give him a nod. "Jason."

"Carter, glad you could make it." Jason swings the door open and invites me in as if it's his own home.

I automatically toe off my shoes beside the door as I take in the space.

It's not at all childlike, except for the video game posters decorating the television wall in the living area. Even those are in frames, so there's a level of sophistication to them. Beneath the mounted television are shelves holding video games and video game consoles.

On the wall across the room, decoratively spaced shelves hold several potted plants with long, viney strands of leaves draping over the sides.

Between the walls is a green, comfortable-looking couch. Emma and Trina are sitting on it, game controllers in hand, leaning into each other as if they want to physically push each other onto the floor as much as they are trying to run each other's colorful cartoon-like car off the road on the television screen.

"Ha!" Trina hunches over her controller. "Eat turtle!"

Emma groans and collapses sideways on the couch as the two cars roll under a banner that reads *Finish*. A large *1* and *2* appear on the different sections of the screen.

Trina does a little victory dance in her seat before looking over at me. "Hi, Carter."

Emma flips over to look at me over the arm of the couch. Her lips curve into a shaky smile. "Hi." I can read the word on her lips, but the sound doesn't reach me across the room.

I smile back and come to stand beside the couch. "When you said game night, I thought you meant board games."

"Oh, I did." She waves at the television. "We're just killing time until Michael and Victoria get here with the pizza." She bites her lip. "Do you, um, want something to drink?"

"Sure."

I follow her to the kitchen area, which is a long counter with upper and lower cabinets along one wall and another counter with cabinets beneath separating the cooking area from the dining area.

Jason is leaning against the island counter, thumbs flying over the screen of his phone.

"Hey." Emma points at him as she opens the fridge. "No work stuff. Game night."

He looks up from the phone. "How do you know it's work stuff? I could be texting a girl."

Her eyebrows are lifted in skepticism as she looks over her shoulder. "Are you? Texting a girl?"

"As it so happens, yes."

"One that doesn't work for you?"

He sighs, punches out a few more words, then slides the phone into his pocket. "Happy?"

"Of course." She looks into the fridge and frowns. "I can offer you five kinds of water. When did we get old?"

Curious what five kinds of water looks like, I come stand behind her and look into the fridge. Aside from bottles of regular water, there are two racks of cans in four different colors. "Sparkling water?"

She nods. "Are you a fan?"

"I don't know that I've ever tried it, really." I take a note of the brand and flavor, though, so I can add it to my next grocery order.

She pulls out a pink can. "Try grapefruit. If you don't like it, you can grab a bottle."

"You don't have a cup I can just fill from the tap?" I prefer filtered, but using a bottle seems unnecessary when I'm in a home.

Jason shakes his head. "No clean-up on game night. Trash and recycling only."

I pop the tab on the can and give it a swallow. It feels like soda, and yet it doesn't at the same time. My taste buds don't know what to think about it. It's not awful, though, so I take another sip. "What other rules should I be aware of?"

"What happens at the game table never stays at the game table." Trina helps herself to a blue and red can of water.

"Especially winner's bragging rights," Jason adds. "But you can only keep those until the game gets played again."

Michael and Victoria arrive with boxes of pizza and introductions are made. I try to sit back and let the conversation swirl around me while we eat, but Victoria is one of those people who insists on equally including everyone in the conversation.

Normally I think it's a noble trait for someone to have, but tonight I want to observe and learn, not participate.

By the time we box up the remaining pizza, I think I've gotten a basic handle on the personalities in the room and the connections.

Michael and Victoria are dating and seem to be more Trina's friends than Emma's, though everyone is certainly getting along well enough.

On the other hand, Trina and Jason are each better connected to Emma than anyone else.

I can't remember the last time I really sat back and observed the dynamics of a particular group of people. It's something I used to do with Frank as we talked about what sorts of paintings were capable of really displaying an idea people often lived with and recognized, even if they never consciously saw it. The skills are still there.

Everyone pitches in on clearing the table and cleaning up. They all have their roles and the whole thing takes approximately four minutes, so I stand to the side and watch it like a ballet.

I expect us all to move back to the table to play whatever the game is meant to be, but instead they stream toward one of the doors that opens off the large, open main room. I fall in behind the line and find myself in what can only be Emma's office.

It's a full-size version of the controlled sort of chaos she creates each afternoon in my living room. If this is how she functions best, she must be giving up some productivity to be around me so much.

Another large television is mounted in here, though it's used as a large computer monitor if the wireless keyboard and mouse stacked beneath it are anything to go by. Color is absolutely everywhere, from the papasan chair cushion to the three different throw blankets, to the sticky notes plastering the wall. For a person who makes their living with technology, she seems to utilize an awful lot of paper.

My mind immediately starts adding up how many different pigments I'd need to put on my palette to paint this scene on canvas, even ones I'd do no more than dip my brush in the top of the tube to collect. I lose count after fourteen because the group has crowded in and around the room's walk-in closet and their game debate is growing louder.

My six-foot-two frame is easily the tallest in the room, so it's easy enough for me to see what's causing the commotion.

The closet is an odd sight. One half is full of designer clothes and home decor items I would have expected to find when I first met her, but now know Emma wouldn't choose in a million years.

The other half of the closet has an assortment of baskets and bins with masking tape labels that have things like *cables*, *plates/cups*, *gift ideas*, and *mementos* scribbled on them.

I shift to see if I can get a peek in the mementos box. Also crammed on this side of the closet is a collection of board games.

Trina is deepest in the closet, clutching a box for *Trivial Pursuit*, all but stomping her foot in insistence. "But we have an even number of people."

"You just want to make it guys versus gals," Michael complains.

"Well, yeah. What fun would it be otherwise?"

"Fine, but I'm also taking this one as an option." Victoria snags a pink box I can't quite read from a low shelf.

Jason shrugs and pushes a shoulder into the closet. "If that's how we're doing it." He pulls out a blue box with the name *Telestrations* on the side.

"Are you planning on spending the night?" Emma asks. "What happened to our rotation?"

Three people unanimously say, "It broke."

As one, the group leaves the closet and I step back so they can pass me on their way to the table. Emma falls behind and gives me a hesitant look. "You doing okay? I hadn't realized quite how loud we get before. I'm surprised the neighbors don't complain."

"You're having fun at"—I glance at my watch—"seven on a Friday night. I think you're safe."

"True." She lets out a large sigh. "But we're—you're good?"

"Yes, I'm good." I drop my arm around her shoulders as we follow everyone else. "We are good. I like seeing you like this. It suits you. Like your hooded sweatshirts."

"Hoodies, old man. They're called hoodies."

"And what do you think that's short for?"

She gives me a cheeky grin. "Adorable?"

I have an almost overwhelming urge to pull her into my arms. To just hold her, at least for a moment. The desire to kiss her is there—it's always there—but I know once that happens, that'll be it for me. She keeps creeping into my soul in ways I didn't expect. Holding on to that last known quantity is my only defense.

Although in that moment I don't know what I think I'm defending myself against. This is Emma. What else could I want?

The idea almost knocks me sideways, and I let her slip away when someone asks her to grab a pencil and some paper for keeping score.

"Of what?" Emma asks even as she moves to her jumbled desk. "None of those games need it."

"Pies are not enough. I want statistics," Trina calls.

Out at the table, the chairs have been grouped on each long side instead of around the ends. The girls are on one side, the guys on the other, and the round board with its colorful squares sits in the middle.

An hour later, I'm no longer allowed to sit on the outside and observe. I've been moved to the center seat on the guys' side, though the chair to my left is empty as Jason paces behind me and Michael. He occasionally grabs my shoulders as if I'm preparing to go three rounds in the boxing ring, but he's clearly excited by the new set of knowledge I bring with me.

For someone who insisted on playing this game, Trina is remarkably uninvolved. I look over at her while Jason and Emma argue over whether Roosevelt is an acceptable answer, or the girls have to narrow it down by first name.

She smiles and gives me a wink. Did she do this for me? As much fun as everyone seems to be having, the core of this game is Jason versus Emma.

When the debate is finally settled and Emma is slipping her blue pie piece into her team's holder, I look between the two of them and ask, "Do you ever go to trivia nights?"

Victoria snorts. "They got us kicked out of Pete's Pizza Parlor once because Jason argued that the facilitator's answer was wrong. Emma was sitting there, scribbling backup points onto napkins and passing them over so he could keep arguing and finally they just told us to leave."

"That was actually the start of game night here," Michael adds.

The guys win, although Trina's tally shows the girls answered more questions correctly. Good-natured bragging ensues on both sides as the game is put away, chairs rearranged, and new seats claimed, or rather *assigned* in this case as Jason tells everyone where to go.

I'm not complaining because he's set me on one of the long sides of the table with Emma to my right. He claims the end of the table to my left, which makes everyone groan that it isn't fair.

My only real concern is that Emma actually looks nervous as the game box is opened and spiral-bound dry erase booklets are passed around.

"Is everything okay?" I ask in a low voice. I know this is my first time meeting her friends, but I'll kick them all out if she needs me to.

"Of course." Her smile is tight. "You, um, you said we're good, right?"

"Yeah." I search her eyes, but don't find a clue as to why she's concerned.

Until the rules of the game are explained.

I get a card with a word on it. I then draw a picture to represent that word. Jason will look at my picture, flip to the next page, and guess what the word or phrase I drew is. He'll pass that to Michael, who will draw a picture based on Jason's guess. And so on it goes around the table.

That means my pictures are going to Jason.

And Emma's drawings are coming to me.

While Trina might have been helping me out, Jason has put me in a position to fail spectacularly if I make a wrong step.

What he doesn't know is that this professional artist has spent a lot of years interpreting cubist and abstract art. I actually understand what's happening in *Nude Descending a Staircase.* Both versions.

As long as Emma's not as jumbled as early Picasso or vague as Piet Mondrian, I think I'll be okay.

And despite the fact that I prefer hyperrealism, I've studied and tried a lot of other styles as well.

Dry-erase marker certainly isn't my first choice of medium, but at least it's an ultra-fine tip. I do okay in the first round, passing Jason a decent depiction of Mount Rushmore.

Emma's blushing as she passes me a picture of a stick figure holding a smaller stick figure that has a tree coming out of its leg and a flower coming out of its head.

She's looking at me out of the corner of her eye and I don't hide the booklet as I write *Mother Nature.*

Her mouth drops open. "How?"

"Hey!" Victoria points her marker at us. "No looking! The fun is in the final reveal."

We pass the booklets around the table and for this first set, I give Jason exactly what he thinks he's going to get.

Victoria is correct in that the fun is flipping through the chain with everyone at the end. Mother Nature did not make it past Jason, who tried to draw a tree in a nun's outfit, but it looked more like a candy bar.

I've gotten a good feel for how much time I can safely take with each drawing now, and in the next round I draw like an old-world Baroque painter, giving Jason a picture so busy and with so much detail, he can't begin to know what to focus on.

After that, I switch to a little abstract minimalism with stick figures and combinations of basic shapes.

I try for cubism, but the lines bleed together too much, so I switch to the curves of expressionism.

He kicks me under the table for that one.

After I send him some comic-book-style pop art, he throws his marker down. "I surrender."

No one else knows what he means, but I do. I don't care about impressing him. I'm here for Emma and I've managed to guess every one of her drawings correctly. Even the weird blobby one that was a golf course and everyone—Emma included—accused me of cheating to guess it right.

When the night draws to a close, I won't lie that I don't relish the clean peace of my car as I drive home. But as I walk through my house, making sure everything is settled for the night, I can't help but notice how much it isn't like hers.

As much of her as she's shown me the past few weeks, she's still holding back when she's here.

And I want her here.

At least, I think I do. But can I handle having game nights in my own space? Am I okay with cables going everywhere and colors that don't blend and enough throw blankets to weigh down a horse?

There's only one way to find out.

22

**EMMA**

I suppose it shouldn't be a surprise that beings made in the image of a humanly incomprehensible God would be complicated, but I still get baffled by how much I don't understand men.

After the game night, whatever reserve Jason had about Carter disappeared and while I'm certain he's still watching out for me, ready to hold me accountable to living according to the beliefs we share, he isn't frowning at me whenever I leave the office for lunch anymore.

We'd taken to sitting together in church for weeks now, but I had always ended up between Carter and Jason. The two Sundays since game night, I've been flanked by Carter and Trina, as Jason sat on the other side of Carter and discussed everything from graphic design to basketball.

That last one really baffles me, as to my knowledge, I've never seen either of them watch a game and yet they carried on a five-minute conversation about it.

When I asked Carter about that, he just shrugged and said he gets a collection of emails every week that give him recaps on things he often finds himself talking about at social gatherings.

Speaking of social gatherings, my mother wants to know why I haven't attended any with them in a while. I've ducked out of every cultural encounter since Amy's fashion party.

> ME
> I've been really busy with work. The new project is taking up a lot of time.

Not a lie. Also not the whole truth. Of course, I haven't been telling my mother the whole truth for about ten years now, but it didn't start bothering me until I knew how much it bothered Amy.

Speaking of Amy, I open the file in which I've gathered a ton of get-to-know-you questions and copy the next one so I can send it to her.

> ME
> Aside from necessities, what's one thing you can't go a day without?

This is actually a hard one for me because I want to say something that will make me look good, like prayer or my Bible, but I promised myself I'd be honest in this attempt to mend the rift with Amy.

> ME
> My phone.

Looks like I need to take some time and revisit my own priorities. My phone buzzes as Mother and Amy answer at the same time.

> AMY
> Coffee. Although at this point, that might be a ne-

cessity.

**MOTHER**
There's a new opera opening next month. I can get us access to a box.

The good news about a box is she wouldn't be burning money on a ticket for me if I back out at the last minute. I've done it before.

I can't bring myself to commit to doing it again. I'm not sure if it's the fact that Amy would know what I did or the idea that I want to see if opera is something Carter enjoys. If it is, then . . . Maybe?

At some point he's going to have to meet my mother. It might as well be somewhere she can't actually talk to him.

**ME**
Maybe. Can you send me the details when you know? I might bring a friend.

I delete and retype that last sentence twice before hitting send. A chill sweeps over my skin. Am I sweating?

I shiver and toss my phone on the desk. I'll wait to ask Carter when I know the details.

For now, I need to get back to work. I'm behind, but I'm learning how to make it work. I got started at six this morning so I would have more time to plow through tasks with access to all the notes and tools I usually use.

It isn't just my afternoons at Carter's that haven't been as productive, it's the additional mornings I've been spending at the office. I don't know why it feels better to go to Carter's from the office, but it does. Unfortunately, I just don't get as much done there. People are very distracting.

I yawn and rub my eyes before adding a test run to my afternoon task list.

Those are easy to do without all my notes around me. I just jot the issues I find in my notebook and work from there.

After double-checking that I've completed everything anyone else is waiting on from me, I turn to the museum project. Somewhere along the line, this became as much about proving something to myself as it was proving something to my mother.

I wasn't so sure I could do this when I first put my foot in my mouth, but I truly think I've come up with something that's interesting, usable, and, well, cool. The experience isn't making me want to ask Jason for a lateral move or anything, but it's nice to learn I can do more than I thought I could.

By noon I've pushed through most of my tasks for the day and all that's left to do is start loading in the data for the test gallery on my museum tour guide prototype.

There can't be anywhere better for doing that than an artist's studio.

Has Carter thought about giving me a key? Probably. I know I've thought about asking. Having a key, though, seems like a very next-level thing. Maybe even a next-next-level thing, seeing as we still haven't had that what-are-we-doing-here conversation. No longer seeing each other would certainly require a break-up, though.

I park my car and walk to the door. Two steps away, I freeze.

Hanging from the doorknob is a small game controller. The kind that attaches to the side of my favorite gaming console. Above the doorknob is a bright orange Post-it with *It's open* written on it.

How hard does a heart have to beat before it's considered a heart attack because I think I might be getting close. I can't stop swallowing as I remove the controller and the sticky note before turning the doorknob.

I don't even bother with my green Crocs. I just step out of my black ones and drop my bag to the bench because in the opening to the hall is a copy of my favorite racing game. I add it to the bundle in my arms. The second controller is hanging on the door to his studio.

No.

He couldn't have. Getting a console for his living room would have been enough to send me to the moon. If he put it in his studio, that would mean . . .

My stomach drops into my socks. What would that mean?

There's no more swallowing because my mouth is utterly and completely dry as I open the door to the studio. He told me to stop taking my watch off weeks ago, but walking in with my phone in my pocket feels wrong. Then, of course, there's my armful of video game accessories.

The working side of his studio hasn't been touched. Everything is neat and orderly and cleaner than any space that sees that much paint every day should be.

On the other side of the room, though, where his couch once sat as an island of peaceful contemplation, is a whole new world.

The couch is still there. One end maintains an unencumbered view out the floor-to-ceiling windows, but the other end . . .

It's like a miniature version of my office.

A 27-inch flat-screen TV is secured to the top of a low, two-shelf cart. On the bottom shelf, next to a wireless keyboard and mouse, is a cable dangling off the side, ready to be plugged into a laptop. The rest of the gaming console sits in a docking station next to the TV. In front of it are three more of my favorite games. Those plus the one in my hand are the ones I play so often I just leave the cases sitting open on top of my storage console.

He was in my apartment for a single evening. And he noticed all this?

My eyes start to burn, but the tears don't spill over until I realize what the large, multi-paneled screen beside the couch is. I'd first thought it was to block the view of the electronics from the painting area, but the back side of the panels are actually whiteboards surrounded by cork. A basket of twenty-four colored Post-it pads and a box of thumbtacks is on the floor in front of the screen.

This little corner of Carter's world has everything I need.

Except Carter.

I dump the game and controllers on the couch, prepared to go on a hunt for my man. With evidence like this to back me up, I think I can follow Jason's directive to just inform Carter he is now my boyfriend.

As I'm turning from the couch, though, I see a lime green sticky note on the gaming console. *Play me.*

I'm torn. I want to go find Carter, to tell him this is too much, to tell him we can go to the opera or the museum or a gala on the moon, and I don't care how many fancy dresses I have to beg Amy to fit me for. I know he's been skipping events or, when he absolutely must attend, going without me.

No more. If he can bring video games into his studio—even if temporarily since the cart is sized to be pushed down the hall to the office—I can go to a social.

But I also want to honor his wishes. He went through a lot of work and expense to put all this together. If he wants me to play it before I thank him, that's what I'll do.

I turn everything on and load in a game. I could connect to the Wi-Fi and log in to my account, but it feels better to start fresh. This is a completely blank-slate console and I want it to feel as clean and neat as the room it's sitting in.

I'm almost finished with the fourth race in the set when I feel him enter the room. I'm not sure where he came from because I didn't hear a door or anyone on the stairs, but I can feel him there. My orange animated car rolls over the finish line and before the game can congratulate me, I'm looking at him.

The words to say thank you don't come because words aren't enough for what I know this cost him. It's too much, too big, too important. Even as I'm smiling the biggest smile I'm capable of, because I have never felt more seen or cared for in my life, tears are pooling in the corners of my eyes.

"I'm going to have all the high scores, you know." My voice is merely a whisper because I desperately want to convey to him what this means to me, but I don't know if he'll understand. "I've never had a console where I had all the high scores."

"Emma." That one word from Carter sounds almost reverent, and a tear spills over my lashes and rolls down my cheek.

He's smiling, too, as he sits on the couch next to me. "Will you be my girlfriend?"

I look around the nest he's created for me. "I think I already am."

I can't stand looking anywhere but at him, so I immediately swing my head back to face him. "But if you need to hear it, yes. Yes, I will."

One of his hands reaches up to cup the side of my face. He's done this before, looked at me like this before, but always as if the moment caught him unaware, like he did it before he could stop himself. This time, it's very obviously deliberate.

"I'm going to kiss you now," he whispers.

"I think that would be a very good idea."

And then he does. He presses his lips to mine and although I've experienced a few other kisses in my life, I will happily and easily forget them all and consider this the most ultimate kiss that ever existed.

The game controller tumbles to the floor as I reach my own hands up and allow my fingers to comb through his hair. I didn't even realize I'd been saving that for this moment, but I had. Because it would mean his head was close to mine, that he'd gotten down into my space.

His light chuckle breaks the mood and I pull back to look at him, my fingers still trailing through his long hair. "What?"

"You're smiling."

"So are you." He has a massive, big, tooth-showing smile.

"Yeah, but you were smiling while I was kissing you."

"Kissing you makes me happy."

"Then I'll get used to funny-feeling kisses." Then his mouth presses to mine once more and I have to recalibrate because this one is the most ultimate kiss ever.

He sits back a little and wraps one of my hands in his. For several moments, we just stare at each other.

Then he leans down and scoops up the controller I dropped. "You want to show me how to play this thing?"

I hug the controller to me and look from him to the television.

"I don't . . . I can't . . . Why?"

He blows out a long breath and slouches into the couch beside me so that his shoulder is pressed snugly against mine. "I needed to see you in here."

I frown because it doesn't make sense. I've been in his space for weeks.

"Not just you," he continues, pointing at me, "but *you*." He waves a hand to encompass all the new additions.

He shifts so that he's facing me, pulling one knee up onto the sofa. His hands wrap around both of mine and his gaze locks into me as if he's desperate for me to understand what he's about to say.

"Your apartment . . . it's a lot."

I wince. He's not wrong. Compared to his place it's utter chaos.

His grip tightens as he continues. "I need you to know I'm not just dating you for fun. I like you here, like spending time with you, like that we can do puzzles and watch documentaries, that we can have a good time but also be serious."

"I like that, too." I think I know where he's going. And I like it as much as it absolutely terrifies me.

"But I don't want to date forever. Eventually, you, me. Well." He nods his head to the side. "We'd be more than boyfriend and girlfriend. And I had to know if I could handle this, handle you."

He picks up the controller and looks at it. "I had a guy bring all this in this morning. I hadn't seen any of it until a few minutes ago." His gaze lifts to mine. "If I had a chance of being able to handle it, I had to see it as part of having you in my life."

"That's why you wanted me to play it."

He nods.

I lick my lips. I think I know the answer because otherwise that kissing we just did was a bad idea, but I still have to ask. "Did it work?"

"I can't imagine this room any other way now."

I blink at him, because seriously? There's not any part of him that wants his electronics-free space back?

"I'm being serious. When I came in and saw you leaning with the car and yelling at the television, all I could see were possibilities."

I do not remember yelling at the television. I wouldn't put it past me, though.

"With this, I can look over and see you whenever I want. Whether it's during the workday or in the evening or on a weekend. Doing what I need to do won't have to win over spending time with you."

"I'm really behind at work," I admit.

"Me too." He grins at me.

I grin at him.

And the excitement and fear and happiness and worry threaten to make me ill, so I grab the controller back and turn to the TV. "How do you feel about being a plumber?"

**23**

*EMMA*

Why couldn't my official first appearance as Carter's girlfriend be somewhere easy? Like church or the grocery store or maybe the parking lot outside my office?

Honestly, the only thing I can think of that would be more nerve-racking would be dinner at my mother's.

"Relax." Carter laughs as he reaches across the car to shake my bouncing leg. "It's just my grandparents."

"No, it's not just your grandparents," I say, mocking his calming tone. "It's your *grandparents!*"

He sends me the smile he knows makes me melt. "At least it's not my parents."

"As far as you know. You did tell them I'm coming, right?"

"Yes, they know I'm bringing my new girlfriend."

"Then there's every chance your parents will be there, too."

He coughs in an attempt to cover his bark of laughter. "You think my parents, what, got the call last night and decided to take a last-minute flight?"

"They could have driven." I wiggle my phone in the air. "I looked it up. Less than five hours in current traffic."

He grabs my phone and slides it into the interior pocket of his sport coat. "My parents won't be there. Just my grandparents. Although I have no doubt Mom will require a full report from Grandpa when we leave."

"That isn't making me feel better."

"Sorry."

I smooth my hands down my pants, but the wrinkles pop right back in because the fabric is trapped beneath me. I finally took the basket of clothing to the dry cleaners, even though the bill made my eyes water, so I'm in one of the least constricting ensembles from the *Look Book*.

"Do I look okay?"

"You look amazing, but you should have worn something you're comfortable in. I told you to wear whatever you wanted." He pauses a moment, then adds, "Within reason."

I smirk because I'd called his original bluff real quick by sending him pictures of my Eeyore pajama pants.

All too soon, we're pulling into his grandparents' driveway. It's a cute little house a few miles from Appleton's main square.

He opens the door and walks in without knocking, dragging me behind him into a bright, yellow kitchen that smells like the world's best-ever bakery.

I step up beside him, fingers squeezing tight enough to threaten the circulation to his hand, and freeze. Fortunately, I'm wearing a smile when my body completely decides to stop moving.

He was right in that his parents are not in the room, but I was right, too, because they are on a video call and Carter's grandfather is pointing the phone screen right at me.

At least I really hope that's Carter's parents.

Two faces are squished into the screen and in the upper corner I can see myself, wide-eyed, smiling, and slowly trying to disappear completely into Carter's side.

They start talking to each other as if looking at a picture and I can't really blame them because I am not moving a muscle. I don't think I'm even blinking.

"Aw, look, she's darling," his mother coos. "She's so short. Carter, you didn't tell us she was short."

Is that bad? Is there an expected height requirement? Is Carter blowing all their expectations of having seven-and-a-half-foot grandchildren?

Carter reaches out and pulls the phone from the hand of his smiling grandfather. He turns it so that only he can be seen by his parents.

"Hello, Mom, Dad. Goodbye, Mom, Dad." He disconnects the call and slides the phone into his other interior jacket pocket.

Is it healthy for him to surround himself with phone signals like that?

Carter doesn't seem worried about it as he shakes his head at his grandfather. "And here I thought you wanted me to be able to keep my girlfriend."

"Your grandmother thought it wasn't fair that we get to meet her before they did."

The old woman swats the man on the back of the head with a kitchen towel as she moves toward the oven. "Don't go telling stories, now."

He just chuckles as he smooths down the back of his hair. "Come in, come in." He turns to lead us deeper into the house, then stops to look over his shoulder. "The people in town call me Maddox, but this one calls me Grandpa. You're free to take your pick."

I've never had anyone to call Grandpa. Mom's father died when she was a teenager, and while I'm sure my father had parents at some point, I've never even met him, much less them.

I try the word out in my mind, but it doesn't feel right. "Thank you for inviting me, Maddox. You have a lovely home."

That should probably have been said to the grandmother. Not that I believe the woman makes the home. I mean, Carter is clearly the better decorator of the two of us, but she is the one with the kitchen towel at hand and they are several generations older.

"Ah, you too, Mrs., er ..." These are Carter's mother's parents, so their last name wouldn't be Anderson. I can hardly call her Mrs. Maddox. Or maybe I can?

"Gloria, dear. You can call me Gloria." She offers me a sweet smile. "Dinner will be ready in fifteen minutes."

"Come have a seat," Maddox calls.

Carter and I settle around a dining table that looks old enough it'd probably be considered an antique. I bet Maddox and Gloria bought it new, though. If I lean right, I can see into a living room that looks straight out of the 1980s aside from a high-tech television on the wall. I think I spy an entire basket of remotes as well.

There's a voice-activated home automation tower on the counter and a fairly modern laptop next to it. It would seem Carter's distaste for most things technical wasn't learned in this home.

"Carter tells me you work with computers." Maddox glances from me to the laptop.

"Yes, sir." Oh, please no. Don't do it. Don't ask. Because I'll have to say yes and I'm really not that good at tech support beyond turning things off and back on again.

"You see that computer?" He points to the laptop.

Carter groans. "Grandpa, are you trying to embarrass me?"

Okay, maybe I do want to hear this after all. "Yes, sir."

"It's got a problem, and I was wondering if you could fix it for me."

Only Carter's utter dismay is keeping me curious instead of resigned. "I can try."

"It's the email, you see."

Yeah. I'm not gonna be able to do anything with that one.

"I can't seem to get emails from my grandson. Everything else comes through but nothing from him."

I can't stop the giggle as I lean against Carter's hunched shoulders. "Aw, are you not contacting your grandfather, honey?"

The look he sends me says he is very much aware that this is the first time I've called him by a pet name, but he doesn't acknowledge it further as he speaks to his grandfather. "I send you a text every day."

"That's for things like Wordle scores and seeing if Gloria needs anything from the grocery store. You don't share life through texts." Maddox points a slightly crooked finger in my direction. "Just ask your girl. She'll tell you."

My face absolutely flushes with heat as Carter almost folds in half laughing.

"Aw, now, don't tell me you let him get away with just sending you a little text. You let me know if he needs to call more. I can still take him out to the woodshed."

My makeup is going to melt. I'm going to have to change my entire wardrobe to go with my now permanently red face.

And I'm going to need a new boyfriend because I think Carter is laughing so hard he's forgotten how to breathe.

Fortunately, the evening continues with just as much laughter but far less embarrassment.

Maddox can't convince Carter to relinquish his phone back to him, so he snags Gloria's and keeps it with him at the table. Every now and then he slips it into his lap, stares at it a moment, then puts it back on the table.

The seventh time he does this, right after I've answered Gloria's question about where I went to college, Carter sighs. "Do I even want to know?"

"Just getting with the times and doing a little texting."

"To who?"

"Your mom."

I slap my hands over my mouth because it wasn't actually a "your mom" joke even if Maddox had the tone and timing completely right.

Carter glances at me but quickly looks away, the corner of his mouth twitching. "Why are you texting her?"

"Because you disconnected the video call. She feels left out."

I know this should all feel weird and awkward, and Carter is probably going to apologize seventeen times on the way home, but the truth is, I like it. It's real and caring and after this night I don't know how in the world I'm ever going to take my boyfriend home to meet my mother.

**24**

*CARTER*

I've gotten so accustomed to natural, casual Emma that I'd forgotten how beautiful she is when she truly gets dolled up.

She gives a little twirl in the open doorway of her apartment. "Will this do?"

"It's perfect."

I search her face, trying to find that feeling of something being off that I saw when I first met her, but I can't find it. Her wide smile is the smile she always gives me; her sassy responses are right on cue.

She's still a girl of contradictions because I know the moment she gets home she's swapping this blue sheath dress for a pair of pajama pants with cartoon characters on them, but now the contradictions don't bother me. All her different sides are connected by the puzzle pieces I've learned about her over the past couple of months and now it's all just part of the delightful, complex picture that is Emma.

Or that's what I think until we walk into the private room at the restaurant.

The woman greeting the gallery owners and local high-end art collectors is not the same woman who climbed into my car in her apartment parking lot.

I try not to think about it as she trails me around the room like a puppy. I greet some of the gallery owners and curators I've worked with that are in town for a conference, then find the manager of my main gallery in New York, who put this dinner together.

"Todd, this is my girlfriend, Emma."

She practically gives him a small curtsy. "How wonderful to meet you. Are you enjoying the evening?"

Todd doesn't seem to find anything amiss with her behavior as he gives her a polite but genuine laugh. "As the host for this evening, that should be my question."

"A private dining room at the Nourriture Chère? Who wouldn't be having a wonderful time?" Her laugh is equally polite but entirely fake. Todd doesn't seem to notice, though, so maybe his was fake, too.

I don't care about his.

Todd turns to me. "Frank tells me I'm going to like what I see in a few months."

He will. Every artist is their own worst critic, but even I'm excited about what's taking shape. "We might want to talk about an actual show."

Todd's eyebrows lift because he knows what that means, coming from me. A show means spending a month, possibly two, in New York. It means doing the social circuit, teaching a few classes at the local art schools, and basically working night and day to make up for the fact that I'm far more reclusive than I should be.

"I can't wait." He nods across the room. "If we're talking about that sort of idea, we need to lay the land, keep your name up while we collect enough works for an event."

I agree, which is the whole reason I came tonight.

There's a French restaurant half an hour closer to my home that serves equally good food for half the price. Not that I'm paying tonight, but that's not the point.

I make a mental list of the people Todd wants me to make sure I talk to and who it would be beneficial to sit at dinner with versus just saying hello to them. Then my socialite doll and I start working the room.

She says all the right things, laughs at all the right jokes, and is, in short, utterly forgettable. This is the Emma I first met, but somehow I'd made her nervous enough that just a little bit of her true personality slipped through, highlighting the cracks in her façade.

Everyone we speak to finds her forgettable as well because once the pleasantries have been exchanged, they turn all their conversation to me.

Part of me recognizes the value of this tactic as I am, supposedly, the one they need to meet and remember, but I'd much rather be known for enjoying my evening with my charming girlfriend, even if she is a little unorthodox. If an artist can't get away with that, who can?

Before everyone settles at tables for dinner, I guide Emma out into the hall.

"What are you doing?" My question is far more abrupt than I meant it to be, but I can't have Emma crawling back in this shell every time we go out. Events like this are part of my life, just like video games and a little bit of chaos are part of hers.

Her eyes get wide. "Am I doing something wrong?"

I realize then that she genuinely is trying. This isn't her phoning it in or passing the time or checking off a duty box. This is truly how she thinks I want her to act.

"Yes." I lean down a little so my face is on her level so she can see the sincerity in my eyes. "You forgot Emma back in the car."

Her face crumples a bit and my heart aches. "Oh. I don't . . . I thought this . . ." She bites her lip. "I don't think those people will like the real me."

"Why not? I do." I more than like her.

"I know, but . . ." She sighs and looks around as if she'll find the answer in the main restaurant a few feet from the little hallway we're standing in.

Then she takes a deep, steadying breath and looks me in the eye the way she does when we're discussing an interesting opinion she heard on a podcast.

I brace myself for whatever she's about to say, but at least I'm once more talking to my Emma.

"This is what I was taught. I don't know how else to be in there." She sticks out her foot to show me the delicate sandal with the one-and-a-half-inch heel. She points down at the shoes. "These heels come with that face." She points at the room we just left.

"Then take them off."

"What?"

I shrug. "Take them off. You'd rather be barefoot anyway."

The seriousness cracks and she almost giggles. "I think that's a health code violation."

"Probably. Do you have other shoes in the car? I don't care if it's your Crocs. If that's what it takes to get you to be yourself in there, I'll go get them."

She shakes her head and holds up the clutch that can barely contain her giant phone. "This is all I brought."

"Okay. We keep the shoes, then. There has to be something else you can do to loosen up."

Who on earth taught her to act like this?

"Emma? Is that you?"

Both of us turn to see her sister. Richie is behind her, a sport coat over his V-neck T-shirt because the restaurant won't let any male in without one.

I wanted to meet her family, but not exactly like this.

Looking between the two women, my confusion grows. The way Emma talks about Amy, I thought they were close.

Then again, most of the stories I've heard are from when they were younger. There's clearly some tension now.

"Amy," Emma finally says. She's hesitant, as if unsure what could happen, and I reach my hand into my pocket to wrap around my valet ticket, ready to make for the exit at a moment's notice if need be.

The beautiful blonde looks from Emma to me and quirks an eyebrow. "Carter Anderson, isn't it? We met briefly at Richie's show."

I give her a nod. "Nice to see you again."

She looks from Emma to me and back again. "Is this something you do often?"

I don't know how to answer. I probably shouldn't answer. This is Emma's sister, after all.

Emma sighs. "He's my boyfriend."

The silence that falls is heavy indeed. Did she not tell her family about me?

"I see." Amy adjusts her hold on her purse. "Does that mean you'll be bringing him to Mom's for dinner?"

"Eventually. This is still . . . new."

I frown. We're not that new, not really. Officially, yes, but we both know it was real before then.

"I see."

What is it that Amy keeps seeing?

"I'm not keeping him from you," Emma blurts in a rush.

"Aren't you?" Amy slides a phone from her purse and poises her thumb over the power button. "Shall we check the texts? Favorite ice cream, least favorite Mr. Darcy, a few would-you-rathers. I'm pretty certain the word *boyfriend* is nowhere to be found."

"It's not like that."

"The measure of truth is in the reflection of the mirror, not the label on the wall," Richie spouts like a walking, talking Magic 8 Ball.

"Oh, shut up," Amy grumbles before shoving her phone back into her purse. "You're having an event in the private room, so we won't keep you." She turns to me. "I'm not sure what parts of her life she's deigned to show you, but I promise Mother taught us both how to behave in public." Her gaze drifts down Emma's dress. "And at least you're using the *Look Book*."

"I told you I did," Emma says, voice tight, eyes bright.

As Amy walks away, I think I might know where the polite mask came from.

"Just so you know," I say, leaning down so my lips skim her ear and make her shiver, "I never asked you to behave in public."

As I'd hoped, a watery laugh sputters out of her.

"We'll talk about the family dinner later." When worried blue eyes meet mine, I reassure her. "Much later. Not tonight on the way home."

Her shoulders relax and my mind swirls with questions. I'd forgotten that her mother actually lived closer to her than my grandparents live to me and yet not once has she mentioned meeting her.

We talked about family, but it always sounded like hers was as far away as most of mine and I'd assumed we would all eventually get together.

But that's not the case for Emma. Her family doesn't even know about me.

I promised her we wouldn't talk about it tonight so I'm going to do my best not to think about it.

"All I ask of you tonight is that you go back into that room and be yourself." I nod toward her feet. "Just a shoes-stay-on version."

She takes a deep breath and squares her shoulders. "I'll try."

I give her a nod and lead her back into the room. Some of the tables are starting to fill and we find places with the people Todd wanted me to talk to.

Emma doesn't completely relax, but I can tell she really does try. Several times she passes on the opportunity to make a joke or share a smart remark. I know she catches those moments, though, because her foot nudges mine under the table.

Still, she shares a few interesting pieces of trivia, makes an observation about a recent event in the news, and even gives one couple a few suggestions of video games they can purchase their son for his birthday.

It's an improvement.

The drive home is quiet, both of us deep in our own thoughts.

The sudden, determined way she slaps her hands to her thighs creates a sharp crack that sounds all the louder because of the silence. "I know you said we weren't going to talk about it, but I need you to know something."

"Okay."

"Amy and I are twins."

This is information I already knew, but she seems to be telling me something more with the statement, so I just say, "Okay."

"Mother wanted us to really be twins."

I frown. "Like dye your hair blond?"

"No. Like wear pretty clothes and take dance classes and go to work in the boutique."

"And Amy did those things."

"Yep."

"And you?"

"I went to college. Discovered a whole different way of living. But I didn't want to hurt my mother. She raised us on her own with just a little help from her sister. I, well, I guess I thought I owed it to her to preserve her dream."

"And I don't fit that?"

She laughed. "You are probably the only thing I've actually done right. She's going to be over the moon when she hears about you."

I pull into the parking lot of her apartment and turn off the car. We sit, staring into the night. "You do realize that doesn't make sense, right? Trying to make your mom happy by not telling her something that would make her happy?"

My heart hurts for Emma, but it's becoming very clear that whatever is going on with her family isn't about me or even her and me. That doesn't mean we don't have to deal with it, but it does mean we get to deal with it together.

And I'd rather face anything in this world with Emma than without her.

"I know. The thing is, as soon as she learns about us, she's going to want to have you for dinner."

"Is she a terrible cook?"

"No, her favorite caterer is actually quite good."

There's a lot to unpack in the sentence, so I don't even try. "What's the problem, then?"

"I don't want you to see me with her."

I take a moment to think about that. "Because that would look a lot like tonight's cocktail hour?"

"Right."

My contradictory girl, always seeming to be just a little bit different from what I thought I was seeing.

How blessed am I that I'm now behind those walls? If I had to guess, I am currently learning things that not even Jason knows about.

And I'm the person she's choosing to share them with. It reminds me of the times I'd tell Grandpa things I hadn't told my parents. My worries, my concerns. As I got older, the problems got bigger, but he always handled them the same way.

I reach out and start the car again. "You know what we need?"

"What?"

"Milkshakes."

She laughs and it sounds more natural than she's been in a few hours. "Why?"

"Because how bad can things really be if you're drinking a milkshake?"

**25**

*EMMA*

It's done. I stand up, snatch the last light blue sticky note from the wall, crumple it up, and toss it in the small trash can.

I still have to finish testing it across different platforms and hardware, but I have a few weeks to do that before the demonstration party.

The app itself, though, is ready. Narrator files have been uploaded, test paintings have been mapped, code has been optimized. I've added screenshots and demonstration movies to the presentation. I've taped printouts of the test paintings around my office and taken a virtual tour.

I'll present the app to the board in a few days, but they wanted to see the slide deck early, so I attach it to an email and send it on its way.

All that's left to do now is make sure my outfit is ready to go.

I've done a lot of really good work over the years, but it's been a while since I've been as proud of anything as I am of this. Has Mother been right all along? Is there something more powerful about being the idea creator?

I pick up my phone and dance around the room with it, aiming the app at the printout of the jail cell painting and giggling happily when Carter's picture comes up. I didn't know it was his then, but I should have. It would be his art that finally made me stop and look, even if only for a few moments.

I point the phone at another picture and more information comes up, making me dance around the room. Is this what being drunk feels like for some people? If so, I understand the appeal.

I exit the app and shoot off a text.

> **ME**
> I'm done! Want to celebrate?

My victory dance keeps going as I cross the room and close my laptop.

> **JASON**
> You know I do. This is a big deal. Tacos?

Oops. I'd meant to text Carter, but Jason was probably the actual right choice. This affects his company, after all. I can celebrate with Carter later.

I meet Jason at our favorite taco place, and we get two sampler platters of street tacos.

"All done, huh? How's it feel?"

"Amazing." I spread sour cream and guacamole onto my tacos. "I don't think I've got a secret calling for the design team because this was really hard, but maybe I could sit in on more brainstorming meetings? It felt good to be part of the front end."

"Totally doable. You'd probably push our offerings more because you know what the code is capable of doing."

I nod as I chew and swallow my bite of taco. "You're coming to the demonstration party in a few weeks, right? I can't wait for you to see it."

Jason doesn't say anything as he plays with the straw in his drink.

I put down my taco. "Jason? You're coming, right?"

"Yeah, I'll be there." He sits back in his chair. "I think I made a mistake."

I don't want to climb down from my celebratory cloud, but if Jason has a problem, I'm here for him. Maybe it's a good thing I mixed up my text messages. "What kind of mistake?"

His face tightens as if he's in pain. "I was your friend more than I was your boss."

"I don't understand."

"I would never, and I mean never, have let anyone else get away with lone wolfing a project like this." He shakes his head. "But you wanted it so bad, I let you do it."

"And it's great."

"To you."

"Yes, to me. I'm the only one who's seen it."

He lifts his eyebrows at me as if that's his exact point. And I suppose it is.

I crumple up a napkin. "I could . . ." I take a deep breath. "Do you want to go back to my place and look at the presentation? See the app in action?"

The way he's looking at me, I know the boss in him wants to say yes, but the friend in him knows I want him to wait and see the demonstration.

Never before have I put him in this kind of dilemma because never before have I stepped out of our normal team structure.

I slump in my chair and cover my face. "Oh my gosh, you're right."

He leans forward and braces his arms on the table. "Look, you've worked on a lot of apps and campaigns. You know what good looks like."

"But what if it's not as good as I think it is?"

"Then we don't get the job. It won't be the first time."

But I want to get the job. I didn't think it mattered. I thought just showing my family my design at the party was going to be enough.

The party. My family will be at the party. So will Carter. And he and I haven't worked all that out yet.

Okay. One thing at a time. Presentation, boyfriend, family, demonstration. Everything in that order.

I throw my balled-up napkin at Jason. "You've gotten in my head now."

"Sorry." He gives me a half grin. "Look, you've been working on this at Carter's, right? He's seen you working on it?"

I nod. Now that I'm sitting in his studio, the schematics and test plans and notes have been tacked up on the rolling screen panels. I've streamed the app from my phone to the TV a few times as well.

"I mean, he hasn't actually looked at it and used it, but I ask him questions all the time and he's seen the design." I mean, I've been working on it in his studio for three weeks now.

"Have you tested the presentation on him?"

"I . . . no."

He gives a quick nod. "That's what you need to do, then. His eyes are probably better than mine at this point, anyway. He'll give you pointers if you need them. If the app needs a tweak or two, you can fix it in the two weeks between the presentation and the demonstration."

"True." Winning Carter over to the design would mean I really had knocked it out of the park as well as I thought I had. He was so against my idea at the beginning, but now he's seen the light about technology. I mean, I have a gaming console in his studio.

I dig into my last taco, confident that this is going to be the month that I really take charge, make some changes, and take the next step into the rest of my life. Once my family sees my work is just as valid as theirs, I can introduce them to Carter and slowly start blending the different areas of my life together.

I can't wait.

**CARTER**

Five minutes after I finish my morning painting session, my doorbell rings. I glance at the clock. Am I running late?

No. I'm right on my normal schedule, yet somehow I know that it's Emma.

I open the door and she all but bounces inside, giving me a quick peck before she sends her shoes flying across the entranceway.

"I am so excited," she says as she walks backward down the hall.

I can't help but grin at her as I follow. "I can tell. What has you so happy?"

"The app is done. The presentation is tomorrow." She wheels her media cart out of the office and pushes it into the studio before dropping her backpack onto the sofa.

My grin falters. The board sent me the three slide decks to look over as I'm supposed to sit in on the presentations over the next few days. Emma's is scheduled first.

It's not going to go as well as she apparently thinks.

I'm only one opinion, though, so maybe I'm wrong? She certainly seems to think it's amazing. Her confidence is making me wonder if there's something I missed when flipping through her slides.

"I know you have to have an official opinion and all that, but I was wondering if, you know, as my boyfriend, I could practice my presentation for you."

I give her a nod because, yes, as her boyfriend, I will absolutely cheer her on.

And if her design doesn't get accepted, I'll be there to pick up the pieces because as high as she's flying right now, that landing is really going to hurt.

"Okay. Great." She starts pulling things from her bag. "So, I'm going to set everything up. You go do your walk, get your lunch, whatever, then maybe I can present? I was hoping we could maybe shift your afternoon paint session, so I still have time to tweak things if you have any suggestions."

She straightens up from her bag with a frown. "I've lost my pen. Can I borrow one?"

I wave her toward the working side of the studio because she knows which pens are normal and which are special.

"Thanks." She slides her phone from her back pocket and sets it on the television cart before going to my drawing desk to get a pen. Despite the fact that I've made her a little technology corner, she tries really hard to keep it contained, never even carrying her phone into my art space.

I love that she does that.

She comes back, pen held aloft triumphantly. "So, what do you think?"

"About your schedule?"

She nods.

"Sounds great. When do you want to meet? An hour?"

"Perfect."

I go for a walk, as much to clear my head as stretch my muscles. Emma needs me to support her today. No matter what my personal opinion of the project is, Emma's work should be respected. She's like an artist with amazing skill who uses it to make paintings I think are ugly. I can applaud the artist without applauding the art.

Once I make that connection, I hurry through lunch, fully prepared to be what Emma needs me to be.

She works through her presentation and the light in her eyes tells me she believes in her work.

And I can see why. It's a genius piece of technology. In the right place at the right time, it would be phenomenal.

The museum self-guided tour isn't either of those. Not only does it rely on visitors having phones they are willing and able to run the program on, but it also encourages people to look at those phones instead of the museum itself.

She's winding down and I manage not to cringe at the usage video that has museum patrons holding up a phone between them and the artwork. One of the other solutions utilizes an app as well, but only as a controller for playing the appropriate audio files. I didn't care for their usage illustrations, either, but at least the phone wasn't between the visitor and the art.

I hold in a sigh. Any minute now, Emma's going to ask me what I think and I'm going to have to give her an answer.

I'm going to have to tell her half the truth, because if she's got any chance of getting a good response from the board tomorrow, it will be because she talks to them with the same excitement she's talking to me with now.

The final selection won't happen until after the full demonstration, but if her presentation is well received, it might soften the blow when hers isn't chosen. While the board may think it interesting now, actually seeing the phones being waved about at the demonstration party in a couple weeks will make it unpalatable.

She finishes with her question slide, then grabs up her borrowed pen and a notebook.

"Well? What do you think?"

I stand and run my hands up and down her upper arms. "I think you are amazing. To do that entire thing, on your own from start to finish, is incredible. I have seen how much work you put into this thing, and it shows that you really love it."

Somehow, her smile gets wider. "I do love it. I went through the whole thing all over again after I tested it. I've never found art so interesting."

That's because she practically turned it into a video game.

"There are people who are going to love this idea."

I make a mental note to pull Jason aside on Sunday and tell him they should repackage this after the board passes on it and try to sell it to some art education groups. They would love to have their hands on something like this.

Her arms wrap around my middle, and she squeezes with all her might. "Thank you."

When she pulls back, she waves her notebook around again. "Nothing is perfect, though. What do I need to fix?"

"Um, I'd move the video."

She frowns. "Really? To where?"

"The end."

"Why?"

Because otherwise she'll get nothing but checked-out faces from the very start. "It makes more sense to tell them what it is and then show it to them, right? So they know what they're looking at."

"I suppose." She jots down a note. "I mean, that's easy enough to do and you're my target audience."

I'm not. I'm really not.

Because she seems to want them, I find a few other innocuous things to point out, some minor corrections to make. Through it all, I try to make her remember the important things, that she worked hard, this was a new challenge, and somebody, somewhere is going to want it.

As she's packing up her notebook, I wonder if I should warn her about the possibilities tomorrow, but I don't. She's done this before, right? Had proposals get turned down? There's no reason to take computer code personally and at heart she's a programmer, not a designer.

Everything is going to be fine.

"I'm going to head home now."

I shake out of my deliberations. "You aren't staying for dinner?"

"I want to make these changes, go ahead and wash this mop of hair so I can dry it, then get a good night's sleep." She slings her backpack up before going on tiptoe, pressing her hands to my chest, and giving me a loud, smacking kiss. "I will see you tomorrow."

I walk her to the door and remind her to put her shoes back on.

As she drives away, I make my own plan for the morning.

I can get up early and take her to breakfast. That lets us celebrate her true accomplishments before she realizes she will have to pivot. I can even pick her up and drive her, so she doesn't have to worry about driving home distraught.

The board's initial reaction is sure to upset her until she's had time to really digest everything and think about it. Better to do that in privacy instead of in the museum.

With a plan in place to be the best boyfriend and board consultant that I can be, I return to my studio to get in another painting session.

**EMMA**

The outfit on the bed exactly matches the page in the *Look Book*. Right down to the shoes and the necklace.

It's the one I picked two days ago, but now I'm not sure.

My phone buzzes and I grasp at the distraction before I completely lose my mind.

CARTER
Big day! You ready?

ME
Did I choose the right outfit?

CARTER
Yes.

ME
You don't even know which one I picked.

CARTER
Is it from the *Look Book*?

ME
Yes.

CARTER
Then it's perfect. Trust your sister.


He has a point. I reach for the trousers and slide them on.

My phone rings and I can't help but smile as I slide my Bluetooth earbud into my ear and answer the call. "We went over this."

"You're getting dressed; you need your hands free."

I roll my eyes, but he has no way of knowing that. "See, if we were texting, I could send you a gif right now that would perfectly depict my reaction to that statement."

"But we're not, so instead you should let me pick you up and take you to a celebratory breakfast."

I laugh as I shrug into the blouse. "Seems a bit premature unless a certain someone has an inside track they aren't sharing."

"All I know is that the draft presentations were turned in two days ago. The presentations are to clear up understanding and ask questions, but the final decision won't come until after the demonstration party."

"Ugh. I'm already dreading that. My mother received an invitation."

"That's good, right? She can see your work."

"I guess. I've just never . . . my mother and my work have never been in the same room before. I don't know how to take it." I sigh. "Plus, you'll be there."

"That's right, I will be there. Everything is going to be fine."

The idea of Carter standing by me makes my mother's various possible reactions far less daunting. That in itself is both comforting and terrifying. We've only been seeing each other for two and a half months. Even if we do spend far more time together than the average dating couple, how does he know me this well?

"Anyway," I say to redirect the conversation to less volatile things, "what are we celebrating with this breakfast?"

"This app is a massive accomplishment for you no matter what happens. That should be honored."

"Aw, that's sweet." I slide my feet into the shoes and regret the choice immediately. I refuse to change, though, because I need every advantage I can get. "We can do breakfast, then, but I'll meet you there. I'm probably going to need to go by the office after the presentation."

"You sure?" He clears his throat. "I'm happy to drive you wherever you need to go."

I frown down at the phone but it's nothing but a blank black square. "Are you okay?"

"Why do you ask?"

"You're acting weird."

"I think that may be you projecting."

He's probably right. Nerves are jumping around in my stomach. I'm probably assuming everyone around me can feel them, too.

We decide on a breakfast place, and I hang up before grabbing an entire extra change of clothes in case I manage to spill something on myself.

When I get to the restaurant, Carter takes one look at me and declares we will talk about anything but the presentation at breakfast because I already look like I'm about to toss my cookies.

Those are his actual words. *Toss my cookies.*

This man is charmingly delightful.

"How are your grandparents doing?" I carefully lean over the table to take a sip of my coffee.

"Good. Grandmother says you're the best thing that ever happened to me." He smiles as he lifts his own coffee for a drink.

I nod. "Well, for what it's worth, my friends think the same about you."

He gives me a considering look. "Even Jason?"

"Even Jason."

I grin at him. He grins back. This is the perfect way to start a day like this. Spending time with Carter is going to put me in a happy, relaxed mood that is sure to come through during the presentation.

The drive from the restaurant to the museum is uneventful.

I check my phone as I climb out of my car. I've got fifteen minutes until I'm scheduled to present. That's enough time to feel prepared and not enough to feel nervous. Perfect.

Carter's phone rings just as we step into the museum. He frowns at the screen. I look down and see the ID for his agent.

He takes the call and listens for a moment.

"Okay. Give me a minute. I'll call you right back."

He hangs up and slides his phone in his pocket before placing his hands on my shoulders. "I have to talk to my agent. It might take a few minutes because there could be some other calls as well. You've got this, though. My being in there would just make you more nervous."

I take a deep breath. "You're probably right."

He gives me a quick kiss. "I'm proud of you. This was a real challenge you took on and no matter what they say, you should be proud of that, too."

He's right. I should be. I am. My first real design. I'm sure lots of people don't win bids with their first designs.

I give Carter a wave as he steps back outside and pulls out his phone.

As I walk to the board room, I can't help but think how cool it would be, though, if my first design is a roaring success.

•　•　•　●　•　●　•　●　•　•　•

I am not a roaring success.

I am, at best, a whimpering failure.

Jason won't blame me. I'm not a designer, we hadn't planned to bid for this project, and our reputation won't even be hurt because it has been my name on the schedule instead of the company's.

Still, I've failed. Oh, technically they haven't rejected the prototype yet. That will come in two weeks when they're demonstrated in their real-world environment.

That is going to be embarrassing. I can't not show up. Three prototypes are expected, and I signed a contract, but that doesn't mean it's going to go well.

I brought my best work. It was so much better than where I'd started. I mean, two months ago Carter was ready to bury it and yesterday he'd actually been proud of it. I even saw him smile a little when the video showed how the animated guide can lead people through the museum.

I'd been so sure my work would be well-received.

It wasn't.

They'd compared it to a video game. Called it cumbersome and unsophisticated. A distraction. Misaligned with the purpose of the museum. Gimmicky.

I want to go through it all again, walk through it in my head to see where I went wrong, what I can tweak, how I can rephrase the pitch and improve it before the demonstration.

All I can think about right now, though, is how hard this bench is.

It really is uncomfortable. Like a rock or cement instead of a piece of wood. Maybe it's petrified wood. Isn't that essentially a rock?

Did they make it this bad on purpose? Maybe they don't like for people to linger and contemplate life. Or can art only be seriously considered when a person stands around in a self-important pose?

Maybe it's an aesthetic. The straight, flat planks of pale wood do look a little like a piece of a picture frame.

Is this what a picture feels like as it rests in a frame? Maybe art is so unapproachable because it's uncomfortable.

Clearly my emotional avoidance skills are in good working order because my mental wanderings have gone off the fanciful deep end in order to not think about what just happened.

I turn the phone around in my hand, launch the app, and aim it at one of the test paintings. The tour guide appears. If I had headphones in, I'd hear his happy little voice.

Carter enters the room, his face grim, his mouth pressed into a tight line of sympathy.

I frown. Why isn't he happy? Where's the encouraging man from breakfast? Why does he look prepared to offer me comfort?

He's not coming from the direction of the board room. How could he know?

Had I dropped my professionalism while I was in the board room? Did someone from the board text him because they knew I was upset?

He sits on the bench and wraps an arm around me. "I'm sorry, Emma."

I don't say anything as my brain churns through the options, searching for anything but the obvious one—that he knew before we came here today what the board members were going to say. He'd known while I polished my presentation. He'd known at breakfast this morning.

And still, he'd said he knew I was going to do my best.

He'd expected my best to fail.

"You knew." My voice is flat. It matches the feeling in my stomach. "How did you know?"

"Know what?"

"That they were going to hate it."

He sighs. "You're a brilliant programmer, Emma. You know that."

What Carter isn't saying slams into me. He isn't saying he didn't know. He isn't saying he loves the app and he's going to make the board see that.

He isn't even saying that while mine is good, he knows there's a better prototype because he has access to the draft proposals.

I want him to say any of those things right now, because the alternative is that he never thought I had a chance.

His hand rubs up and down my back, offering comfort that feels sticky and cold.

"Your tour guide, well, he's a neat gimmick. I think it would be a great tool to use in an elementary classroom to talk about art styles or history. Maybe even an app or a video game to get children interested in art. But a museum isn't just about education. It's about connection and this doesn't align with that mission."

Gimmick. Elementary. Video game. Doesn't align with the mission.

A weight hits my stomach, rolling and tightening as if it has strings connected to every part of me and is determined to pull me into a crumpled little ball.

He's made it worse. Somehow he's actually made it worse.

Because he didn't just know they weren't going to like it.

He told them why they shouldn't.

"You told them that."

He frowns. "Told them what?"

"What you just told me. You said those same things to them."

"I'm just a consultant, Emma. They asked me what I thought when the drafts came in a couple of days ago and I told them. My words don't carry that much weight."

"How interesting. Because your words were the exact ones they used."

I can hear my blood as it rushes past my ears, and it sounds like my mother's voice telling me I'm an excellent executor of other people's ideas. Then it's my art teacher's voice telling me I don't have Amy's inspired vision. Finally, it's Carter's voice repeating the words my memory has no problem recalling from moments earlier.

The cords pulling me tighter snap, and I no longer feel like I'm collapsing.

Instead, I'm shattering.

I spring to my feet as if I can somehow catch the pieces. "You let me sit in your studio with schematics and design specs and never once thought to tell me you were going to let me fall flat on my face. No, not let me fall. Give me a great big push."

My voice is still flat and calm. I'm not yelling. Shouldn't I be yelling?

"Emma, that's not—"

"You sat through my presentation."

He nods. "Yes, I—"

"And you said it was good."

"And it is." He stands as well and shoves his hands in his pockets. "Just not for this."

Where is the hurt? This should hurt, shouldn't it? Why do I feel nothing but numb?

He places a hand on my shoulder while the other pulls his phone from his pocket. "This isn't sophisticated. You know that. It's easy to think having a visual component in addition to an audio-based guide would be interesting and modern, but asking everyone to walk around with their phones out would be cumbersome. Not only would they not connect with the art. They wouldn't even connect with each other."

And there it is. Every single dagger they'd thrown at my presentation over the space of twenty minutes has now come out of Carter's mouth in less than five.

An iceberg lodges in my chest. I'm the *Titanic* going down and it's just a matter of time before I fall apart. If I'm going to be able to drive home safely, I need to do it now.

I push past Carter and walk toward the door.

He follows. "Where are you going?"

"Home."

"Do you want me to come over? I can pick up Chinese. Maybe a bag of M&M's."

Comfort food. The iceberg creator himself wants to offer me comfort. "I think you've done enough for today."

I push out into the parking lot and stride to my car, Carter half a step behind me the entire way.

"Emma, wait—"

"Out of curiosity," I say as I dig in my bag for my keys, "what are they going to say to the other two?"

"I don't know. I didn't know what they were going to say to you."

"Okay then. What did you say about the other two?"

He shrugs. "They're both audio-based. One's more traditional. People will be familiar with the device. The other seems more cutting edge. It uses a phone like controller but it can be put away once the room tour is selected. Their decision will really come down to the content editing."

The first crack in the ice wall is forming. Fortunately for me, the first emotion to push its way through is anger.

"So it's only mine you had a true opinion on."

"You know I don't like your idea."

"No. I knew you *didn't* like my idea. Back before you knew me, before you taught me about art, before you watched me work on it. Clearly, I was wrong about how you feel about it now. I thought you liked it."

"I like you."

"And yet, you didn't think to warn me that this meeting would be an absolute slaughter."

If I ride this wave of anger carefully, it can get me all the way home before I fall apart. I reach for something to give me another surge of protection and recall the one comment I haven't yet heard Carter repeat.

I pull open the car door and throw my bag toward the passenger seat. With one foot inside, I turn to him. "You no longer have to worry about my work cheapening the value of artistic expression or flattening the potential for human reaction."

He frowns. "I never said that."

"Good to know they can think for themselves, then." I slide into the seat, but Carter catches my door.

"Emma, I never said any of those things about you. I was talking about the project."

"And the *Times* art critic was only talking about your paintings."

"Emma, we are more than this project."

I look at him and my heart aches. "Right now, I'm not sure we're anything."

With a mighty heave, I wrench the door shut and slam my foot on the gas. Unfortunately, my steady little hybrid doesn't make a satisfying roar as I drive away. It emits nothing but a whiny little whir that feels appropriate, as I'm not sure what else I have to give.

28

**CARTER**

I try calling twice, but both calls go to voicemail. The second time I leave a message and then switch over to our text thread.

> CARTER
> Please, Emma, talk to me. I hate that I hurt you.

I read it through, remembering the crushed look on her face when she got in her car.

> CARTER
> I'm so sorry.

Five minutes creep by as I wait for an answer. When nothing comes, I decide to attempt throwing the riot of emotions in my head onto canvas. I've never brought my phone to the studio with me before, but I'm so happy I did when it buzzes with a text from Emma.

EMMA
Can I come over?

My fingers nearly drop the phone in my haste to tell her yes. After the way we left things at the museum, I wasn't certain she'd ever want to talk to me again.

I run up to my kitchen. Do I have the makings for dinner? I can offer it as an apology. She has a point that I should have told her my thoughts before I told the board. I can do it now, explain why as much as I care for her, I can't in good conscience allow her project to be the one that moves forward.

Then we can sit and watch a movie or talk or play one of her video games. I've been practicing the track with the cows. I can get around it without landing in last place now.

When the doorbell rings, I almost run down the stairs to meet her.

My heart breaks all over again when I see her standing on the step. She looks tired. The trousers from her pantsuit are poking out from beneath a T-shirt with a cartoon elf of some kind on it. Her hair is up in a limp ponytail and her eyes are red around the edges.

I pull her in and hold her close, the first full breath I've taken in hours shuddering through me as she hugs me back.

Finally, she pulls away and pushes a few baby hairs out of her face. Her smile is thin. "Hi."

"Hi." I swallow and gesture toward the spiral staircase by the door. "Come on up. I thought I'd make us dinner."

"Dinner is good."

I follow her up to the kitchen, but I don't keep pulling out the ingredients. Instead, I lean against the counter. "I'm sorry."

She turns, standing in the middle of the kitchen, head cocked to the side. "What for?"

"For not talking to you first. For not telling you what I really thought. For thinking you'd never know."

She licks her lips and swallows. "So, you're not sorry for not believing in me?"

Is that what she thinks I meant? Clearly, I should have paid more attention in English class. My communication skills are horrible.

I cross the room and take her hand in mine. It's limp.

"No, baby, no. I believe in you. Your work is incredible. That app that lets you test a paint color in a room? Mind-boggling. You're a genius."

"I didn't design that."

"I know. But you're the one that figured out how to read the different light levels and adjust the colors accordingly so it would be as close to reality as possible."

She nods, but her gaze drops.

"I didn't think you wanted to be a designer."

"You know I don't."

"Then why—"

She breaks away. "My sister is a designer."

"I know." I don't want to frown at her, not when she's so clearly upset, but I truly don't understand what's going on right now. Maybe if I can get to the bottom of the problem, I'll know how to fix it.

"Do you . . . want to be like her?"

Somehow, her face loses even more color and her eyes appear ever bigger. "Do you want me to be more like her?"

"No." I am not dumb enough to step on that land mine. "You know I like you the way you are. I've never asked you to be anything different."

She bites her lip. "But how long will that last?"

"You inspire me, Emma." I'm desperate to get her to see herself as I see her. She's deep and complicated and fascinating and real, more real than anyone else I've met in a long time, possibly ever. "Every time I'm with you, I see something new." I give her a grin. "I've gone through more sketchbooks in the past four months since meeting you than I have in the past four years."

Her smile is small but soft and a little of the tension uncoils inside.

"So that's why you want me around, huh?" She leans in and nudges me with her shoulder. "Keep the ideas flowing."

"I've got enough ideas to keep me painting for the next five years." I wrap my arms around her middle.

Her smile slides a little closer to a grin. "So you've been painting me? Those blobs and shapes are going to turn into me?"

"Not exactly." My face tightens up as I try to find a way to explain. "I paint ideas. Feelings. Not reality as we see it, but a picture that hopefully inspires reality as we feel it."

"You paint metaphors."

"I guess that's one way of putting it." I cup her cheek and run my thumb under her eye, somehow trying to erase every trace of the tears I put there. "I was struggling to find them the last few years, which is why I started painting perspectives. I think I'd disconnected from life too much, got too jaded."

"And then I came along."

I nod. "And then you came along. Full of contradictions that didn't quite make sense, but I found fascinating."

She pushes her lips into a pout. "I am not contradictory."

I laugh, relief coursing through me that we are going to make it through this. "If you say so." Her lips are warm and inviting as I press a light kiss to them before dropping my forehead to hers. "I'll remind you of that next time you try to slip your Stitch into a formal dinner."

Her laugh is real but tired. "It's a Switch, you goof. And it was a joke."

"Only because you didn't think you could get away with it." I kiss her forehead and step away. "How do chicken and vegetables sound for dinner?"

"Good." She pulls her phone from her pocket. "Can I use your charger? My battery's at eight percent."

"Of course." I move to the counter where my phone always charges, but the outlet is empty. "Oh. I took it downstairs."

She blinks at me. "Your charger is downstairs?"

"Yes." I hold up my own phone. "My battery was low, too, and I didn't want to risk missing it if you called or texted."

"Were you in your office?"

"No, my studio."

"You took your phone to your studio?"

"Yes."

"While you painted?"

"Yes. Although I have to admit I didn't get anything done. I'm not even sure I put any paint on the palette."

"That's sweet." Her mouth stays open slightly, as if she wants to say something else but can't.

I want her to say it. I want to say it back. It feels too soon, too impractical, too everything, but I really want to say it.

She clears her throat and breaks the eye contact while sliding her phone back in her pocket. "I'll just . . . run down and get that charger."

I nod and move to the fridge to pull out the food.

I've got the chicken marinating and the peppers sliced before I realize she hasn't come back upstairs.

After wiping my hands on a towel, I cross the great room to look over the railing into the studio. "Did you find it?"

She's standing in the middle of the studio, phone in one hand, charger in the other, staring at the painting on the easel.

Her face isn't happy. It's frighteningly blank.

I run down the stairs. Which painting is on the easel? What is she seeing? Why does it scare her? Because I do think fear is what I'm seeing on her face.

I swing around the end of the stairs and see the easel as I cross the room. The picture is discernable now. All the shapes and features are in place and recognizable. I need to add details, shading, and texture to bring it all to life, but the base of the image is clear.

A woman is sitting on the floor. All around her people are standing. They're actually dancing, but since you can't see any of them above the waist, it might be hard to tell.

The standing people are all in elegant evening wear. Gowns and tuxedo pants. Heels and sequins.

The woman on the floor, though, is in casual clothes. A long-sleeved T-shirt and a pair of joggers. She's curled into herself, looking defiant. A phone in her hand is in the process of shutting down from a low battery. Her other hand grips half a tiara. The other half is on the floor next to her feet.

"Emma?" I come to stand next to her, looking at her now instead of the painting.

"I'm your inspiration."

I frown. "What?"

She points to the easel. "Is that how you see me?"

I turn to look at the painting. "In a moment, I suppose." There was a time I saw this in Emma, and I still see a glimmer sometimes. At the Eyes and Ears Gala. At the gallery owner dinner. It didn't take much getting to know her to realize high-society functions left her drained, but still she soldiered through them because they mattered to people she loved.

When I drew this, I was thinking that can only continue so far. There will come a time when either the façade will break, or she will. She'll have to make a choice about who she wants to be.

"A moment." Her voice is flat.

This feels like an odd sort of reversal. She's the one looking at art and feeling all the emotions and I'm left standing there, staring at the same painting, wondering what in the world she sees in it.

Because I don't think we see the same thing.

I take a deep breath and try to explain. "You didn't want to be there."

Her shoulders stiffen. "You mean I didn't belong there."

"No, that's not it at all. You belong with—"

"Then why is it broken? Why is the phone dying?" She crosses the room, jabbing a finger at the painting. Is she going to destroy it? I'll let her if she needs to.

"Why is she lost?" Emma stands in front of the painting now, not touching it. That eerie blank calm has come over her again.

"She's not lost. She's . . . determined."

Emma shakes her head. "She can't be. Because she's got nothing left."

"She has herself."

"She doesn't even have shoes on."

"Neither do you, half the time." As soon as the words are out, I know they're wrong. I just don't know why.

"Is this how you see me?" she asks again.

Once more I don't understand the question.

"I didn't paint you, Emma."

"No, you painted a metaphor of me. Something that represents me. I'm a contradiction, remember?"

"You're twisting my words. That's not what I meant." I push my hands through my hair. "Emma, you know you don't understand the nuances of art. Why won't you believe me when I tell you what they are?"

"Because you see me better than I see myself?"

I drop my arms wide in a gesture of surrender. "Maybe."

We stand in silence for several moments.

Finally, she gives a sharp nod. "You should be happy."

"Believe me, right now I am not." I'm frustrated. Almost angry. Certainly confused. Anything, really, but happy.

"For the past two months you've been trying to get me to feel something when I look at art. Congratulations. I finally feel something."

Her eyes turn to me. The tears have returned.

"I feel betrayed. Goodbye, Carter."

She's walking away from me.

I go after her, but I don't know what to say. I'm not sure what went wrong.

I'm halfway down the hall when the door slams and I know it's too late.

**EMMA**

I'm in the middle of collecting the spoils from my latest video game battle when my apartment door opens. I don't look up.

Chances are it's Amy, but if it's a mad man come to put me out of my misery, I'd rather spend my last seconds of life playing a game than screaming my head off.

"Wow."

It's Amy.

"I have no words."

"Good." I hit the save button in case my character doesn't make it through the next quest, then send him plunging through the dark door into the temple.

"Is this a who's who of which restaurants will deliver to this address?"

"I thought you had no words."

"Yeah, well, I have a nose and the stench of this place fixed my vocal cords."

"It's not that bad." I try to take a discreet sniff, but my head is buried in my blanket hoodie and all I manage to do is tickle my nose until I sneeze.

She steps over a pile of takeout bags and settles onto the couch beside me. "Can we at least play a two-player game?"

I'm not far into the temple so my last save point is good, and I exit the game. I slide out from under my fuzzy blanket and cross the room to put *Mario Kart* in the console. Silently, I return to the couch and toss a controller to my sister.

Her eyes are wide as she takes in my outfit.

The giant, fuzzy blanket hoodie falls to my knees and is wide enough she could easily climb in here with me. My leggings were black at one point but they're faded to whatever color "almost black" is called. You can't see much of them anyway, because huge fuzzy socks cover my feet and go halfway up my calves.

"You're like the abominable snowman," Amy whispers in horror.

I glance down at my clothing. My socks are two different colors. "The abominable snowman is white. Not blue, black, pink, and orange."

"Fine then. What's blue, black, pink, and orange, covered in fur, and wallowing in self-pity?"

It's me, but I refuse to acknowledge that.

Instead, I return to the couch, snuggle back under my blanket, and prepare to leave Amy in the dust.

Unfortunately, I can only put distance between our characters on the screen. In real life, she continues to be less than eight inches away.

"Why are you here?"

"Because your boss called me. Apparently, you haven't been showing up for work."

"I turned in my vacation requests."

"And then unplugged your phone."

I point across the room to where my phone sits on the counter, the charge cord connecting it to the wall. "Not unplugged."

"Not being answered." Amy's car gets rescued by Lakitu for the third time this round, but she doesn't seem to care. She just keeps pressing buttons and running into walls until the game takes pity on her and declares her the twelfth-place finisher.

We play in silence until the screen displays the menu again. Amy snatches the controller from my hand before I can start a new game.

"What's going on?"

"I . . ." I want to say I got dumped, but I've had enough miserable introspection to admit that it's possible I technically still have a boyfriend.

I frown at Amy. "How do you know if you and your boyfriend break up?"

Her eyebrows rise. "Usually my screaming *I never want to see you again* is a pretty good clue." She sighs. "At least that's how it went when I broke up with Richie."

I lie there, waiting to see if there's more. There's not. "Do you need some ice cream? I signed up for the free delivery membership."

"Of course you did." She laughs. "But no. I'm surprisingly good with it."

She wraps her arms around herself and goes back to the original question. "I don't know that it has to get said in a particular way, but it needs to be obvious. Did you and Carter break up?"

I sigh and burrow deeper into my hoodie. "I think so?"

Amy kicks at the pile of fast-food bags the DoorDash drivers have been so kindly leaving in front of my apartment. The way her foot bobs, I think she might be counting. "You know, most girls get wine and ice cream and chocolate."

"Well, I eat French fries. I guess I'm not a normal girl, which, now that I think about it, could be the whole problem."

"Did you get milkshakes, too? You dip the one into the other, right?"

"No. Milkshake cups smell when you leave them lying around." Plus, they're what Carter got me when I had a bad night. "May I have the controller back now?" I stick my hand out, palm up.

Amy shoves both controllers behind her and down into the crevice between couch cushions. "No. Not until you've showered and put on clothes."

"These are clothes. I could put on my Crocs and go to Walmart right now without getting arrested."

"That is a remarkably low bar to set for an outfit."

"Well, your *Look Book* doesn't cover grocery shopping. Might want to think about that next year." Wow, I'm evil when I'm grumpy. Or sad. I'm sumpy. Ew, no, that sounds like a gross disease. I can't be grad either for obvious reasons. I'll be grud.

Apparently, I'm mean when I'm grud.

She snorts and leans in toward me. "Since you clearly don't actually use it, maybe I won't make the *Look Book* at all."

"Maybe you shouldn't."

"Maybe I won't."

"You're repeating yourself."

"At least I have a self."

By now we are nose to nose, yelling at each other loud enough to disturb the neighbors if it wasn't the middle of the afternoon.

"That doesn't make any sense." I thump her in the forehead.

"Oh really? Answer the question, then."

"You haven't asked one."

She rips the hood off my head, sits back on the couch, and points at me. "Who are you?"

The fight drains out of me. I flop back onto the couch, then keep melting until I slither down to the floor.

Amy lies on the couch and leans over the edge, her face looming above mine as her hair drapes around us like a curtain.

She repeats the question, but this time with a painful curiosity instead of anger. "Who are you, Emma? I feel like I don't know you at all anymore and now I'm not even certain you know yourself."

She's right. "I don't."

How long has it been since we talked? Like really, really talked? In high school we sat in each other's beds long after we were supposed to be asleep, talking about teachers and boys and friends. She would lay my clothes out for me each morning and I would make our breakfast.

Now, we're all but strangers.

"What happened to us, Ames?"

Her little shrug looks strange from this angle. "Life, I suppose. I think you moved on but I'm not sure I ever did."

"You're the reason the boutique has become one of the most exclusive fashion destinations in four states."

"Yeah, the boutique Mom and Aunt Jade own."

I frown. "They haven't made you part owner yet?"

"No." She groans and rolls off the couch, landing on top of me and crushing my will to breathe if not my will to ever get up again.

She keeps rolling until we're lying side by side, staring up at my ceiling.

"I own the line and the customizations, though. And my styling business. I'm not sure they realize how it's set up but, technically, I'm renting space from the boutique."

"That doesn't sound like standing still."

"It's the path I was on ten years ago, though."

"Wait a minute." I push myself into a sitting position so I can see her face. "You think there's something wrong with you because you kept going down the path you chose as a teenager?"

"Well, yeah, I mean. Look at you." She sits up as well, shoving aside the other balled-up orange sock so she can sit flat. "You couldn't be further from that girl."

I spread my arms wide to indicate my giant plush hoodie. "I'm not sure that's a good thing."

"True."

We both fall silent. I don't know what she's thinking about, but I'm wondering what teenage me would think of my life now.

I don't think she'd be happy about it.

I think she'd say I'm just as stuck as I've always been, but I've managed to build a life that lets me pretend otherwise.

I don't want to live like that anymore, so I break the ugliest, most painful lock I've created for myself, and I start talking. I tell my sister everything.

"When I went to college, it seemed like I'd stumbled into a whole new world. I went to class with people wearing last night's pajama pants. People wore hoodies and jeans to sports games. My roommate loaned me a pair of yoga pants when we went out one day to play frisbee on the green."

That was a day I remember clearly because it was the first week of college. We were tossing the frisbee around with a group from our freshmen orientation class and at the edge of the green I saw a group of girls walking toward a sorority house. They were in dresses and heeled sandals. Their hair was curled, and even as far away as I was, I could see the lipstick and nail polish and false eyelashes.

It felt like I was supposed to be over there, like that was where Mom and Aunt Jade and Amy would want me to be.

But I didn't want to be there. I wanted to be wearing yoga pants and tossing a frisbee.

"I started going to church with my roommate and attending an on-campus Bible study. That really changed things for me. Knowing Jesus changed what I wanted in life.

"When I graduated, I told myself it was a fresh start. I was going to build the life I wanted."

"But we didn't let you." Amy's voice is soft, mournful.

"I didn't let me. The first time Mother saw me in a college hoodie she nearly fainted."

"That might have had something to do with the fact that it was eighty-five degrees outside." Amy's voice is still sad, but she at least has the beginnings of a grin now.

"Perhaps. Either way, it scared me. I told myself it didn't matter what I wore. I could still be me. But that didn't work either.

"I found myself talking differently at family gatherings than I did with my friends. It wasn't just you, though. I kept my hobbies from the people at work because the games I like to play felt childish. I didn't tell my friends at church about attending galas and the theater."

I didn't fully realize how bad it had gotten until I saw that painting in Carter's studio.

He can say all he wants that he didn't see me in that picture, but I know the truth. He saw the real me. And he painted her.

"What about Carter?" Amy pulls at the toe of my red sock, and I let her slide it from my foot.

"He knew."

"About the deceit?"

I shake my head. "About me. I don't know why but I didn't hide it from him."

She pulls at the other sock. "He's a lucky guy."

"Yeah. I gave him fresh inspiration, but I don't think it's because he liked me. I think it's because he found me odd."

"Who needs him, then?" She stands to her feet and extends her arms down to me.

I take her hands because she's my sister and while there's still some mending to do, the rift between us has been bridged more easily than I would have imagined.

"What am I doing?"

She grabs my shoulder and pushes me toward my room. "Getting a shower. But don't wash your hair. I'm calling in a favor at my salon and taking you down there this afternoon."

I smirk at her. "Isn't getting a post-breakup haircut one of those cardinal no-nos?"

"You just spent forty-five minutes telling me you aren't like other girls so you can't go claiming the rules apply to you now." She gives me another shove. "And just for that, I'm telling them to give you bangs while they're at it."

When I get out of the shower, I see that Amy has gone through my clothes and pulled out an outfit for me. It's lying on the bed like when we were in high school.

I put on the faded, ripped jeggings and the slouchy T-shirt. She didn't give me shoes so I slide my feet into my Crocs.

When I come out, I find Amy's spent my shower time straightening the apartment. A tied-up trash bag sits by the door and the array of blankets I spent the last few days wallowing in have been folded and laid over the back of the couch.

"Let's go." She wraps an arm around my shoulders, gives me three squeezes—two short, one long—and leads me out the door, grabbing the trash as she goes.

I know where her salon is, and that isn't the first place she drives. "Nordstrom?"

"We are going shopping."

Before I can collapse in a fit of groaning, she holds up her hands, palms facing me. "Hear me out!"

"Fine," I grumble.

"This isn't a boutique. It's a department store."

"I'm aware."

"I get it. You don't like fancy clothes and belts and scarves and basically everything we sell at the boutique."

A wince scrunches up my face, but Amy seems unbothered by my dislike of her chosen fashions.

"However," she continues, holding up one finger as if she is about to make a life-changing declaration, "I refuse to believe that we cannot find something as comfortable as your beloved hoodies that doesn't make my eyeballs hurt."

She snatches the keys from the ignition and pushes open her door. "I am a woman on a fashion mission and you, my dear twin sister, owe me this one." She takes a deep breath. "And I owe it to you as well."

I climb out of the car. "What do you mean by that?"

She looks at the sky as she jiggles her keys in her hand. Finally, she looks at me. "Is broke college student on the five-year plan the impression you want to give the world, or is it what you default to because you think it's that or dressing like me?"

"Ah . . ." I've never thought about it, but there's a chance she's right. Still, I'm not convinced there is a good middle ground. "You might have a point." Besides, if following her around as she combs through the racks and then trying on clothes will make Amy and me close again, I'll gladly go along.

She stalks toward the store like a woman who is indeed on a mission. "Now. Let's figure out how to show the real Emma Trinket to the world."

I can't help but grin a little as I follow her.

Amy gets recognized by the workers in the women's clothing section and soon a personal shopper is trailing after us, taking everything Amy selects to a private dressing room. For an hour, I'm asked if I like how this shirt feels and how tight I want to wear my pants. Do waistbands cause a problem or is it the way trousers fit?

Half of her questions are things I've never thought to consider, and I have to tell her I honestly don't know. That gets the item sent to the dressing room.

Finally, she calls a halt and we're taken to wherever the clothes have been drifting off to.

I stumble to a halt in the giant dressing room. A sheet has been tacked over the mirror. "What is that?"

"My special request. If you cared about how the outfit looked, you wouldn't be in those shoes, so all you get to be concerned about today is how it feels. I get to worry about how it looks."

"Um. Okay."

I start trying on clothes. As we narrow it down, Amy makes me sit, stand, stretch, and even lie on the floor to decide what's most comfortable.

Finally, she shoves a pair of backless leather flats at me. "Wear these."

"You don't want me to wear the rest of the clothes out?"

"No." She pats the bag containing her final choices. "These can wait until after your hair's done. But these"—she shudders as she drops the Crocs into another bag—"just no."

We get to the salon and are met by a guy with a Greek accent. I've never had him do my hair before, even though Amy's dragged me here before events on more than one occasion.

Amy waves at me as if I'm a gift. "Here she is, Nicolo."

The man mumbles to himself in Greek.

Amy pulls out her phone and shows him a picture. "I was thinking something like this? Do you agree?"

"No, no, no." The man shakes a finger at the picture. "You say she is simple, yes?" He looks to me for confirmation.

As if I would know how to answer that.

"Wash, dry, go, no?"

"Ah." I give him a nod. "Yes. I'm not going to do much more than brush it."

He returns my nod and waves away Amy's phone. "No sense doing something like that if she won't do anything with it."

Now I really want to see Amy's picture.

There's no time, though, because I'm plopped in a chair and strands of my hair are folded into strips of aluminum foil. I've seen them doing this at the place I get my hair trimmed, but I've never experienced it. The gunk they put on between pieces of foil is cold.

Then I sit under the heat while Amy gets her hair washed and blow dried. It's a little boring, but totally worth it when my head is dunked into a sink and given the most blissful head massage known to mankind.

I then sit as my chair is turned this way and that and I'm treated to a monologue about the wonderful new traffic circle going in at the end of the street but the horrors of the construction traffic in the meantime.

A blow dry and a brush later and Amy is whisking me away to the back room with the Nordstrom bag hooked on her arm.

Both me and the bag are pushed into a closet.

"Get changed. I want you to see all of it at once."

The outfit is simple. A pair of tailored jeans made with some sort of stretchy fabric that practically makes them feel like yoga pants, a light blue and white cotton shirt, and a cardigan sweater made of neutral-colored stripes that falls to my knees and has a hood. As I slide my feet into the shoes again, my heart starts to race.

This is it.

When I step out, Amy and Nicolo are standing next to a large mirror, both grinning like proud parents. I cross the room, careful to keep my gaze away from the myriad of other, smaller mirrors I pass on the way.

I step in front of the big mirror and see nothing.

My eyes are closed.

And I can't seem to change that.

Amy squeals. "Oh my gosh, don't you love it? Emma? Oh, for goodness' sake, Emma, open your eyes."

Her command has my eyes flying open and I almost don't believe it's me. My hair is still straight, but somehow doesn't seem as flat. Streaks of dark blond flitter through the brown, and wispy bangs cover my forehead.

The clothing is neat and fashionable, but I have no desire to claw it off and run for my hoodie.

I look . . . cute. Grown-up. Put together.

I look like me, like all of my parts have come together and decided to show themselves at one time.

Just gazing in the mirror is healing something in me I didn't even know was broken, but it isn't just the vision in front of me. It's how everything in the mirror represents part of the journey it took to get here. It's not an abandonment of where I started. It's a completion.

Is this what Carter sees when he looks at art? Does he see how the snapshot of the moment captured in paint represents so much more than just what we see?

Amy lifts her phone and snaps a picture of our combined reflection, and it jars me because I know that picture will never be the same as being in this moment.

And just like that, I know exactly where my museum design went wrong.

**30**

*EMMA*

"I need your help."

To Jason's credit, he doesn't jump when I burst into his office. Nor does he panic despite the urgent breathlessness in my voice.

I can discount the breathlessness because of my run from the parking lot, but the urgency is far more, well, urgent.

"I like the hair."

"Not the point."

"As you've given me nothing else to go on, it's all I've got."

I drop into the chair in front of his desk and prop my elbows on my knees as I lean forward, holding his gaze in a desperate attempt to get him to understand the seriousness of this moment. "My design is terrible."

His eyebrows lift but somehow, he doesn't really look surprised. "You said it was under control and easier than you expected."

"I lied."

"I know."

I sit up and frown. "How can you know?"

He points at the computer. "Your presentation and your app are on the shared server. I took a look."

I want to fall through the chair. No, I want to fall through the floor. Who rents the office space below this? Do they need a programmer?

No. I can't slink off in a pile of embarrassment. I need to make this right.

"I have an idea." I pull out the sketches I pulled together after getting home from my outing with Amy and throw them on his desk. "But I don't know how to do it."

Jason looks over the sketches and then holds them in the air. "This is a different design."

"It's a different concept, yes." I take a deep breath. "But design is more than that."

I bury my head in my hands and go from talking to my boss to talking to my best friend. "Jason, I messed up. And Amy made me get a haircut, and it doesn't look ridiculous, and that means everything doesn't have to be in different little boxes, and I don't know who I am, but I finally feel like myself."

His fingers wrap around my wrists, and he pulls my hands away from my face. I open my eyes and look into his. The way he's kneeling in front of my chair puts his face at eye level.

"Two things, well, three." His voice is gentle, and a small smile is tugging at his lips.

"Okay." I sniff and rub tears from my cheek with my sleeve. When did I start crying?

"One"—he lets go of my arm and grabs a tissue box from his desk—"I can't understand you when you talk into your hands."

"I'm not sure I was making sense anyway." I grab a tissue and blow my nose.

"Two, I'm calling Trina to come over here with pizza or whatever because while I am here for you no matter what and will sit through anything you want to tell me, I have a feeling another woman might be helpful in this case."

I frown. "Maybe. Probably."

He nods. "And finally, I'm going to clear my weekend. It's going to be you and me in that conference room and we're going to redo this prototype."

I groan. "There isn't time to start over."

He tosses the tissue box at me. "Crazy girl. Do you know what else is on the shared server?"

"What?" I pull out another tissue and dab at my eyes.

"Your code. Unlike your design, your code is elegant and efficient. Most of it can be repurposed. We're tweaking. Not starting over."

He drops back into the seat behind his desk and pulls out his cell phone. I assume he's texting Trina.

"Tell her I want bacon."

He nods.

"And pineapple."

He pretends to gag.

"You aren't a designer either."

"I'm better than you are." He finishes his text and drops the phone on the desk. "But if it makes you feel better, I'll see if anyone on the design team is available to give us a few pointers before they leave for the weekend."

I nod. "If they go over hours, you can take it from my paycheck."

"What did they use to make those blond streaks?"

"I don't know. Why?"

"Because I think it fried your brain." His laughter joins with the click of keys as he types out an email. "You do remember we have salaries around here, right? No one is paid by the hour."

A few more keystrokes and a click of the mouse, and he folds his arms on the desk to lean toward me and grin. "I will, however, let you pay for all the takeout we're about to have delivered."

By the time Trina arrives with a giant stack of pizza boxes, most of Digital World Solutions' employees are packed into the conference room.

The white board is covered with the design team's ideas for how to organize the menus and handle the layered imagery. They are in the middle of a heated debate on how long the delay needs to be to accommodate people just strolling through so the software isn't constantly trying to remap to paintings the user isn't truly taking the time to look at.

On the other side of the room, the junior programmers have brought in a projector, and the wall is filled with line after line of code as they determine which objects can work as is and which need to be adjusted for the new plan.

The intern is digging through the supply closet to find our stash of smart glasses that we use for testing.

Even our two marketing guys are here brainstorming names for the new design.

Trina places the pizza boxes on the table, and everyone stops in the middle of their work to descend upon the food.

Moments later a box slightly smaller than the others is shoved at me. "Here's your pineapple monstrosity," Stephanie says with a shudder. "If that's what heartache makes you eat, I'm never dating again."

"Wait, Emma got her heart broken?" Zach, one of the junior programmers looks up from his slice of pepperoni.

"Yeah," David from marketing answers. "That's why we're doing this. He thought her design was bad."

"He wasn't wrong," Stephanie mumbles.

I'd like to feel offended, but she's right.

"We are doing this because the museum visitors deserve the best possible self-guided tour, and we all know that's augmented reality." I try to keep my voice firm because this does not need to devolve into a discussion of my personal life.

Nor do I want anyone here as some sort of vendetta against Carter. It isn't his fault. He never pretended to care about my job. I just wish caring about me had been enough to cover it all.

"Aw, man, she's crying. Who's got some tissues?"

"Good job, David."

"What did I do? Stephanie was the one who called her design bad."

"My mom says when girls cry it's always a guy's fault."

"I think it's time to get an apartment of your own, Zach."

I can't help it. Laughter bubbles out through the tears and I sink to the floor, still clutching my bacon and pineapple pizza.

Trina prods me with her foot and my laughter approaches hysterical levels. "I think we broke her."

"Good," Jason says as he rescues my pizza and then nudges me in the shoulder, so I roll completely onto the floor. "Maybe she'll start to see reason, then."

I cough and choke and roll over to lie flat on my back as I try to get control of myself enough to talk. "I'm completely reasonable."

"Falser words were never spoken." Trina sits on the floor near my head.

"Hey!" I lay my head on her knee and she strokes my hair.

Jason kneels, making sure to stay out of kicking range. "I get this is a girl thing, but I'm a guy so let me give you something to think about. That guy is crazy about you. Maybe even stupid crazy. You remember what you were mumbling in my office?"

I try to think back, but it's all a blur. "No."

"I didn't get all of it, but I know something about this haircut made you see things differently."

"It's really cute." Trina fluffs the hair on my forehead. "I like the bangs."

"What's your point, Jason?"

He shrugs. "Maybe this guy just needs a haircut."

I frown. "I like his hair long."

"I'm being metaphorical here, Trinket. Keep up." Jason stands and points to my sketches. "Let's help him see things a little differently, shall we? It's what we do."

Conversation bounces around the table as we eat the pizza. Most of it seems to center around me and before I know it, I'm showing them pictures of myself and Amy in formal wear, Carter's paintings, and my string of high scores on his new gaming console.

Jason gathers the empty pizza boxes into a stack as everyone gets back to work. He leans over to whisper, "Do you get it yet? All these people think you are worth helping, just as you are."

I throw a napkin into my box. "I never said I was unloved."

Trina leans in. "Everything they just learned about you hasn't sent them scurrying, either. It's just interesting trivia. I really like that green dress, though. Can I borrow it?"

"I'll see if I can find it." I grin at her.

"Good. Now. Go code a pumpkin or whatever needs to happen to make this fairytale work." She leans back in her chair, props her feet on the table, and pulls out her phone.

I can't help the smile that splits my face. "What are you doing?"

"Y'all are gonna need a food runner." She snags my purse from the back of my chair. "And I'm putting all of it on your credit card."

"Be sure to include a tip for the delivery driver." I'm still grinning as I join my coding team.

The smart glasses are plugged in to charge. Code is ripped apart and put back together. Ideas are erased and rewritten on the board. When late night milkshakes arrive, a few people, primarily the marketing and testing people, call it a night. Before they leave, they make Jason promise to text them if there's anything they can come back and help with.

The looks they give me as they do this say they don't trust me to be honest about it.

They're probably right.

Finally, Jason calls it for the night and everyone else heads home. It's just me and him in a conference room that looks like the command center for a world disaster movie.

"This really is a good look on you." He pokes at the bun on top of my head being held in place by a couple of pencils because I couldn't find a hair tie. The layers make it messier than it used to be, as strands have come loose and are poking out in all directions.

"Thanks." My tone is dry.

He laughs. "I mean it. You look like . . . you. The real you." He groans and runs a hand through his hair. "I'm so bad at this. Where's Trina?"

"Hopefully asleep since she promised to bring everyone coffee and donuts at eight AM tomorrow." I gather up my purse. As much as I want to keep working, I'm not a college student who can run on catnaps and caffeine anymore. "I think you're doing a good job, though."

He hits the lights and secures the locks before we head toward our cars. "As a former boyfriend, may I say—ouch!"

I pinch him in the side. "It was what, four dates? And we spent most of them talking about how weird it was and deciding we would just spend the evening as we usually did. Can those even really be called dates?"

"Did you discuss outfit ideas with your friends?"

I laugh hard enough to need to lean against my car for support. "Is that what makes it a date for you?"

"I dunno." He leans against the car next to me, and we both look up into the sky. There are too many streetlights around for us to see many stars, but still we look.

"What I was going to say before I was so rudely interrupted was, I like what came out of that time."

"Our non-dating dating time?"

"Yeah. I mean, do you really think we'd still be friends if we hadn't done that?"

I consider it and have to admit the answer is no. If we hadn't tried, there would always be the pressure of what if. "I guess not."

"So I'm glad. We both came out of it with something better than what we went into it with."

"What's your point, ex-boyfriend?"

He flicks at my hair again. "My point is, even if this is the end with him, even if you cry into your cornflakes for a few weeks, you're better for this time you had with him. Don't count it all bad."

I look at the stars, contemplating his words. They're true. I have a new confidence, a new relationship with my sister, a new understating of life.

But I still want to have Carter, too.

"Okay, you're taking too long." Jason presses the unlock button on my key fob and opens my car door. "Focus on driving, then ponder philosophy as you go to sleep."

I climb in and give him a salute. "See you in a few hours."

He salutes back and walks to his own car.

Saturday is a blur of code and tests and takeout. I'm surprised by how much of my stuff was usable, how close I came to getting it right. All it took was a few people looking at it from a different way.

Maybe I'm not so far off with Carter either.

On Sunday, there's only a handful of us in the conference room. Me, Jason, and a couple junior programmers are running tests and configuring the mapping graphics.

We take a break mid-morning and use the projector to throw our church service's livestream on to the wall.

It's peaceful after the frantic pace of the last few days. I'll have some clean-up work to do before the demonstration, but the hardest parts are almost complete.

By mid-afternoon, it's just me and Jason in the conference room running one more functionality test. Tomorrow I'll need to go to the museum and make some final measurements and tests with the real thing, but so far everything looks good.

When Carter's painting comes up, my breath shudders.

"Is that his?" Jason asks quietly.

I nod.

"It's good."

I nod again.

"What's the tour going to say about it?"

"I don't know. I didn't look." I had deliberately passed the loading and mapping of this painting off to someone else. The cold facts aren't what I think of when I see it.

I think—I feel—something else entirely.

Something I really want Carter to know.

I take the glasses off and consider them. "I'm borrowing a pair of these."

Jason's eyebrows shoot up. "Okay?"

"I've been doing a lot of thinking."

He coughs and looks around the disaster of a room. "When did you find the time?"

I wave his question away. "Not important. The important thing is, I'm not done."

"With the project? No, it's still got some finishing work, but it's doable."

"No, with Carter. If it's over, I want to be able to say I gave it everything I have." I hold up the glasses. "And it starts with these."

Jason doesn't ask, but I can tell he's curious. "What else is part of this plan?"

I slide my computer over and click into an online dress store. "Going shopping."

**CARTER**

There are many comforting things I associate with my grandparents' home. The smell of home-cooked Southern food. The jingle of the wind chimes on the front porch. The hazy bits in the air when the sun hits the living room just right that I'm fairly certain are small pieces of the ancient upholstery on my grandpa's favorite chair. How that thing hasn't disintegrated and fallen apart yet, I'll never know.

What I am not accustomed to seeing is a man's face blown up to twice its natural size and speaking in a British accent.

"You got a new television?" It's flat, wall-mounted, and at least twice as large as the old box one that used to sit on a coffee table pushed up against the wall.

"Do you close your eyes when you come here?" Grandmother swats me on the arm with a towel as she goes to check on something in the kitchen. "We bought that ages ago."

I come for dinner at least once a month, but that doesn't require coming into the living room. Dining room, yes. Kitchen. Front porch. Occasionally the bathroom.

Grandpa raises his arm and wiggles the remote in the air. There are dozens of buttons on it, some of which have been circled with a silver permanent marker or colored in with a black one.

"Got one of those newfangled smart TVs." Grandpa laughs in triumph. "No more flipping the cable channels. I can pick what I want whenever I choose."

He points to the TV. "You know those British shows we like? Well, there's more of them. And they've got a whole channel dedicated to them."

"It's an app, dear, not a channel," Grandmother calls.

"You got a television." I don't know why I can't quite wrap my mind around my grandparents purchasing new technology, but I can't. I don't know if I'd have reacted this way before Emma, but probably not. It seems like having more technology in my life has brought nothing but problems.

Grandpa waves me toward the couch as he pauses the show on the television. He points at the screen and gives me a wink. "I can stop it whenever I want, too."

"Yeah." I understand the concept of television and apps. I just don't equate them with my grandparents. They're supposed to stay . . . old.

"Had to do something with that extra fifty dollars a month." His grin is wide and proud.

The oven slides shut and a few cabinet doors are closed before Grandmother walks back into the room, looking around with a frown. "You didn't bring that nice Emma with you?"

"Ah, no."

"Messed it up, did you." It's more of a statement than a question and I glare at Grandpa.

"Why do you assume I messed it up?"

"Because you look more confused than sad. I'm guessing she's the one who walked out on you and, given the way she was making goo-goo eyes at you while she was here, you'd have had to do something spectacularly bad to make her do that."

I gape at Grandpa. Emma was making goo-goo eyes at me? Wait. "What are goo-goo eyes?"

Grandpa looks at Grandma and she giggles and swats his arm before coming to sit by me on the couch.

Does she actually use that towel to dry dishes in the kitchen, or is it a special one she carries around just to hit people with? Hopefully it's the latter, but I've never paid attention to it before.

"What happened, sweetie?"

I sigh and fall back into the couch. If I'm honest, this is why I'm here. My heart hurts and I want someone to take care of me. I'll pour out my story, Grandma will whip up a batch of brownies, and when I drive home tonight, things will look just a little bit better.

"She doesn't understand me."

"Course not. She's a woman."

Grandma glares at Grandpa. "Maddox."

"What?" He spreads his hands wide. "A woman ain't gonna understand a man until they've been married thirty years, raised a family together, gone through thick and thin, and renovated a bathroom."

He points at me. "Even then, she's still ahead of you. We've been married fifty-seven years and I still can't predict if bringing her flowers will make her happy or sad."

"Don't listen to him." Grandmother turns to me. "What doesn't she understand?"

"Art."

"I see where that could be a problem." Her wrinkled hand reaches out and takes mine. Her grip is stronger than it looks like it should be.

I should paint more elderly people.

"Is it all art or just your art she doesn't get?" Grandpa points to the painting I made for them when I was just starting out. "Because that is beautiful, but Picasso is just weird."

"My art. She was . . . well, you could say she's been a muse of sorts." The words come spilling out. How we met. The inspiration. The project. The fight at the museum and then again at the gallery.

At one point, Grandmother goes to the kitchen and brings back a glass of iced tea. I've talked so much my mouth is going dry.

Finally, I stop talking and drop my head to the back of the couch.

Grandmother is the one to finally break the silence with a sigh. "I'm afraid your grandpa's right on this one."

I turn my head so I can see her. She isn't smiling.

"You've got a man's lack of understanding."

Grandpa laughs.

They were supposed to be on my side. I came here for comfort, not to be made to feel worse.

"Allow me to enlighten you, boy." Grandpa leans forward in his chair. "You want this woman to be your partner in life, you've got to realize she's just as important as you are. It's a two-way street. She supports you. You support her. Both of you win."

I frown. "What are you talking about? I support her. I bought a gaming console and a television."

"Why?"

"Because I wanted to spend more time with her."

He points at me. "So it wasn't really for her, then, was it?"

When I look at him, confused, he sighs. "You gotta value her skills as much as you value your own. Your Grandma makes the best biscuits in town, but it takes her three tries to get a polarized plug in the socket right and she still puts batteries in backwards."

As Grandpa had been an electrician for forty-eight years, I can only imagine how much Grandma's ineptitude bothers him.

"I should send you to the Cracker Barrel for your biscuits." Grandma smiles as she throws the towel at Grandpa. He catches it without seeming to look.

"No need for that, dear. I'm just trying to make a point."

"And what point is that?" Without her towel, Grandmother folds her arms in front of her and glares.

"That our grandson is being an idiot."

Her anger fades as if it was never real in the first place, and she turns her pitying look on me. "He is that."

I love my grandparents. They've supported me when my own family didn't know how, but they don't understand the struggle I'm having with Emma being not just indifferent to my art, but misunderstanding it to the point that it causes her pain.

My agitation works through me until I can't sit still anymore. I push to my feet. "Thanks for the tea."

Several beeps and clicks come from the television. Grandpa's fingers press the buttons as easily as Emma's with a game controller. Finally, he points at the screen. "See that?"

I turn to see the screen filled with the placard for a movie I watched as a child. It's an adaption from a classic fantasy adventure book Grandpa and I had read together. "I do."

"Which is better, the book or the movie?"

I look at him like he's lost his mind. We've talked about this before. "Neither. They're both amazing."

"And yet, people think books are more refined than movies."

I almost agree that they are, but I stop myself because I learned to spot one of Grandpa's traps a long time ago. It may seem like a simple question or observation, but the moment I agree, he'll spin it around and disrupt my whole life.

Grandpa doesn't let me wiggle out, though. He points at me. "You need to figure out if you're thinking of your work as a book and her work as a movie."

"It's not the same."

"Your grandma makes those biscuits from a recipe." He points across the room to a lamp that is, in its own way, a work of art. A long branch reaches nearly to the ceiling as a light bulb shrouded in a tan shade dangles from one of the limbs. "And I made that lamp out of whim and whimsy."

I search his face, but I can't find the connection he's trying to make. He sighs. "Which is better?"

I frown. "I can't compare those two."

"Your girl thinks you can. And she thinks you put the biscuits in second place. If she didn't, it wouldn't have mattered what she saw in that painting because she'd have known it wasn't the same thing you saw when you look at her."

I don't know what to say. I want to ask him what I should do, but I know he won't answer. Grandpa has always said a man who doesn't make his own choices won't have the conviction to see them through.

"You can think about that awhile." Grandmother pats me on the shoulder as she moves toward the kitchen. "I'll make you a sandwich to go."

I drive away, munching on turkey and Swiss between slices of fresh wheat bread. A bread maker I hadn't noticed before sat on the counter, but I didn't say anything. Whether it was brand new or had been there for years, I didn't want to know.

I try not to think about biscuits and lamps and classic fantasy stories, but the conversation keeps plaguing the back of my mind. It feels like when I read the Bible and God keeps prodding me with the verses until I learn what He wants me to see. It wouldn't be the first time God used

Grandma and Grandpa to teach me a lesson, but this time, I think it's just guilt.

Or hurt.

Because I don't have a reason to feel guilty, do I?

Emma is the one who refused to listen about the painting. What she saw in it is what hurt her, not what I painted. How can I fix a problem I didn't cause?

Needing another voice to ponder, I stop at Frank's gallery before going home. As an art lover, he'll understand. Even though he doesn't create it, he's built his career around an appreciation of it.

I almost walk right back out the door when I see Frank fiddling with a large tablet built into the top of a decorative pedestal. There's a projector built into the pedestal, splaying an image of a piece of framed art onto the wall.

"What's this?"

Frank puts his hands on his hips. "An experiment. Smaller galleries can only keep a certain amount of art on hand. While I'm ideally choosing the things my customers want, if I get it wrong, I lose the sale."

His explanation only raises more questions. "You're going to sell projectors now? Help people shine whatever they want onto their walls?"

My sharp tone almost makes me wince. Clearly, I'm prepared to take out my pain on anyone around me.

Frank ignores my tone, though. "Don't be a snob, Carter."

A snob? "Because I prefer real art to virtual?"

"This connects to a network of independent galleries." He points at the tablet. "We can put whatever stock we wish into the system, and it can be sold at other galleries. The two galleries then split the commission at an agreed-upon rate. It's less than I would get if I sold it on my own, but more than if I didn't sell it at all." He shrugs. "Plus, it expands the options I can give people, making my gallery a more appealing choice. Win-win."

It makes sense. I know it does. But it also feels . . . cold. "Don't you think that takes away from the experience? I mean, this isn't the same as seeing the piece in person."

"No, but not everybody needs art to feel something or have a deep meaning. Sometimes they just like it because it's pretty."

I don't know what to think about that. Even the enjoyment of something pretty causes a certain type of emotion, doesn't it?

Frank looks over my shoulder and gives someone a nod. "Hold on a moment. I need to wrap this up." He steps around me. "Everything get settled?"

"The pieces are ready to ride the winds of destiny to find their rightful place in the world."

I spin around because a statement like that can only be made by one person. Sure enough, Richie Reynolds is standing there, extending a clipboard toward Frank. I recognize the shipping labels because Frank often facilitates packing and sending my pieces to New York for me.

Whatever didn't sell here must be going to a different gallery.

Is he still dating Amy? Is there a chance he's seen Emma? Not that they ever spent a great deal of time together, but I crave any knowledge I can get about her. I haven't gone six days without seeing or speaking to her in almost three months.

If this is what withdrawal feels like, I'm grateful I've never done drugs.

"How are things going, Richie?" I step toward the duo.

Frank looks at me with wide eyes and gives a sharp shake of his head, but it's too late. Richie is already sighing.

"Despair is a muse like no other. I fear too much heartache will elevate my work beyond the understanding of others."

Heartache, huh? Did both of the Trinket twins dispose of their romantic partners? "Bad breakup?"

Frank groans and starts scribbling signatures onto the packing slips.

"Only when love is lost can we feel the depth of its roots. What is ripped from the ground displaces more dirt than that which simply rots."

Richie's eyes go glassy, and he stares at the ceiling until a tear forms on the tip of his eyelash.

I raise my eyebrows and look at Frank, who just shakes his head and extends Richie's copies of the slips.

Suddenly Richie snaps back into reality. "I must go. The muse of greatness has deigned to visit me once more."

He runs out without taking the papers and Frank clips them back onto the clipboard. "I'll just mail them to Greg. Probably safer that way."

"Do you think it's exhausting to talk like that all the time?"

Frank snorts. "I think it's exhausting to live like that all the time." He shakes his head. "Artists are weird."

"Present company excluded?"

"Nope." Frank returns to the tablet and the pedestal.

"Wait a minute," I say as I trail after him. "What does that mean?"

"Don't get me wrong. I like your brand of weird, but you still get in your own head."

I frown. "I've never understood that phrase. Aren't we all in our own heads?"

"One would hope." Frank leans against the wall and purses his lips in thought. "Are you going to the prototype demonstration next week?"

A shudder runs through me before I can stop it, but I nod. "The board expects me there. I have an obligation."

"But you aren't happy about it." Frank points at me. "You aren't happy about the entire project."

I shove my hand through my hair. "Art should speak for itself. The connection between a person and the painting is what matters."

Frank looks at me and then moves to the pedestal to flick through a few things on the tablet. Moments later, a new image is being projected onto the wall. "What do you think?"

It's an artist's table. Paints, brushes, palettes, and rags are scattered over the surface. On one side, an easel sits empty. The edges are soft and without detail, but it's still easy to recognize what is what.

Looking at it, I feel a ghost of the anticipation that rises before starting a new project. Even when I was struggling for inspiration, a clean, new canvas held a world of possibilities. There isn't a canvas in this picture, but the idea is the same.

Frank is looking at me expectantly, so I try to put the feeling into words. "I suppose I'm excited to see what is about to be made. It's a moment of infinite potential."

"If you want it to mean that, sure." Frank points at the wall. "You can buy this painting today, take it home, and have that be what it means for the rest of your life."

"Or?" I don't want to ask it. This feels like one of Grandpa's traps.

"Or you can know the story behind it. The painter has Parkinson's. He's been in steady decline, his pieces taking him longer and longer to do and becoming more and more delineated. His daughter had to help him finish this one."

That empty easel looks different now. It terrifies me. Because one day it could be me looking at my brushes and not being able to create. It could be me relying on others to understand my vision.

"The way you see the world isn't the only way to see it." Frank taps the pedestal. "And a creation isn't bad just because it runs on electricity. You should see the code diagram for this system." He shakes his head. "I asked them if I could have a print for the wall in my office. They laughed, but I was only halfway joking."

I can see it. The scribbled pages of Emma's notebooks strewn around a screen holding the polished finished product of her design.

Frank clears his throat. "I saw Emma yesterday."

My heart stalls. "You did? Where?"

"The museum. She was measuring things."

So she's still working on her design. Despite everything I said, everything I gave the board to say, she still believes in her work.

"Did she look happy?" The words almost choke me, but I have to know.

"She looked focused." Frank claps me on the shoulder. "I don't know what happened, but I know you. I've been your friend for years and it's easy to work around your blind spots as a friend. A girlfriend might find it a little harder."

"My blind spots?" Again, the words come out of their own volition. Again, I don't want to know the answer but I desperately need it at the same time.

"Competence is its own form of art. Order and function is a type of creativity. The bridge between vision and reality must be at once strong and delicate. It takes a talented sculptor to forge it. If you can't see that, maybe it's you who needs to change his definitions."

Frank presses a button and the image on the wall disappears. "Do you need to talk further? We can . . . I don't know . . . go get pancakes or something."

"Pancakes?" Despite the way my brain seems to have been completely upended, the idea makes me laugh.

"Well, neither of us drinks and going to get a Coke sounds like a date from the fifties. So, yeah. Pancakes."

"Thanks, but I just need to think."

He nods. "Call me if you need me. There's a Waffle House on the exit I take to get to your house."

"They don't sell pancakes."

He shrugs again. "Maybe you can learn a little flexibility there, then."

It's by God's grace alone that I make it to my car and find my way safely to my garage, because the next thing I really know, I'm staring at the wall and listening to the click of my car engine as it cools.

Is it possible I've been looking at everything wrong?

32

*EMMA*

"I bought a dress."

Amy pauses, one foot poised to step into my apartment, her arms full of packages and bags. I still have a week and half before the demonstration, but Amy is here to make sure I have a suitable outfit and don't need to go shopping this weekend.

Her eyes fall from my face to the still-sealed plastic shipping bag in my hands.

It arrived yesterday, but I haven't been able to bring myself to open it. What if I'm no good at elevating my own appearance? What if this looks horrible on me?

But also, what if it looks great? What if I could have been doing this all along and simply didn't try because I didn't want to dress like the rest of my family?

Basically, I'm holding an existential crisis emblazoned with the bold logo of an online clothing retailer.

Amy seems to be having her own crisis with the bag.

I frown. "Are you turning green?"

Her head pops up and her forced smile does not help the look of ill revulsion. "Nope. I'm great."

"Did I do it wrong?"

Amy pushes past me with an exaggerated eye roll. "You haven't tried on the dress yet, so how can we know if you did it wrong?"

I kick the door closed with my foot and follow her toward my bedroom, where I did at least go through the effort of making my bed this morning. "Because you look like I asked you to kiss a snake."

"Been there, done that, it wasn't the kissing that was the problem."

"I . . ." I stumble to a halt as her words process, then continue after her, laughing.

She dumps everything from her arms onto my bed. Most of the bags are actually empty.

"What's with the bags?"

"We start prepping for the trade-in sale in two weeks." She shrugs. "I'm going to gather up everything you don't want to wear so I can go through it and see what I want to keep before adding it to the sale stock."

How had I not realized that when Amy said she was all-in on helping me find myself that she'd really meant it? I drop the dress and lurch forward to wrap her in a hug.

There's a pause before her arms wrap around me and squeeze because I'm not usually the one who initiates hugs.

She rubs one hand up and down my back. "Also, I need to sneak things into the storeroom a few pieces at a time because if Mom and Aunt Jade find out about this, they're going to freak out."

I pull back. "Will they be mad? What do I do on our birthday?"

"First," she says as she walks into my closet, "I think it's time you stop using that as a decision-making benchmark." Her voice gets muffled as she goes deeper into the closet.

"Second, it might be time to develop a new birthday tradition." She pokes her head out the door, items of clothing already draped over her shoulder. "Although I can guarantee it will probably still include shopping."

After my experience with Amy last week, that doesn't sound as daunting as it once would have.

"And third, I think Mom and Aunt Jade are going to be more upset about us doing this without them than they are over you getting a makeover."

She exits the closet with several items of clothing and starts folding them neatly into a bag.

"Should we have called Mother last week?" The idea makes my stomach clench, which only adds to my growing sense of guilt.

"Last week was about what you needed, not what she needed. It's not a crime to consider your own needs every once in a while." Her gray-green eyes find mine. "And if you tell me this church and God business means wrecking your mental health and self-confidence so someone else doesn't feel bad, we are never talking about it again."

"Of course it doesn't." My words are automatic because I will not have Amy closing me out on this now, but my brain slowly comes behind and realizes it's true.

When I was a kid, making everyone else happy was just a way to avoid an argument. Later, though, I think I took Paul's idea to be all things to all people the wrong way. It isn't about being like my mother and sister and aunt the way I was trying to do. It's about being the appropriate version of me for the setting the way Carter had me do at the patron dinner.

Carter.

Tears spring to my eyes and before I can blink them away, Amy's there. "Aw, honey, what is it? Did you wear that shirt to dinner with him? See a bird that he's painted fly by the window?"

She turns her head and sniffs. "Is this one of his shirts? Did you smell his cologne?"

Confusion brings me out of emotional crumble. "What? No. This is mine." I pull the shirt up to my nose and sniff. "Do I smell like a guy?"

As she takes a step back, she gives a little shrug. "No, but I'm not going to judge him if he uses strawberry body wash."

I plop onto the bed. "I was just remembering that fancy dinner we went to. The one you saw us at? We were outside the private room because he was telling me that he'd wanted to bring his girlfriend to dinner, not a socially pleasant robot."

Amy blinks at me. Is she about to cry, too? "That's really sweet."

"I know." I sigh. "Do you think he'll be at the demonstration?"

"If he's not, I'll go find him and drag him there myself."

I laugh at the image. It feels good to laugh with Amy. "You don't know where he lives."

"I'm sure Richie could get the information from Frank." She crosses the room to pick up my dropped dress package.

The mention of Richie momentarily drives every other thought from my mind. "I thought you broke up with him."

She rips open the pull tab on the plastic package with a flourish. "Exes are always good for at least two favors if they think it might get you back into bed."

I can't even begin to decide how to answer that.

The dress emerges and the color is just as rich as it was online. The bundle of flimsy dark green fabric spills into Amy's hand and her full concentration is on the fabric. "This is really soft."

"I know." I bounce off the bed with a grin. "I went to the fabric store and just started feeling everything and making a list of what made me want to claw my skin off and what didn't."

"You'll need to share that with me."

"I thought you weren't doing my shopping for me anymore."

She glares at me. "That does not include presents, you ninny. Christmas. Birthday. Twin sister day."

"There actually is one of those. And a National Twin Day, too."

Her grin is crooked. "Let me guess, you heard about it on a podcast?"

"Actually, no. I looked it up once because National Middle Child Day made me curious if there were other sibling days."

"Well, there you go. Two more reasons I might buy you a gift."

"They're both very close to Christmas."

"Of course they are." She unfurls the dress and holds it up by the shoulders. "So, what kind of fabric is this?"

I wince because she isn't going to like this. "Bamboo lyocell."

She blanches a little.

"I know you said to try natural fibers, and this is some weird semi-synthetic rayon blend, but hear me out." I grab the skirt and rub it in my hands. "Feel this. It's amazing."

"I was thinking we could look at cotton or there are certain wools—"

"Yes, but this is cheap."

Amy gives me a flat, blank look. "I'm aware."

"And if I'm going to experiment, I'm not going to waste a lot of money doing it."

She blinks at me. "That's why stores have fitting rooms."

I snatch the dress from her hands and retreat to my bathroom. Her laughter is the only sound that follows.

I slip the dress on and nearly dance around my bathroom. It's not too tight nor too loose. The skirt has a little more fabric and weight to it than I would prefer but it's better than heavy satins and unbreathable silks, so I'll take it.

The sleeves stop at the elbow and the only thing keeping it from being a total sack is a decorative twist at the waist that sends pleats up the bodice.

I open the door and stand there, waiting for Amy to notice.

She looks me over quickly, then stares at my face. Slowly she smiles, gives a little shrug, and says, "Long live bamboo lyocell." Then she ruins the moment by shuddering.

Laughter spills from both of us as I twirl into the room. This may not be the prettiest dress I've ever owned, but it's one I feel like I can be myself in. That's got to be worth more.

"Let's talk shoes." Amy grabs a box from the bed. "And accessories."

My smile drops. I hate heels and those little bags she makes me carry.

She presses the box into my middle. "These probably cost five times as much as that dress, but for now, we're gonna roll with it."

I slide open the box lid and gasp. Sneakers. Granted, they are very fancy sneakers with woven layers of white leather, but they are sneakers nonetheless.

"And this." She pulls a purse from one of the packages on the bed.

It's truly a purse. Not a clutch or a pack-of-gum carrying case. If I packed it right, I could even fit my tablet in there. Not that I would often need to, but I could.

The bag has a woven leather pattern similar to the shoes but instead of being all white it also includes gold and silver leather strips.

I slide on the shoes and hook the bag's strap over my shoulder, then turn to look in the mirror. Amy comes up behind me and rearranges my hair.

Neither of us say anything as we stare at my reflection. I never knew I could look like this—could feel like this. Now that the fabric has been on my body a while, it feels a little dry, but unless they start making formalwear in the same material as my favorite leggings, this is as good as it's gonna get.

What is Amy thinking? What will Carter think? Despite Amy's assurances, I'm not certain he'll come to the demonstration party. If he does, he's skilled enough at these events to completely avoid me if he wants to.

"Mom is going to flip." Amy's grin says she can't wait. "But not as much as Carter."

I'm counting on the project redesign to give me a chance to say what I want to say to him.

I'm counting on this dress to give me the confidence to actually say it.

33

**CARTER**

F rank was right. Grandpa was right. Even Richie Reynolds was right.
I am an idiot.

The sun sets while I sit at my desk, staring at the painting still resting on the easel. She inspired it, it's a part of her, but it isn't her. It's not what I think of when I think of Emma. The idea is merely a facet of what I see in her or, more accurately, one that once was in her.

Lately, she's seemed less isolated. Whether it's because I know her better now or because she is actually relaxing into her life, I don't know.

What I do know is, I did a terrible job of explaining that to her.

This isn't the first time I've sat in my studio, considering a painting until the natural light fades from the sky, but instead of leaving me sitting in total shadow, a collection of tiny red lights pierces the swollen darkness.

The television and gaming console didn't get put away after Emma showed me her presentation. She'd been so excited, she forgot to shut everything down.

I look at the bright dots within the shadowy blocks. If those aren't a sign of how far Emma settled into my heart, I don't know what is.

It's been so easy these past few weeks since I gave in to the urge to have her with me, to make her a space, to lure her in. Painting hasn't been this enjoyable in longer than I can remember, even before I lost the spark of inspiration.

The phone calls with my agent and the calendar requests for time in New York weren't bothering me anymore. I might even say I was excited about the week of events and parties and appearances he'd lined up in a few months.

I'd envisioned asking Emma to go with me. I'd even made the reservation for two hotel rooms.

When had it changed? When did she move from something interesting to someone essential?

My gaze falls on the tiny red lights once more.

That was the day I fell, or the day I started to. That was the day I knew I was all-in on this relationship.

She'd sat on the couch, game controller in hand, grinning up at me, gleeful that she would have all the highest scores on someone else's console. There'd been a hole in the sleeve of her sweatshirt, her legs were curled partially beneath her, and strands of hair were coming out of one of her braids.

The vision is so bright in my head, it's as if I'm back in that moment, looking down on her in the full sun, right before I kissed her for the first time, already thinking in the back of my mind that I could picture making moments like this forever.

It burns from my visual memory into my chest and out through my fingers.

I spin in the chair and nearly knock my lamp from the desk in my haste to turn it on. My sketchbook is still lying open on the desk but when I snatch up a pencil, it feels wrong in my hand.

My fingers fumble with it, trying to make it work like a palette or a brush, and the marks are wrong, the picture refusing to even form the basic necessary shapes.

I stride across the room and hit the light switch, sending a soft glow through the room from a set of wall sconces. It isn't enough to paint or work by, but it's enough to allow me to safely set up the studio lights I use in the dead of winter.

When was the last time I painted in the middle of the night? College? Doesn't matter. I'm doing it now because I have no other choice.

I remove the painting from the easel, barely stopping myself from tossing it away and destroying it. Part of me recognizes that it's still a good idea, still an amazing painting, still has the potential to impact hundreds of people.

If I can ever finish it.

If I can't get Emma back, I don't think that will ever happen.

I pull the canvas that had been prepped with gesso for a different painting and secure it to the easel.

Without a plan and relying purely on instinct, I wheel my cart over to the paint wall and start snatching up colors and tools. My fingers are moving faster than my mind can consciously decide, but it all eases that coil of fear that's been threatening to destroy me, so I keep going.

I paint. Deep into the night, I paint. When exhaustion threatens to overtake me, I clean up enough to keep any tools or paints from getting destroyed and then fall onto the couch.

The sun is shining again when I finally blink my eyes open, and I take a little time to see to my hygiene and get something to eat. As soon as possible, though, I'm back in the studio, back at the painting.

It goes like this for days, though I do seek out my bed for the other nights, my thirty-one-year-old body protesting the hours spent hunched over a canvas enough that I don't want to risk stiffness from another night on the couch.

It's been a long time since I worked with wet-on-wet techniques without letting the layers dry in between. I make mistakes and scrape them off with the palette knife or wipe them down with the rag and move on.

I don't know how many hours I paint. I'm not sure I know how many days it's even been. Eventually, though, I stop. I step back.

It's beautiful.

Not because I'm an amazing artist, but because she is an amazing person.

I clean up my tools, taking deep, slow breaths the entire time. A rabid monster has been inhabiting my body and mind, but it has been satiated by the finished product.

Finally, my studio is set to rights, the completed painting sitting on the easel like a centerpiece. I locate my phone and find a name in my contacts. Time to call in a favor.

I may not be able to find the right words to tell Emma what I think of her, but I can find a way to show her.

**EMMA**

I don't know what I'm feeling.

Just when I thought I'd considered everything, prepared for everything, and was ready to put myself on the line for a chance at happily ever after, he had to go and change the game on me.

"Wow." Amy comes to stand beside me. I don't turn to look at her. I can't.

I physically can't look at anything but the painting on the wall in front of me. I blink a few times. The view doesn't change. "I'm not crazy, right?"

"Debatable. But if you're asking for confirmation that we are indeed looking at a perfect depiction of your face, the answer is yes. Yes, we are."

Where the large jail cell painting once hung is a portrait.

A portrait of me.

There are no bangs, obviously. Carter has yet to see them or my new wardrobe. Yet despite the fact that the woman in the painting looks like the old me, she feels like the new me, like the woman who decided to be herself—or at least try to be herself—no matter where she is.

This is a real moment in time. I remember wearing those braids, that sweatshirt, those leggings. I recognize Carter's couch and the table and the basket of sticky notes.

My right hand is pressed to the couch behind my leg, mostly hidden from the viewer, but I can see the corner of the game controller.

I know this moment.

I know what happened five minutes later.

What I don't know is how this painting came to be hanging on the wall in the McGrary Museum of Art.

"How . . . why . . . I don't . . ."

"Feeling eloquent, I see." Amy nudges me in the arm before leaning down to look at the plaque title and description. "He painted it."

I frown at her. "Of course he painted it." I wave one hand at the painting. "He was the only other person there."

She grins at me over her shoulder. "Don't you want to know what it's titled?"

Do I? "Yes. No. What do you think?"

"I think you might be mistaken about how he really feels about you."

Somehow my heart falls into my stomach because I can feel it pulsing there and it's making me nauseous. "What, is it called *Goodbye* or something like that?"

"No." She drags the word out until I contemplate smacking her over the head.

Instead, I push her out of the way and look for myself.

The first thing I see, though, isn't the title. It's the note beneath it that says to please be careful because the work is not fully dry yet. I look back to the painting, fighting the urge to reach out and see just how wet it is. When did he do this?

"It's called *The Beginning*."

That voice is so achingly familiar, and I spin around so fast I almost lose my balance. He's standing there, one hand in his pocket, the other holding a pair of the tour guide smart glasses Jason and I have been working on. "Hi."

I give a little wave because the choice of hello as a response seems too casual for this moment. It's the first time I've seen him since I practically kicked him out of my life.

Well, the first time I've seen him in person. I've performed plenty of internet searches and scrolled through my phone gallery during coding breaks.

I want to go back and change what I said then. Instead of accusations and demands to be left alone, I would say we couldn't go on ignoring how each of us felt about the other's occupation and dreams. That we needed to grow and learn and become something different or stronger or better.

But I hadn't said any of those things, hadn't even realized at the time that I wanted to mean them. One thing I've learned in the past two weeks, though, is that the past can't be changed. It can only be learned from.

Which means this meeting needs to go in a way I'll be okay remembering tomorrow, even if I don't like the outcome.

He holds the glasses up and looks at them before returning his focus to me. "This is nice." His mouth compresses as he clears his throat. "I don't know how practical it is, but I like the redesign."

Using the glasses as a pointer, he indicates a painting across the room. "I didn't realize that was the only woman Klimt painted twice."

"That's the point of a self-guided tour, isn't it?" I swallow hard and curl my hands into determined fists. A decision made in the quiet of the night with just me, a mirror, and the soft droning of the audio Bible is hard to maintain a few days later.

"Learning a few facts about the artist can make you look at the painting differently," I continue. "Who was she? Why did she matter so much? Why only twice?" I shrug. "Makes you think."

He considers me a moment before turning back to the canvas of me. "And this one? What do you think the artist was doing when he painted it?"

My courage has stretched as far as it can and I'm afraid to say what I hope it means. I can't take having my heart ripped out in this room one more time.

Instead, I point to the glasses in his hand. "I think he's messing up the tour because I don't have this painting programmed into the system software."

His smile is a little chagrined as he rubs a hand across the back of his neck. "Sorry about that."

I don't know how to respond so I stand there. A glance to my left reveals that Amy slipped away some time after Carter appeared. Part of me is grateful, but the other part of me would very much like someone to run interference until I know how this is going to end.

Her blonde hair catches my gaze and I see her on the other side of the room, locked arm in arm with our frowning mother. I can only handle one difficult confrontation at a time, so I turn back to Carter.

"I can honestly say I wasn't thinking about the tour," Carter says with a shrug. "I was just looking for a way to keep you in my life. I knew you'd be here today, so I convinced them to trade it out for the event."

It's a big gesture. And unlike mine, he receives no potential benefit from it. How long did it take him to paint this? What did he have to promise to get them to switch out the paintings? Unless Mr. Leonard is a hidden romantic softy, it would have taken more than a sweet sob story. This painting is far from Carter's usual philosophically intriguing style.

I take a deep breath. How many times have I said I wish I could go back and do that last conversation differently? This is as good a chance as I'm going to get. He's being vulnerable so I can be nothing less.

The glasses I made just for him are in my woven leather purse, calling to me. Without the jail cell painting, they're all but worthless, but it's the only thing I have so I pull them out.

"I have a special set of glasses for you. They have a slightly different version of the tour on them, but I'm afraid they won't do any good now." I wave a hand helplessly at the canvas but don't look at it. It's weird to see myself that way. "Nothing is keyed to this painting."

He takes the glasses from me. "I know where the other one is."

Once again, I'm torn as the many possible responses vie for supremacy. I could say we should go find it together, or I could tell him to go without me before running away and pretending none of this ever happened.

One choice guarantees I spend the evening crying into a bag of French fries. The other merely risks it.

I take a deep breath. "If I had put this painting into the tour, what material would I have gotten?" He has the glasses. If he wants to hear my heart, I won't be able to stop him, but I'd like a little more reassurance before I go there with him.

"It's done in oils. A wet-on-wet style." Carter leans toward me as if he's about to let me in on a secret. "It's been a while since he used that method exclusively and there was a great deal of wiping and scraping involved to correct some small mistakes." His gaze meets mine and I can't look away. "It's easier to fix mistakes on canvas than it is in real life."

Fear and hope form a drum line in my chest.

"There were no sketches," he continues.

"There weren't?" But he always uses sketches. They're works of art unto themselves, but he only considers them an essential part of the process.

He shakes his head. "I didn't need one. I just started painting from memory. When a man thinks he's lost the most important thing in his life, it becomes all he can think about."

I'd imagined him showing up today and shouting across the room that he loved me.

This is better.

I slide my hand into his outstretched one, the one that's been hanging out there, waiting for rejection, offering acceptance. His fingers grip mine tightly, and his palm slides securely against my skin.

"You said you know where the jail cell painting is?"

"I do." The smile he gives me is wide and happy and reaches his eyes, making them sparkle and wrinkle at the corners. "Come with me."

35

**CARTER**

Whether this moment was orchestrated by my subconscious, a loving God with a sense of humor, or straight-up dumb luck, I don't care. All I know is that my heart is pounding hard enough to make my vision blur around the edges as I lead Emma to a door.

She looks different tonight. Not just the hair and the clothes—although I love the way the bangs frame her face and make her eyes look bigger and the way she actually seems to be comfortable out in public. It's as if she's standing taller, or maybe looser? I can't put my finger on it, and at the moment I don't care because she's still my Emma under it all.

Her cough of laughter as we pass the *Employees Only* sign eases a little of my tension and brings a smile to my lips.

"Please tell me you don't have a $200,000 painting leaning against the wall in an employee breakroom." Her voice is a rough whisper, but I can hear the smile in it.

"Not exactly."

We walk down a short hall to the reception area outside Mr. Leonard's office. *Longing for Freedom* is partially covered in sheeting and leaning against the wall behind his assistant's desk.

With great reluctance, I let go of her hand and move about, turning on lights and adjusting the protective cloths so we can see the painting. "So, I just put on the smart glasses and look at the painting?"

She nods and clasps her hands tightly. "Once it recognizes what you're looking at, it will give you the option to hear about the painting."

Unfortunately, I'm holding both pairs of glasses—the one she gave me and the one I received to test the tour guide system. "I don't suppose you know which is which, do you?"

Her eyes widen as she, too, looks at the pairs in my hands. "Ah . . ."

"Never mind. I'll figure it out."

I slide one pair onto my face and wait for the system to walk me briefly through the usage instructions before signaling that it's ready to work. My breath freezes in my lungs as I turn to the painting. I've no reason to think there will be anything bad on this recording. If she hated me now, she wouldn't have come back here with me or made me a special pair of glasses.

Small graphics in the edge of my vision offer me options to learn about the history or style of the painting or learn about the artist.

If these are the special glasses, she'll have put the information in the artist section, right? I follow the instructions to select that option and wave a hand at that icon.

A voice seems to echo straight into my head from the earpieces of the glasses. It shares my official biography, and my more famous works seem to appear on the wall beside *Longing for Freedom*.

The experience is both interesting and a little disconcerting.

And not the one I'm looking for.

I take the glasses off, blinking rapidly as my brain adjusts to no longer seeing the other paintings.

"It's not these." I wiggle them in the air as I give Emma a nervous smile.

"Okay." Her breathy voice and pale face mean she's just as nervous as I am.

"I don't have to do this." I offer her the second pair of glasses. "You can have them back if you'd rather I didn't.."

She shakes her head. "No. I want . . . You should see it. It's my painting for you, if you want to think of it that way." Her head jerks to a point over her shoulder that is probably meant to indicate the portrait hanging in the museum but really aims at the parking lot.

"All right, then."

I take a deep breath and slide the glasses on, but I keep looking at her as the system goes through the opening process.

The way she's standing three feet away, trembling, is about to kill me. I extend my hand and she takes it immediately, sending a thrill through me that is both exciting and calming.

My girl of contradictions.

"No matter what," I say, "you and I start over tonight."

Her nose scrunches as her face tilts up to mine. "That means we had an end instead of a bump in the road. Maybe we continue tonight?"

"Even better." I lean down and drop a kiss on her nose before twining our fingers together as I turn to the painting.

Instead of three options this time, there's only one, and it simply reads *Play*. I click the button on the side of the frame.

The voice in my head this time is hers and it nearly brings me to my knees.

"Before I met you, I didn't realize that I'd locked myself in a prison. I thought I'd structured a life that miraculously let me live in all the available worlds."

A few pictures of her dance around me. Her in a college sweatshirt, in an evening gown, in a church T-shirt on some sort of mission trip, in a linen pantsuit in front of a Christmas tree.

"Everyone was happy with these pieces of me and that made me happy. Then you came along and somehow you saw them all. You saw that I was a puzzle that hadn't quite been put together yet."

My sketches seem to cover the wall now. When had she even taken pictures of those?

"You made me see that I had locked myself away, limited myself by putting life into closely guarded buckets.

"You didn't seem to care which puzzle piece you got. You wanted to spend time with them all. That was both wonderful and terrifying."

I have to blink to clear away the tears in my eyes so I can see the pictures of us she's included in the display.

"I have a lot to learn now. It's a long journey out of a prison of my own making, but you've opened the door and I'm taking that first step."

For a moment I think everything digital has cleared and then I realize she's edited my painting. The cell door isn't closed anymore. It's open.

Tears spill over and roll down my face. *Thank you, God, that I am watching this in private.*

"If this is it for us, I'll always be thankful for that. I hope, though, that maybe it isn't the end. You said I was full of contradictions, and maybe this is simply one of those where we start a happy relationship from a place of sadness."

Her voice fades away and slowly the painting returns to the original.

I turn to her, trying to hug her to me, but she's still standing sideways, facing the painting as if she were watching with me, and we end up in some sort of weird standing tackle.

We both laugh as she turns to me and wraps her arms around my middle.

I know she doesn't need my answer—it's hanging in the museum as we speak—so I lift my hands to cup either side of her jaw, my fingers extending along her cheeks, and bend to kiss her.

Before my lips can touch hers, though, my wrist starts to vibrate and emit the most horrible, tinny tune imaginable.

I close my eyes on a groan of agony as I let my forehead rest against hers. It's a shaky perch as she's suddenly laughing and it's only growing in violence.

"What is that?" she asks through the laughter.

I pull away from her and straighten my arm to lift the sleeve from my wrist before pulling it back in between us to show her my new watch. The bright face sends an eerie green and blue glow onto our faces.

"I thought I'd turned off the alarms, but apparently I just keep making new ones because it keeps doing this."

"You got a smartwatch?" Her hands trail over my wrist as she does something that makes the device stop stabbing our ears.

I sigh. "Yes. It seemed like the thing to do if I'm going to date a technology nerd."

Her smile is wide as she carefully removes the watch from my wrist. "This technology nerd doesn't need you to change any more than you need her to." She lifts her own wrist to show off her watch, glowing softly with its sedate shades of gray. "I can tell you what time it is."

"Oh?" My smile returns and I rest my hands on her shoulders. "And what time is it?"

"Time to kiss me, of course."

I most emphatically—perhaps almost too emphatically—agree.

Several moments later, we're once again standing there staring into each other's eyes.

"I really need to get back," she says with a sigh.

I grin. "You mean you're going to drag me to an event at an art museum?"

Her shrug is cute as a light pink washes over her cheeks. "I guess I am. It's, well, it's not so bad when you know how to appreciate it." She steps back and thrusts one foot forward to show me her white dress sneakers. "And when you have comfortable footwear."

I flick a finger across the new strands of hair decorating her forehead. "I can't wait to hear how this came about."

"It's all part of my discovery of the new me."

"Sounds like a journey I can't wait to take."

I drape my arm around her shoulder as we walk quietly back to the gallery. My fingers can't seem to stop sliding across the soft fabric of her sleeve. "What is this material?"

"Bamboo," she all but shouts at me before going into detail about the podcast she listened to that described how they turn the hollow tree into fibers for clothing, sheets, and more.

My smile is wide enough to hurt my cheeks as we get to the door that will take us back to the party.

She pulls me to a stop before I open the door, though, and her face is serious.

It doesn't make my smile fade, though. If it could, it would get bigger. I'm confident we're not about to go backward, and we've simply encountered the next curve on a journey forward.

Life with Emma is never going to be boring.

"What is it?" I ask.

"You have to recuse yourself from the tour guide system selection."

I frown. She has a really good system now. I especially like the potential it has to show how an artist's work changes over time or links together. "Why?"

"Because having a girlfriend in the running really presents a conflict of interest."

My wide smile returns. "That it does."

And I open the door to a room full of art and technology, friends and family, and a bright and happy future.

# ACKNOWLEDGEMENTS

When I started pursuing publication back in 2011, I one day wanted to be writing both contemporary and regency novels. For far longer than I anticipated, it wasn't something I could manage. To see *Pixels and Paint* become a reality is definitely a dream come true.

I couldn't have managed it without my family. To Jacob, who always patiently listens when I say my book is horrible during rewrites, thank you for pushing me to keep going. To all my blessings, but for this book, particularly Blessing1, your strength and ability to embrace yourself as you are, despite the difficulties that brings, is an inspiration.

To my Voxer girls, who read excerpts and discussed edits and brain-stormed plot twists, you are the best support team a writer could ask for.

To Angie, for helping me define my characters' styles, to Rebecca, for being the type of fan authors dream of finding, and to both of you for showing me how artists actually draw, thank you. To the rest of our lifegroup, it's an honor to do life together.

To my readers and Instagram followers who pitched in with their knowledge on oil painting, grant distribution, and the struggles of being single, I am forever in your debt. My deepest apologies for doing a terrible job at keeping a record of your names so I could thank you all individually.

A huge and likely never-to-be-seen thank you to the artists who put tutorials up on YouTube, particularly Andrew Tischler. Thanks for teaching me how Carter would paint.

# ABOUT THE AUTHOR

Kristi is the award-winning author of romance novels from a Christian worldview. Her books include the Hawthorne House, Haven Manor, and Hearts on the Heath series, set in the Regency era, as well as the contemporary rom-com, *Pixels and Paint*.

She is also a speaker, teaching classes in writing as well as Biblical and spiritual topics. She has spoken to writers' groups, schools, and young women's church groups.

When she is not writing or interacting with her readers, Kristi spends time with her family and her church. A graduate of Georgia Tech with a computer science degree, she knows that life rarely takes the turns we expect. While she still spends hours a day on a computer, now she's living out the dreams of her childhood and creating stories for others to enjoy and be inspired by.

Learn more at KristiAnnHunter.com or by finding Kristi on Instagram @kristiannhunter.

### A NOBLE MASQUERADE
### HAWTHORNE HOUSE, BOOK I

Lady Miranda has spent her entire life trying to conform to the expectations of a proper lady. When her private exasperations get sent to her childhood crush, she opens a connection that might be far more than she bargained for as he turns out to be a spy for the Crown.

### A DEFENSE OF HONOR
### HAVEN MANOR, BOOK I

Miss Katherine FitzGilbert knows life is unfair, but she's spent her adult years trying to make its consequences a little less detrimental for some stumbling innocents. When her path crosses with Graham, Lord Wharton, her heart may be in just as much danger as her secrets.

### VYING FOR THE VISCOUNT
### HEARTS ON THE HEATH, BOOK I

Hudson, the newly titled Viscount Stildon, is out of his depth in Newmarket society. Fortunately, Miss Bianca Snowley is willing to help him acclimate if he continues to let her ride his horses. By the time they recognize what they truly want in life, their mutual matchmaking efforts might have gone too far to be easily unraveled.

Made in the USA
Middletown, DE
17 August 2023